THE GIRL WHO FELL FROM THE SKY

Stranded Hearts Book One

VIVIEN JACKSON

REBECCA ROYCE

The Girl Who Fell From The Sky (Stranded Hearts #1)

Copyright @ 2020 by Rebecca Royce and Vivien Jackson

Ebook ISBN: 978-1-951349-56-1

Print ISBN: 978-1-951349-57-8

Cover art by Amanda Pillar of Smoking Hot Covers

Content Editing: Heather Long

Copy Editing: Jennifer Jones at Bookends Editing

Final Proof Editing: Meghan Leigh Daigle

Formatting: Ripley Proserpina

Published by Rebecca Royce

www.rebeccaroyce.com

BIANCA

I'd always found space travel to be mind-numbingly dull. This trip wasn't proving to be any different. The ship I was on offered lots of entertainment, a paid staff to keep us amused, and yet...every day was the same. If I had my way, I'd never take another six-month trek across the galaxy ever again. I walked the track, my fifth lap—it was important to keep muscle mass up—and stared at the stars outside. Just a whole lot of nothing interesting to look at.

It would be nice to be able to run. I looked over my shoulder. If the monitors weren't looking, maybe I would. My last three heart scans had been decent. I was probably safe to run a little bit. Like maybe a mile. I scanned the wall, and the tell-tale red light that followed me, monitoring my heart rate at all times, presented itself. Yesterday, I'd had a break. A little boy on deck five had broken his leg. That had temporarily taken their attention off of me. But it looked like it had returned.

And that sucked. A lot.

When we got to Jooron Five, my brother's personal physicians would replace my beating heart with a mechanical one that would mean I could run as much as I wanted. Of course, I'd be doing it with a fake metal heart that would have to be replaced every three years. I shook my head. I was lucky to be alive, lucky to be here, lucky I had a family with enough currency and political connections to make this possible for me at all.

Most people would have been euthanized at birth for my kind of defect. I'd gotten twenty-two good years with little interference

I had to remind myself on a daily basis to count all the ways I should feel grateful. Thinking about others helped me to not to dwell too much on myself. I just wasn't that good at it.

My wrist dinged, and I looked down at it. My brother reached out from Jooron Five. This was his daily phone call, albeit three hours later than usual.

"You okay? I thought you forgot me." I spoke as his face twisted into existence on my holowatch. The images were never perfect, but they were better than nothing.

"Forget you? My twin? Never. No, I had to put down some rebels. Took all morning. Paperwork and all that. Why can't people stay where they belong?"

I shook my head. "You know I have no head for politics."

It made little sense to me. We'd technically taken over the rebels' planet...so weren't we the ones not where we belonged? If I asked that, I got a long-winded answer about destiny and rights. I'd quit asking. Give me a school where I could teach literature and art; I was happier that way.

"How are you feeling? What are you doing?"

I rolled my eyes. "I'm on the track. If you wait three hours to reach me, you get me where you find me not waiting for your call."

The fuzzy image projecting from my watch looked like it

was frowning. Or constipated. "On the track? Bianca, tell me you are not running."

"Of course I'm not." Unfortunately.

He sighed over the tiny speakers in my watch. "It's just a day and a half now, and then we'll get you all fixed up."

Fixed. With a metal heart. Right. "Yeah," I said.

"Bianca..." My brother could sound gentle when he tried. Most of the time, his voice boomed, instructing people on how they ought to live, behave, believe, and vote. He took his authority seriously as the youngest enforcer ever elected to the inter-planetary coalition—the Union. But right now, he was just my brother—my worried brother—when he said, "Let us pray together."

Oh, not this again. I closed my eyes to keep from rolling them all the way back in my head.

"Ancient and holy ones, log our plea," he intoned, and I gritted my teeth. "Protect my sister on her voyage, and bring her safely to Jooron Five. Wrap her in your gracious mesh of grace and grant—"

All at once, his voice sliced to silence. I opened my eyes. His holo was gone.

"Miss Cervantes?" came the normally placid voice of the ship's captain, who was currently not placid at all. I could hear voices in the background shouting. "Please strap into the nearest impact web immediately. Might be a good idea to fill your chamber with fluid, too."

I couldn't fill my chamber with fluid. My body—my heart —couldn't handle the added pressure. But if the captain had forgotten my special health accommodations, she must really be distracted.

"What happened? My brother's call got cut off."

"We were pulled out of hyperspace," the captain said. "And had to put shields up. Now really, the impact web."

On the bridge, two people were arguing. I could hear

their shouting match clearly, though I had no idea what they were talking about. What was the Everlock, why couldn't it exist, and why the heck was it obstructing our route to Jooron Five? This was a known spacelane. From the sound of the crew, though, they were as confused and horrified as I was.

Plus, the captain was no longer paying me the least bit of attention, though she'd left a channel open. I heard her screaming, "No, Lieutenant Godfrey, to port! You expose our flank, and those plasma cannons are going to light us up. Talley, don't flood the bridge! The plasma. No, just do it! All ancient and holy ones..."

Emergency lighting glowed blue on the floor panels, and I chased them at a run, which felt like a vise squeezing my chest. I couldn't stop. The lights led me to a pressurized containment chamber that doubled as a shower area for people using the track. If we lost gravity, for whatever reason, this chamber could be pressurized and filled with fluid, just like the bridge, to keep a fragile human body safe from violent impact. It also contained impact webbing rolled up in easy-access cabinets. I released one web, fitted it around my body, and secured the clasps, all with trembling hands.

Just in time, too, because right then, the deck lurched. If I hadn't been hooked into the web I would have slammed into a wall, or worse. The room went sideways; I could feel the oblique angle in my guts, even though the protective web kept me from crashing into anything.

The channel on my holowatch wasn't transmitting voices anymore, just alarms and the whooshing of protective liquid as it filled the bridge and presumably all the cabins where the other passengers were strapped in.

Or at least, that was what I assumed the sound was. Except down the corridor, still lit in emergency blue, that didn't look like a fluid surge. It looked like fire, and then the chamber locked. And the lights went out.

Without warning, the entire ship jolted onto its side. I cried out.

I wasn't sure what happened after that. I had a sense of falling, of floating. Darkness. Pain. Pressure. Then nothing. The sweet relief of oblivion.

I woke up flat on my stomach. And on fire. Without thought or reason, I rolled, slapping at my clothes, smothering the flames, but realizing too late I'd traded burning pants for burned hands.

Tears flooded down my face, and I screamed at the top of my lungs. Where was I? And oh *holies*, my fingers. Had I burned them off? What was...

I had died. That had to be it. I'd died, and I'd refused to say the prayer with Brent. The Holy Ones had sent me to the underworld to roast in flames for all time. Movement caught my eye, and a second later, I stared up at a man.

At least I thought it was a man. He wore a covering on his face, blocking me from seeing anything but his brown eyes as he stared down at me. His hair was dirty blond and hung slightly over his eyes. I didn't recognize his uniform as any from the empire, but I didn't know all of them.

Not sure what to do, I lifted my hands so he could see they were burned. "Help."

He bent down toward me, lifting me from where I lay on the ground. Carnage was all around me. Debris from...well, it had to be our spaceship. It was everywhere. My lips trembled.

He stepped over metal pieces, carrying me away from it. Where were the others? I couldn't possibly be alone. My earlier idea of the underworld fled. I didn't think the Holy

Ones would bring the broken remains of our transport with us there. This had to be... Well, I had no idea.

My hands throbbed with pain like I'd never felt before—and believe me, I'd endured pain. This was different. Worse. I didn't want to look at them, but then I did. Red, raw, bubbling. Oh no, this was bad. Was I going to lose the use of my hands?

The man set me down on the ground as a gust of wind brought sand flying into my face. I choked on it.

He took a pack from his bag. All of this, it felt almost dreamlike, as though it couldn't possibly be happening. From his bag, he removed a green scarf and wrapped it once, then twice, around my face, covering my mouth and nose. It was the same color as the one he wore.

Once again, he went into his bag, this time producing a jug. He set it down next to him before he stared at me one more time. With fast hands, he tore at my pants. I gasped. What was he doing? The air hit my skin there like an assault. I was burned on my legs? Well, of course I was. That's where I'd been on fire.

He poured some of the liquid from the jug on my injury. It was a red color, and as it hit the burned skin, the pain immediately cooled. Seconds later, he did the same with my hands. Sweet relief. Tears fell from my eyes.

"Thank you," I spoke through the muffled scarf.

"Your tissue will regenerate in time, but only if I remove you from the scouring effects of the sand." He hesitated, as if he were having some kind of internal argument with himself, and then finally looked down at me. "You require shelter, but if you have fractured bones, movement could worsen the injury. May I ascertain your condition?"

Okay, one, his accent was bizarre, soothing and lilted, like it ought to be reciting classical poetry all the time. And two, no curriculum in the Union taught kids vocabulary like that.

He almost had to be a nerd. Looking like he did, with a jug of magical healing goo at the ready, a voice that rubbed the air like Iolian silk, and a general air of nerdishness? Clearly, I'd been almost right to begin with—I had died, but far from being sentenced to everlasting punishment, it seemed I was now receiving some sort of bespoke karmic reward. Go me. I closed my eyes, leaned back on my blissfully painless elbows, and said, "Sure. Knock yourself out."

He frowned. "I must...put my hands upon your person."

Was he serious? Doctors had been poking me my whole life. I had no sense of personal privacy left. "Please do."

"You are a female."

"Ah, yes?" Was that a trick question? And was he blushing behind that face-scarf?

"But you're... No matter. If you grant permission, I shall be swift and circumspect."

"I, uh, grant permission?" I meant it as a statement, but it kind of did sound like a question. I wasn't sure anyone had ever asked me for permission before for anything. Most people told me what to do and expected me to do it.

His frown deepened, but he leaned in to the examination. Clearly, he had some medical or military field training. First the long bones—legs and arms and the odd "press against my hand" or "can you move this extremity?" When he checked my ribs, he managed to find every single ticklish spot, which was funny to me but seemed to embarrass him a lot. His hands were gentle but applied firm pressure, and when he moved them up through my singed hair to check my skull, it was everything I could manage not to sigh.

He might have been a trained medic, but if he weren't also a masseuse, he'd missed his calling.

He cleared his throat, and I sighed. "Do you think you can walk, or shall I carry you?"

I could probably walk, but being carried like a sand-glass

doll sounded really good. Although the magical goo had taken away the most immediate pain, I still felt vaguely sore, like I'd just taken a pretty bad fall. Which...yikes. If I wasn't in the karmic afterworld, and if that was a real planet beneath my ass, I must in fact have fallen. From the sky. In a burning wreck of a starship.

"I can walk," I said, scrambling to my feet. My entire body felt like one giant bruise, and there were patches of still-red skin—tissue, he'd called it, which would heal—but somehow, I was still functional. "My name's Bianca, by the way."

We started picking our way free of the debris field, and I wobbled a little. He caught my elbow. Steadied me.

"I am called Nox." He bowed his head for a second. "We need to hurry. Your transport fell from the sky. As we are in war season, others are out scouting for the best location to create our battlefronts. Our City-State will win this year and take most of the land offered. To whom do you belong? And how did your transport get up in the sky?"

I swallowed, trying to think about what he'd just said to me. Truth was, I didn't understand a lot of that. My transport? He must have meant spaceship. I didn't know what a City-State was. Did he just mean city? Or was that the name of his city? My father had been insistent that all the colonies speak the common language, and my brother had certainly pushed that even further since he'd been in office. I'd never before encountered someone whom I didn't fully understand. And yet this man, Nox, was gentle, easy with me, and I didn't mind listening to him. He'd asked me a question.

"Um...I don't belong to anyone." This was a source of discomfort in my family. Betrothal was still a thing among the upper crust, although the lower castes did get to marry for love, something Brent scoffed at as ridiculous. Who cared about feelings when there were political alliances to make? He'd had three different fiancée arrangements that had fallen

apart thanks to shifts in the socio-economic climate. If she couldn't hold the planets Hadlock and Rosin for him in elections, she wasn't worth his time. We'd officially canceled three weddings. I'd never been betrothed because of the heart issue. I was not considered an appropriate wife at this point. After the heart transplant, maybe. I shook my head. My savior hadn't said a word since I'd spoken.

I blinked. That was because it had been a two-part question. He waited on my response. By the Holy Ones, had I hit my frickin' head?

"My, ah, transport flew because it's a space vessel." That was the best I was going to be able to do here. I didn't understand the mechanics of space flight any more than I could explain how carbon-pulsion worked. Nope. Not my thing.

Nox tilted his head slightly to the side. "I'm not familiar with that term. If you belong to no one, and that seems unlikely—I find it more believable you wish to just not tell me for some reason—then I will bring you back home and our leader Torrin can decide to whom you will go."

To whom I will go? "Hold on. What I need is the closest Union ambassador. They will reach my brother. I'm sure you even know who he is...Brent Cervantes." Usually, I hesitated to tell people who he was right off the bat. That was awful and I'd never deny him, but he wasn't beloved everywhere. Sometimes, it was simply easier to leave his name out of conversations. Now was not one of those times. Not if I wanted to get home.

"I don't know what either of those things are. Come." Nox held my arm. "My transport isn't far."

I dug in, refusing to move. "That isn't possible. There is an ambassador on every planet affiliated with the Union." And at last count, everyone was affiliated.

"You speak words I simply don't know. What I do know is the Reamers may soon return to the wreckage, and if they find us, they will attempt to kill me—and likely will succeed since I am alone—and take you back to use in the most deplorable ways."

His words brought out images that made my head spin. Yes, I knew what those ways were.

His long legs ate up space better than mine, but he slowed so that I could keep up. That part wasn't odd at all. People had been slowing down for me and treating me with kid gloves all my life. No, the strange thing was that this time, I didn't mind it. He didn't seem inconvenienced or begrudging, and his preternatural patience soothed some of my worry.

Not that I was going to lollygag. I couldn't quite stop my brain from imagining those deplorable uses by...Reamers, was it? I had no idea what a Reamer was, but the way Nox had said the word made me never want to encounter one.

He pulled up short next to a hunk of heat-welded metal that at first, I thought was just another piece of wreckage. But the closer I looked, the more I could discern this wasn't part of just one wreck. It was a soldered-together vehicle with metal bits from at least three distinct sources, and instead of landing gear, it had tracks, like a robot server at a cocktail bar. Only, well, bigger than a cocktail bot.

Nox lifted an overhead accordion-style door and pulled out a short set of metal steps. At his gesture, I climbed into the dark cabin, and he followed. There was a bench spanning the width of the transport, and I sat there, letting my eyes adjust to the change in lighting.

After dropping his bag on the bench by my hip, Nox moved past me and into some sort of cockpit-like control area at the front and started flipping switches. The patch-work transport rumbled to life, which sounded more like a beast growling than the sleek whine of an ion engine coming online. Combustion engine, then? Who even used those anymore? Come to think of it, hadn't they been outlawed throughout the Union?

Maybe the better question wasn't *where* I was but *when* I was, because it felt like I'd fallen from the sky and into the last century.

I could only see the back of Nox's head at first, but when he drew some curtains back—made out of the same soft green cloth that still covered both our faces—dingy light flooded the cabin. I peered outside just as the transport lurched into motion.

Without looking back, he said, "Under your seat is a container with more of that salve. If you slide the lid aside and put your hands directly into the solution, I believe it will help."

How kind. But really, I had a high pain threshold, and his first application of the goo had taken away the worst of it. "How far is your home from here?" I asked.

"Only three kilometers, and the terrain is flat."

Another sensation of time travel assailed me. I knew what a kilometer was, but only because I'd taught an academy course in old-Earth folktales. Transportation technology had become so swift that most transit distances were described in terms of time. Nexus, the capital world of the Union, had a mathematically perfect orbit that was close enough to old-Earth's as to fit neatly into three hundred days in a year, thirty hours in a day, sixty minutes in an hour. Brent swore three was a holy number, but pretty much everything was about faith with him. It did make the math easy.

We seemed to be creeping over this planet's surface, so even though a kilometer was a fairly short distance, by my best guess, our travel time would be...ten minutes? "I can wait till we get there. Your treatment back at the crash site really helped. Thank you."

He said something under his breath, but it sounded

grumpy, so I didn't ask for clarification. Doctors, in my experience, hated when I refused treatment or pushed the limits. But I'd been in this body longer than they'd been studying it, and I knew what it could handle.

I peered out the dirt-filmed window at the end of my bench. A tower of smoke rose from the wreckage, but we were moving steadily away from it. There was, as I'd already experienced, a lot of sand or dirt in the air, and much of the rolling topography was sand-dusted. I could see the odd shrubbery here and there, and some interesting reddish rocks roughly the size of this transport. As we got closer to Nox's home, the wreckage smoke grew smaller and the shrubs became more frequent. It was hard to see clearly, but I thought some of them might have white flowers.

When we slowed and then rumbled to a stop, I turned and looked out the front window, and the sight that met my eyes caused me to gasp.

CHAPTER ONE

He'd called where we were headed a City-State. I knew what a city was—I'd been in more than I could count in my life—and I knew what a state was. Usually we placed *the* in front of it. *The* State. It referred to the government and what they wanted. This place where we headed was completely unrecognizable to me. I'd never seen anything like it.

The buildings were old, beaten up by weather, or maybe other things, and falling apart. Most had been patched with various bits of metal or wood, and they were tiny compared to the skyscrapers I was used to. There were no roads, no highways, just trucks and tank-like vehicles like this one going all over the place. What had happened here? Had it been through some kind of...quasi-apocalyptic event?

Dirt lifted into the air, and for a second, seemed to form a twister before it dissipated and floated on like the whole thing had never happened. I'd been going along because I had no other choice. Injured. Terrified. I didn't think I'd grasped the severity of my situation here until that very second. I was somewhere foreign, and everyone I'd been with was dead.

My watch! I'd not even considered it before. There was a universal contact button on it. I could reach Brent, and he'd come. Or he'd send people. Wherever I was, my brother would find me. But when I looked at it, I found the watch was cracked. Shattered would be the better word. These things were supposed to be resistant to being destroyed, but I supposed that didn't apply to falling out of the sky.

"Excuse me, Nox." My voice shook. "I...I need you to explain to me where I am. Please. Right now."

He glanced back at me. "I found you in what will be the field of battle, and now you are safe in our City-State. Where else would you be?"

That told me nothing. "No. What planet is this? What is its designation?"

"I'm sorry, Bianco."

"Bianca," I corrected him, and he winced.

"Apologies, Bianca. It is a foreign name to me. I apologize, Bianca, I don't know what a planet is or a designation."

I was in so much trouble.

"Okay. How about a bigger city? Bigger than this?"

He shook his head. "There aren't bigger cities. Why would there be such things?"

It was possible he was completely crazy. Or maybe he'd never left this strange corner of his world. If either of those things were true, I had absolutely no idea what to do about it. The vehicle started to bounce on rough terrain, and I held on for dear life, which made my hands start to burn again. Where was that jug he'd mentioned?

"I am going to stop." He pulled the green scarf off of his mouth for the first time. There was no mirror for me to see him in, but I could finally make out his ear. It was pierced and set with a tiny jewel. Men didn't do that where I was from. That small detail distracted me temporarily from the pain in my hands.

I wasn't sure what to say. "Okay..."

He nodded. "I feel we should go see my friend Astor. He is...more versed in things than me. Truth, he is the smartest person I know. I am obligated to bring you straight to Torrin, and I may take a lashing for not doing so, but once you are with Torrin, he will make a decision and that will be that. Better to know what to do with you before we go to him so that we can give him all the information he needs."

I leaned forward. "This Torrin, is he going to...hurt me?"

Nox was quiet for a long moment. "I hope not."

My stomach tightened. "Nox..."

"When we get to Astor, do not stare. He is unusual."

The bright blur beyond my window had darkened, and once Nox lifted the accordion door again, I realized why. He had piloted the whole transport into some sort of hangar, just on the ground. Or maybe underground? It was a poorly lit space, thick with fumes that made me cough when I tried to climb out, but at least there wasn't any dust in the air.

And it was cool. The change in temperature licked me all over, and I shivered in delight. I hadn't realized how the heat had aggravated my burns, but being out of it was a relief.

Nox set his pack down again, rummaged for a moment, and pulled out a wad of that green cloth we'd used for masks. The original shape had been small, compressed, but when he shook it out, it could almost have been a rug. He draped it over my shoulders and clasped it at my neck, all without so much as brushing my skin.

"You trembled," he explained sheepishly.

"No, I'm not—" I started, but he looked so confused and possibly embarrassed that I just forced a smile and said, "Thank you."

He nodded and indicated that I should follow him, so I did.

Off the main hangar, we took a tunnel whose walls looked

like someone had dug them out by hand, maybe with a spoon. Every surface was rough, including the uneven floor, and tiny electric light bulbs had been strung at random-seeming intervals. The farther we got from the hangar, the more breathable the air became. I even got to a point where I wasn't struggling to pull in breaths, which alerted me that I had, in fact, been struggling, probably since the crash.

I didn't want to think of what the stress and trauma of the crash were doing to my stupid, fragile physiology. Thinking about it wouldn't help, after all, and from the looks of this place so far, there weren't any diagnostic units to hook into anyhow. No emergency surgeries or metal hearts, either. Why was that thought the exact opposite of panic-inducing? Being in this strange place was freeing, somehow. I concentrated on slowing my breaths, taking in as much of this cool, clean air as I could on an inhalation and then releasing it completely.

Until Nox pulled up short at the mouth of another tunnel and I almost ran into his back. He tapped out a pattern on the metallic door, and a voice inside said, "Quit scratching on my door already and get in here. I can't wait to show you..."

Nox swung the door open on complaining hinges and stepped inside. I followed. And the voice faded into a...sort of a purr? A trilling, questioning, surprised sound that I could almost feel on the surface of my skin.

I blinked against the change in light—it was brighter in here and smelled like everything savory and delicious in the universe, and my stomach reminded me that I hadn't eaten in a really long time.

Long tables and benches were littered with vials and glass bottles and metal scales and jars of seed-looking things as well as liquids, some of which bubbled. Behind a bank of steaming blue fluid stood a man taller and leaner than anyone I'd ever seen. His night-dark hair was glossy in the bright lights, reflecting the blue of the fluid, and his laser-green eyes were tip-tilted and incinerating in their intensity. The first word that floated into my mind when I looked at him was *slinky*.

Which was exactly descriptive of the smile that eased onto his face. "Oh, my brother, what delicacy have you brought me this time?"

Those breaths I'd been monitoring and modulating? Stopped. Instantly. I caught my bottom lip between my teeth.

"She is a Bianca," Nox said. "Do not eat her."

The sleek one with the black hair rolled his eyes. "You know I only do that on the day of rest."

Nox laughed, and I let out the breath I held. Oh, they were joking. Yes, he'd said Astor was off, but he hadn't said cannibal. Surely this was a joke. I'd known Nox for half a second, but he wouldn't have brought me here after saving my life just to eat me. Right?

"Bianca." Astor smiled, and it lit up his face. He looked... less severe. "Who do you belong to? What faction has Nox stolen you from that he is now afraid to tell Torrin about so that he brings you here to me instead?"

Nox shook his head, dropping his bag on the couch before he threw himself down beside it. "See? I told you. He's smart."

Okay. Astor was smart. Maybe he could help me, or at least understand what I said to him. "My name is Bianca. Nox didn't steal me. He saved me, actually." I was speaking slowly, as though if I enunciated every word, he would simply be able to make sense of what I said based on the effort alone. I held out my hands to show him. "Treated my burns. I was in a crash." I pointed at the ceiling. "The spaceship I was traveling on fell out of its trajectory. I don't know why. It crashed. I survived. I'm here. I need to get home."

Astor looked at Nox, who nodded. "I found her in flames. There is wreckage. Right where the battle will be fought. That's all I know."

The black-haired man shrugged. "Then one of two things has happened. She is either insane—and we know that happens with some of the factions, with the way they abuse women—or she is a trap. Decide which one she is and turn her over to my brother."

Nox stared at Astor for a long moment. "Just one problem." He nodded toward me again. "She has no markings. None. She has smooth, unmarred skin. No numbers. No tats. Nothing."

This seemed to get his attention. "Let me see your arm. Everyone, even the most remote tribes, are marked at birth. It is the way. Everywhere."

"I know." Nox threw his hands in the air. "I'm not stupid."

Astor didn't so much as wait for me to roll my sleeves up as grabbed my arm and did it for me. His gaze scanned up and down my arm from my wrist to my elbow and back again three times. "This makes no sense. How do you not have the marks, girl? Speak to me."

I yanked my arm back and stumbled in the process. I might have gone straight backwards into the table with all the vials if he hadn't caught me.

I breathed heavily, which was not a great sign for me.

"Easy." Nox was on his feet and rushing over to us. "He isn't going to hurt you."

After a long beat, Astor spoke again. "Are you okay?"

I stepped back, pulling my arm free. I was great at pretending to be fine. "I...I don't have whatever mark you want to see because I'm not from here. I need to get back to my people. Okay? Can you help me do that?"

They exchanged a look.

"I'm not crazy," I repeated. "I'm just lost and hurt and tired and confused and...hungry." Somewhere in the middle of that litany, I started crying again. This day was turning out to be an unending nightmare, and I just wanted to wake up. Enough trying to make the best out of every hellish thing the cosmos threw my way. I was done, so done. So...pissed.

Suddenly, I was also sitting down. Where had the chair come from? A cup of something cool and refreshing was offered—clearly from the same magical place—and held to my mouth so I wouldn't have to grasp it with my injured hands. It smelled vaguely minty, and although drinking strange things proffered by men was generally on my nope-not-ever list, I did it anyway. I leaned forward and gulped down the better-than-water—and how'd they even do that?—stuff, hiccupped, and kept right on sobbing.

Someone touched my shoulder blade, and when I didn't flinch away, the slight pinpoint of pressure became a soothing circle, working calm into my sore back.

"So you see, we've something of a conundrum," Nox said.

"Tell me something that isn't blazingly obvious," Astor replied. Oddly, he was the one stroking my back. Not Nox. Huh. Nox paced distractedly around the laboratory-like room, and Astor went on, "Torrin will assume she's some kind of Reamer trap, and he will be right to think it. Protecting us, that's what leaders do."

"I know, but she literally fell out of the sky."

"Did you see it? The crash? Tell me everything."

"I saw only from a distance at first. As you know, I had the watch while we were preparing for the battle, and I spotted Reamer scouts swarming in that area. A fire lit up the horizon, and I went to investigate, but the Reamers got there first. I waited for them to clear out and then approached. They had picked over the wreckage and took everything of value, all the larger pieces of metal and material—and all of the wires and such, because I know you will ask—and then apparently, they set fire to the rest." He looked at me when he said that last bit.

Because that was me. The stuff of no value left behind. The stuff good only to be burned.

Nox met my eyes with his gentle brown gaze. "I am thankful they thought you dead. I only wish I had gotten to the site sooner—before you woke to such horror."

The circles on my back widened, became slower. My panic had lessened, too. Was I also thankful? Being captured by Reamers still sounded terrifying, and I hadn't forgotten the "deplorable uses" comment. But if they hadn't discarded me, maybe they wouldn't have burnt me, either. Maybe I would be whole and safe. I wondered if the Reamers had better technology or understanding of the universe. The fact that they took electronics from the wreckage implied some level of tech. Could they get me home? But did I sincerely want to throw in my lot with violent unknown aliens on the off chance they could contact Brent and the Union?

Or just stay here in this cool, simple place with its cool, minty water and let these two take care of me?

"Hmm." Astor was still drawing comforting patterns on my back, but he didn't sound convinced.

"We have been tracking them for a season, and they have shown no sign of having flying units," said Nox.

"What if this was the first, albeit unsuccessful, test of one?"

"That makes no sense. Why would they have left her behind? A female, unclaimed, unnumbered?"

"Dead," I reminded them. "I must have looked dead. Before my ship crashed, I strapped myself into impact webbing, which is probably the only reason I survived. But whoever found me first disentangled me from it, and when I didn't respond or wake up, they probably assumed I was dead."

The two men exchanged a look again, and it was cooler than underground air.

"Also, they didn't take all the, er, wires and metals." I held up one arm, the one with the broken holowatch. "They left this."

Astor instantly stopped rubbing my back and grabbed my wrist. "What is this?"

"It's my holowatch. We could fix it and contact my brother. He'll come get me. Then you'll be done with me." I smiled. "Can you fix this?"

"I've never seen anything like this."

A knock pounded on the door and they both stilled. Nox stepped forward. In a hushed voice, he said, "Are you expecting anyone?"

"I'm never expecting anyone." Astor's reply was equally as quiet. "Here. Take her to the back."

CHAPTER TWO

Nox grabbed my hand and pulled me with him toward the back of whatever this crazy place was. I looked around. It turned out to be a bedroom. In fact, the whole thing looked like some kind of bunker with the front serving as a living room, kitchen, and lab and the back as this tiny bedroom. This was how he lived?

Seeing me stare, Nox shrugged. "He's Torrin's brother. That gets him more space than the rest of us."

This was more space than the rest of them got? This was the tiniest home I'd ever seen.

"It's okay," Astor shouted. "It's Mattis. We're safe."

"And what"—a man appeared in the doorway a second later—"are you people doing that you are nervous about discovery? Ah...I see. You have a new female, Nox? How unusual for you. When was the last one? Five? Six years ago?" He sauntered toward me. "Pray tell, new female, what do you charge, and do you offer group rates?"

Astor grabbed him by the ear and pulled him back. "The female has a name, and she is not a whore."

The new man—Mattis—had sun-bleached hair and bright

green eyes, and he winced and shouted as Astor tugged him back into the main room. "Ow. Okay. Stop. Apologies. I just assumed. I'd never seen her before, so she can't be high ranked. Where did she come from? Stop, damnit."

Astor let go of his ear. "That is what we are trying to determine. Bianca, come back here and show me what is on your wrist again."

Nox sighed. "Bianca, this is Mattis. He owns the bar in our City-State. I'm not sure what he is doing out of his bar on this fine day, considering he is never short of patrons."

Rubbing his ear, Mattis sat on Astor's couch. "Actually, I came to see if Astor had heard from you, Nox. I heard there was a huge Reamer presence and got worried you might have gotten yourself killed. I was going to see if Astor wanted to look for you with me."

Nox motioned at the three of them. "These are my friends. The two of them. If it had been anyone else at the door, we'd have had more trouble. Bianca, would you mind showing Mattis your arm? That way, he can comprehend what we're talking about. I do plan on taking her to Torrin, Mattis. I'm just... Well, you'll see."

I held out my arm for Mattis to see. What was the deal with these numbers? What was I supposed to have, and why did they matter?

The man who'd wanted to pay me, presumably for sex, widened his eyes. "Shit."

Astor hit him. "Language. Bianca, please, your wrist device."

He indicated my holowatch. It was broken, and any expectation I had that it might ever work plummeted. Wherever I'd crashed, it was like stepping into a past with no technology that I recognized and a population of men who made no sense at all. Even if they were all three ridiculously, ruggedly handsome in a slightly dirty, unkempt sort of a way.

They all smelled clean. It was just the dust in the air that clearly got all over everything.

I unclasped my broken watch and handed it to Astor, and his face lit up in a smile. "Here. I will return your gift with another gift." He rushed to the other room and came back with a thermos that he put in my hand. "It keeps things cold or warm."

Mattis was on his feet. "I've been trying to trade you for that for years. And...how does she not have designation?"

Nox rolled his eyes. "This again..."

"That's what you get for bringing her here first instead of straight to Torrin. You have to re-explain it to everyone," said Astor. "Not that I'm criticizing you."

"Nah, he wouldn't," Mattis chimed in. "I mean, who'd criticize a man for bringing a beautiful, unmarked, unowned female to an unoccupied bedroom?"

An *injured*, unowned, unmarked woman, I almost snapped out loud, but the other word gave me a slight pause. *Beautiful.* I'd been described lots of ways—clever, defective, privileged, tough, brave—but I couldn't think of a time when someone had called me beautiful. It seemed like such an old-fashioned term. No one in the Union defined their worth by physical beauty anymore, and I guess when we all moved past that, we stopped mentioning it to each other. Which meant that I was completely unprepared for the feeling such an offhand compliment sparked inside my chest.

My body still ached, and I was still tired and confused and a little scared, but I wasn't scared specifically of these guys anymore, not even Mattis, despite his swagger. Here, in this room, I felt...valued? I glanced down at the thermos—Astor's prized gift.

"She's hurt," Nox said in his gentle voice, though with an edge to it now, "from the crash. So perhaps you should delay any aggressive wooing until after she is fully healed and rested."

Like *beautiful*, the word *woo* was old and long unused. It also produced a similar giddy effect inside my body, like a silent, delighted giggle erupted there and could not be stifled. I knew all these words, mostly from poetry, from the classics and ancients. I didn't recognize the feeling they evoked at all, but I wanted to examine it.

Mattis looked abashed, which was kind of difficult for a man who was so large and scruffy and...wild. He reminded me of a bear variant I'd once seen at the free habitat on Darny-sis. He could probably be just as dangerous, but there was something about him that made you want to pet him. Or snuggle.

"Oh, you don't have to delay all that long," Astor said smugly.

Nox frowned. "Yes, he does..."

Mattis made a wordless noise of protest, but Astor gestured toward my lap. Or rather, toward the thermos I was still clutching between both of my hands.

"You used my calathari salve on her as soon as the burns happened, right?" he asked Nox, who nodded. "Well then, have a look."

I flipped my hands over so they could see, and sure enough, they were no longer injured. Even our most modern burn methods didn't heal skin that fast. "How did you do that?"

Nox elbowed Astor. "He's spent his life learning all about the plants and herbs on this planet. He can do amazing things."

"Don't get him wrong, he only started doing it as a means of trying to figure out which ones were safe and would make him high." Mattis laughed.

Astor shot him a look before he turned his attention back

to me. "For what it is worth, Bianca, I don't think you're a Reamer spy."

Mattis shook his head. "Who thought that? Look at her skin. She's been taken care of. You know what they do to their women. Who do you belong to?"

I swallowed. "I don't want to know what the Reamers do. I know that the things I say to you don't make sense, but I don't belong to anyone. I am just my own person. I live with my brother, Brent. Or I used to. I am going to have to again, shortly. I'm having... Never mind." They didn't need to know about my heart issue or why it was forcing me to leave my job and live with my brother like he was my parent and not my twin.

"You're right." Mattis sighed. "It makes no sense. So now what?" The last question was not directed to me.

Astor scrunched up his face. "We take her to my brother. What choice do we have?"

Nox nodded. "I'll go. I hoped...well, I took a shot there might be another way."

Dread pooled in my stomach. "That's Torrin, right? The one you guys keep avoiding. The one you think might hurt me."

"I hope not," Astor and Mattis said at the same time.

"And he might do that because he might think I'm a Reamer spy? Even after you explain to him, Nox, that you found me."

He linked my fingers with his. "I'm going to be honest with you. I believe you've come from the sky, but most of our people will not. The idea...it's too much, I think, for most people. Whether or not Torrin believes will greatly depend on what kind of day he is having. We all grew up together, and we live by his protection as we once did by his father's."

Astor laughed. "Better him than me. Can you imagine if you had to live by mine?" He held up two fingers. "He was born two minutes before I was, and then our mother perished."

I gaped at him. "I'm a twin, too." I put my hand over my heart as joy flooded me. There were so few twins out there in the universe. We were always an oddity wherever we went. "I'm sorry about your mother."

"Hard enough to live through one baby, let alone two." He shrugged, but there was an edge to the way he held his back now, the stiffening of his spine that spoke more than the words he said.

I reached out to touch his arm. "I lost my parents, too." I supposed it didn't really matter now. "And Torrin has great responsibilities and he might be in a foul mood, which could mean I'm in big trouble."

Astor swung around. "I don't suppose you've decided to marry Dreama? That would greatly improve his mood."

Mattis paled. "Your older sister does not wish to marry me any more than I wish to marry her, and I wish you'd stop suggesting it. I'm afraid she might kill me in my sleep if I were to agree to it."

"Getting Dreama out of his house would put Torrin in a much better frame of mind. Nox? You?"

He shook his head fast. "That was never an option. Dreama hates me. Ever since the incident with the crossbow."

"Ah, yes. She almost lost that toe. Then there is nothing for it. We go to Torrin, and we hope. Perhaps it's a good day. It is almost battle time, and that always puts him in a good mood. We go and we see." He touched the side of my face. His fingers were callused, but they felt nice there. "Bianca, who fell from the sky, you are very unexpected."

They all went with me, like a ring of protectors—Mattis, Astor, and Nox. They didn't appear to be armed, and Nox left his bag of magical healing stuff behind. I didn't know how far the protection of their mere physical existence would extend or whether they'd seriously intervene if Torrin decided I was a problem he didn't have time for, but their gesture was nice.

After the crude—and, let's face it, backwards—structures and vehicles I'd encountered on this planet so far, I almost expected Torrin to lounge half-naked atop a throne made of antlers with a bunch of beast hides at his feet. And then of course, being me, I felt bad for making such assumptions.

Well, about the antlers and beast hides. If he looked anything like his brother, the half-nakedness might be something to see.

As it turned out, I wasn't entirely wrong about Torrin's quarters. It wasn't a chamber of governance or a throne room proper, just another rough-hewn corridor with a plain metal door at the end. Only this time, when Mattis tapped out his special secret-code knock, we weren't called inside by a disembodied voice in the room beyond. Instead, we were met with a guard.

Okay, not a guard. A warrior. Female, almost as tall as Astor, wearing some sort of animal leathers and armed to the teeth. I counted a spear and three knives on her person, and those were just the weapons I could see. Thank the ancient and holy ones she didn't have access to plasma weapons.

Could this be Dreama of the crossbow toe incident?

"About time you returned from your scouting, Nox," she said. "He's been waiting for your report. I'd get right in there if I were you."

Her gaze glided over Astor, deepened into a slight frown

when she saw Mattis, and went full grumpy when she beheld me.

"What the fuck is this?"

"A who, not a what," said Astor, grinning like this was the best prank ever, which, considering they were most likely siblings, it probably qualified. "Our guest is called Bianca, and though she is currently unnumbered and unclaimed, as far as you and your knives are concerned, she's under my protection."

"All our protection," Nox added. He hadn't gone into the room yet and still stood with the rest of us out in the corridor. Mattis loomed there, too.

I wanted to hug them all for standing with me and sticking up for me.

Dreama scanned me from the top of my hair to the soles of my feet, and I'm pretty sure she missed nothing, including the half-burned, half-missing pants. And my so-scandalously unmarked arms.

If Torrin was the leader of this group, and she was his older sister, that would make her some kind of princess, right? Well, I might not know a whole bunch of primitive warrior women with crossbow issues, but I knew how to greet hereditary royalty.

Right there in the dirt-delved tunnel of this filthy backwater planet, I inclined my head and sank into a deep curtsey. The last time I'd done this had been for a planetary Empress. That had been two years earlier, but it felt like a lifetime.

A strong hand yanked me up. Nox shook his head fast. "Don't do that. You could easily be killed in such a vulnerable position."

My cheeks heated up. They were probably bright red. My pale skin tended to lend itself to that kind of thing happening. My mother had been a redhead, and although neither Brent nor I had inherited her hair color, I still had the pale,

pale skin that showed every moment of embarrassment I ever felt.

"I was trying to be polite. She's a...princess, right? That's what you do for royalty."

Astor laughed. "You didn't do that to me. Wouldn't that logic also make me deserving of your bows?"

Dreama hit her brother straight in the arm. He jumped, rubbing the spot. She turned to me, rolling her eyes as if to apologize for her boorish brother. "Thank you for trying to be polite, Bianca. Thank you for trying to be respectful. But we're very casual here, very uninterested in most protocols. Where did these two dig you up?"

But Mattis didn't seem interested in a long chit chat with Dreama. He placed his hand on the small of my back and nudged me forward. "Moving along. Come."

Instead of being offended, Dreama threw her head back, laughing. "What's the matter, Mattis? Afraid we're about to get married?"

Was that even a possibility? If so, I didn't really see what the problem would be. Dreama was strong—clearly a trait that was valued here—and funny, and she seemed to be kind. Why not marry her? I supposed that was something I really shouldn't ask, given my current circumstances.

Still, she had been nice to me, and Astor had as well. Maybe Torrin wouldn't be so bad.

I let my guard down just a little and dared to hope this would all turn out to be a short, peaceful, temporary adventure.

Big mistake.

CHAPTER THREE

We found Torrin, the leader and de-facto king of the City-State, sitting on a throne made of bones with heads hanging all over the room, like some kind of shrine to death. My worst nightmare could not have made up such a scene. *This* was the man who would decide my fate? For a second, I couldn't breathe. My chest tightened, and I rubbed it, fast. The pain lessened, but the man who sat on the throne of bones, leaning forward so that his elbows were on his knees, didn't miss the movement. If anything, he was even more intimidating than his gory, barbarian throne, with an aura of power that made me want to either whimper or run. Or just keep looking at him, because for all his imposing presence, he was also incredibly attractive.

His dark gaze seemed to track me instantly.

I doubted he ever missed anything. Like his brother and sister, he had jet-black hair, but unlike his siblings, his eyes seemed to match.

The room wasn't solely decorated with heads. There were also weapons and bones piled around and a cage in the corner.

Empty, but still...a cage. What kind of leader sat on a skull throne and kept a cage handy?

"Nox." Torrin's voice boomed through the hallway. Although he addressed Nox, he continued to stare at me. Shivers ran through my body, followed by a heat I couldn't make sense of. What was wrong with me? "I am glad to see you are not dead. I see you have collected a group to come visit me today. I expected you hours ago, and you know how I worry, my friend. Who have you brought me?"

Nox performed the same introduction he had for the others—my name, where he found me, my "designation" as unclaimed and unnumbered. It was starting to get a little annoying, honestly. I still didn't know why the number was such a big deal, and the whole notion of claiming ownership of another human person offended my modern sensibilities. But deep breathing, right. These people clearly weren't modern. Possibly weren't even sensible—exhibit A, this room full of weapons and skeletal remains.

Throughout Nox's introduction and explanation, I tried to keep my chin up, projecting strength and confidence. I also tried to hold Torrin's black-eyed gaze, but that was harder. He didn't just look at me as if he saw everything about me. He looked like he saw into me, into my past and my motives and my... Brent would go on about souls and cosmic connections at this point, and I wasn't quite there. Still, the intensity of that stare was excruciating. I wanted to hide from the implicit judgment of it, even though I hadn't done anything wrong.

"Thank you," Torrin told Nox. "Kaden returned from his patrol in a timelier manner and confirms your account of the crash. However, he then followed the Reamers back to the base they had chosen for their muster. Apparently, their arrival was met with some excitement, to the point that the entire base cleared out immediately. They even left their food stores and medical supplies behind. The entire Reamer war party has returned over the mountains and sent word by slave messenger that they are canceling their participation in the seasonal battles."

Dreama made a sound like a growl. "They can't do that. It's tradition."

"Well, if they concede, we can claim all their ground, right? So go us!" said Astor, who I was beginning to believe could be counted on to take literally nothing seriously.

"I don't think he's implying concession," Mattis said in a slow voice. "Are you thinking that they will besiege us here, in our fort?"

"They wouldn't dare," said Dreama, dropping one hand to a sheath.

Torrin was still looking straight at me. He hadn't stopped the whole time others were speaking. I'm not sure when I started trembling, but it grew difficult to hold my mouth firm. I didn't dare attempt to speak.

"Bianca," he said in a deceptively calm voice. "What exactly was on board your sky transport?"

I swallowed. "Well...it's, was, a huge ship carrying me and at least two dozen others across the galaxy. Sorry, not literally across it. You don't want hyperbole right now. Sure. It was taking us several light years from one planet to another."

He tilted his head. "Other than people. What was it carrying?"

"Luggage." I'd had a lot of clothes. "Food. Technological things."

He nodded. "Weapons?"

I opened and closed my mouth. "All ships carry weapons. Space pirating is a rare thing but not unheard of. And then there are ungodly factions that do not worship the holy ones and always want to go to war." They particularly hated my brother, which made sense because he particularly hated them. He and his faction in the Union wanted them all killed. It was a brutal, bloody mess. Convert to our way of thinking or get out. I hated every second I had to hear about it. Not that I'd tell him that. I'd probably be sent to do penance and some kind of religious therapy if I did.

One of the books on the floor caught my gaze, and I gasped. "Is that...*The Lady Mardigral and the Third Dance of Melbey*?"

Everyone looked where I pointed. Yes, it was. I could see the title from where I stood. That was my favorite book when I was a teenager. A classic text. We used to teach it in school before it was determined only religious texts were to be taught there, effectively putting me out of a job.

Torrin rose from his scary throne. "Can you read that? You recognize it?"

"Yes, and you know what that means? If you have it, then you're not so far outside of Union space. I mean...we must not be too far if you have it?"

He picked up the book and brought it to me. "These words? You can actually read them?"

"Of course."

Something was going on here, and I had no idea what. Everyone stared at me with open mouths and no words coming out of them, except Torrin, who was so still I couldn't see him move at all.

"These are ancient texts. Not one of us can read them. The language is lost. We hold on to them to honor our ancestors. Reading is a skill long gone."

Now it was my turn to stare. "What?"

He turned to Nox. "Make arrangements to raid the Reamers. We're going to follow them and take their weapons before they can use them on us or blow the entire quadrant to smithereens. I want a full-scale attack plan by morning. We are going with our new secret weapon."

Next to me Nox nodded. "My lord, as you say."

"Your new secret weapon?" Astor's face was serious, as though he was now made of stone. "You mean Bianca."

Torrin nodded. "Yes. The Reamers have the weapons, but they won't know how to use them. She will. Mattis, get the girl branded. She now belongs to me. And no one is to know she was ever anything but mine. Dreama, I trust you to make the questions go away."

"How do you expect me to do that?" She snorted and looked around.

"Manage it." A muscle ticked in his jaw. "Mattis, after you're done, bring her back to my quarters. She'll stay there with me, where I can watch her to make sure she isn't up to some trickery."

Astor shook his head. "I'm not willing to give her to you, brother."

All movement stopped, and Torrin turned around. "Excuse me?"

"I'm making a claim on the girl Bianca. I wouldn't be surprised if Nox and Mattis are as well."

Nox looked from one brother to the other, his uncertainty obvious. It occurred to me that he was junior to the rest of them, either younger or lower born, maybe both. Oh sure, they liked him and respected him, but he wouldn't have been able to argue successfully against Torrin on his own. This was why he'd brought me to Astor first, to prevent me from going into Torrin's cage and becoming his weapon, or worse. But Nox also had a duty to the war planning, and a loyalty to his leader, which was pretty obvious by his unquestioning acceptance of Torrin's commands. Poor conflicted Nox, I really did get the sense that he wanted to do what was right. Sometimes, the world and our circumstances made that impossible.

Torrin's mouth hardened when he turned to Astor. "Must

you always lead with your heart, little brother? It's bad tactics."

"Must you always lead with tactics," Astor flung back, "to the exclusion of your humanity? Claiming a woman only to throw her at our enemies is not just bad logic, it's cruel. She has more value than that, and you know it."

I quickly revised my earlier opinion of Astor. He might have been a tad silly and a natural trickster, but clearly there were some things he took deadly seriously. Lucky for me, the safety of females appeared to be one of those things. I wondered if it had something to do with his mother or his sister. Or a lover?

"Look, I don't have time for your sentimental nonsense," said Torrin. "I do not claim this woman in expectation of setting up household or breeding her. I only want to protect our people, and she can make that happen. If she is useful as I suspect and we survive this battle, you can do whatever you wish with her. I won't stop you. But right now, you will stand down."

"Swear it," Astor said, not moving, "on the bones of our fathers, after the battle, you will cede her to me. There will be no use of her person until that time, only of her knowledge."

"And in return, little brother, what will you give me?"

Nox's eyes were glass green and just as hard. "Exactly what you want."

"Say it."

Astor reached into a fold of his tunic and retrieved something that glinted in the meager light but was too small for me to see. A signet? A coin? A key? He handed it to Torrin, who took it.

"Mattis and Nox will accompany her wherever you're taking her, to ensure you don't harm her," Astor said. "You will be held to your promise."

"Oh, I'll do better than that," replied his brother, pushing past Nox and striding to the doorway and not sparing a glance back at any of them, as if he had complete confidence they would do as he commanded. "I'm putting all three of you in charge of her for the duration. I'll let you know when I require her and for what purpose. Don't make me regret this. Dreama, with me."

His sister hurried to catch up with him. On her way out the door, she looked over her shoulder at me. I didn't know her well enough to understand what the look she gave me meant. It wasn't alarming, just different.

Mattis took my hand. "Come. We have to get you branded and fast."

I didn't pull away. I'd be crazy to try. Where could I even go? Still, I searched for Astor before I left. "Thank you. Whatever you just did, you saved me. That much I gathered."

He nodded at me. "I'll see you soon."

We were a distance away, Mattis dragging me through the halls of Torrin's scary palace, when we ended up outside. The dust hit me in the face, and I pulled my scarf up to cover my nose and mouth. Mattis didn't bother. Maybe he was used to it. Walking with his head down, he eventually slowed his steps when he realized I wasn't keeping up.

I tugged on his hand, and he indicated that we should walk through a door. I looked around. The place was well-furnished and not much different than other bars I'd been in. Not that there had been many. Tables and chairs filled the center of the room, with the chairs currently upside down and dangling off the sides of the table.

Taking off my scarf, I had to catch my breath before speaking. "What happened back there?"

He ran his hand up my arm. "Torrin ordered me to brand you. I'm sorry. I wouldn't hurt you for anything in the world."

That part I'd understood. "Look, I handle pain very well.

I'm not thrilled about it, but it is what it is." Not to mention when I figured out how to get off this planet, I was getting the brand off first thing. Brent would probably want to pray over it. "No, the rest of it? What happened?"

"Astor and Torrin?" He sucked in an audible breath. "Torrin is having me brand you with his numbers. That means that you will have the City-State on you here." He indicated where that would go. "And Torrin's number beneath it. Astor took exception to that, and Torrin promised to turn you over to him afterwards, which I suppose will mean you will have to have it changed. But that won't be hard. Torrin has a zero and Astor is an eight. Adding the line. That's lucky."

We were getting off track. "What does it mean that I'm Torrin's number?"

He blinked. "You belong to him. You are his woman."

"In what sense?"

Mattis ran a hand through his hair. "In every sense. Please don't tell me that you don't know what—"

I held up my hand. "I know."

"You will be safe." He put his hand on my cheek, cupping it. "Astor had Torrin swear you would not be harmed, and in return, Astor gave him his sacred jewel. That is in an unbreakable oath between them. Because of Astor's gesture, you are under the protection of the City-State, and no outsider may harm you."

I had to understand... I had to somehow get a handle on this, before the reality knocked me on my rear and I couldn't get up. This was a primitive place. Torrin had heads hanging from the ceiling, he sat on bones, and they couldn't read books. They said *woo* and *beautiful*. All of them hated monsters called Reamers, and yet it was a real planet. Their planet. Of course they'd have customs different from what I knew or was comfortable with.

"Mattis..." I forced my breathing to slow. "What happens

to women here? I see that Dreama is a warrior. Do women and men fight together?"

Instead of speaking, he took my hand and showed me the street. "Dreama is indulged because she is Torrin's sister. She guards him, but she has never seen battle, and never will. Women have many roles. They cook, they clean, they tend to the men in their lives. And they..." He pointed down the street. "They sell their bodies. The whorehouses on this street are high-priced. The women live well."

A headache formed between my eyes. Whorehouses? Premarital sex? That was...unheard of. "They have clients like you? You asked me how much I charged."

"My apologies. I...I shouldn't have said that." He put his hand on my waist. "I will take care of you. I promise."

He hadn't finished what he was going to say to me. "And further down the road? What happens to those women?"

His voice was soft. "We are often at war. When we don't win, they don't live very long."

I'd been keeping it together, mostly. But tears flooded my eyes and fell down my cheeks. I never thought I would miss Brent, but I did. Oh...how I did. What was this horrible place, and what had I done to the holy ones to deserve this?

CHAPTER FOUR

When I was younger and my immune system was fighting so hard my heart couldn't keep up—that's how my mother had described it—I often had to be isolated, which meant a lot of downtime, alone time. I spent a lot of that time reading and learning, of course. Also, when my wardens and doctors and teachers weren't around to see, I watched sensory vids. Tons of them, on every topic imaginable. I knew I'd never climb a mountain or pilot a star fighter through planetary ice rings, but I ached to know what those things were like, what they *felt* like, and sensory vids eased that yearning a little.

When I was fifteen and in an especially rebellious phase, I watched a whole lifetime of itinerant pan-galactic artists, true heathens and hedonists, musicians and dancers and resistors of everything the Union stood for, and all-ancients, how I wanted to be one of them.

Even when they marked their bodies. The pain and patience they endured to get those tattoos and piercings and brandings wasn't a small thing. It was real pain, a thing I understood very well. But when I endured a surgical procedure or a chemical treatment, often the only result was that I didn't get sicker or weaker.

When those pan-galactic heathens went in for body alteration, the result was often pretty, always liberating. Always courageous.

Only later did I hear that those troupe members had been "reclaimed" by the enforcers and made to see the error of their ways. All of the beauty on their bodies had been scoured off, repaired by forced procedures.

But in the dingy room behind Mattis' bar, squeezing a wad of soft cloth in my fist while he burned the shapes into my skin, I remembered the beauty of those black-market sensory vids. And I remembered also how much I had wanted to live them.

At last, he leaned back and hung the brand on a rack to cool. He dipped a length of soft green cloth into a bowl and then held it against the raw welt on my arm.

"I'm sorry, Bianca," he said for maybe the hundredth time.

"Please don't be. The heat burned past the nerve endings almost right away, and there weren't a whole lot there to begin with. Not like my hands earlier." I paused and asked, "Can I see?"

He moved the cloth away, and I peered down. The mutilation was too red and angry to be discernible yet, but I could see where it had taken skill. The figure for their City-State was a stylized pack of beasts in profile.

"What does it mean? The figure?"

Mattis looked ready to put the wet cloth back over my arm, but I waved him off. I couldn't stop staring at it.

"It's the pack, the brotherhood. See how we're in a circle and connected? It means we're unbreakable as long as we are together."

"But they're facing the wrong way," I said. "Shouldn't they be facing out, back to back?"

"No. When it heals, you'll see the shape of the void in the center. You can sort of make it out, see how it's like a flower? Like the white blooms on the calathari plants. That's what they are all focused on, the thing they protect. There's only one good, fertile piece of land on this rock, and clans fight for the right to care for it for a season."

"You fight over a piece of ground? When you could be protecting your women instead?"

His smile was fast. "That is how we protect our women. We can't feed them if we can't grow anything. A good portion of our clan that are currently acting as military are actually farmers. When we beat the others in the battle, they drop their weapons and care for the land for the season. Then the winter comes, we step away and do it again next year."

This was the strangest concept I'd ever heard. Mattis readied another brand. This one would have a bunch of numbers on it; the last one would represent Torrin. They couldn't read, but numbers they understood perfectly.

"I'm sorry to do this again."

I waved my other hand. "You guys do this as children?"

He held out his own arm. "Everyone gets the City-State markings. Then the boys get their numbers right away. The women get theirs when they marry to match their husband's or plural husbands. Sometimes, a woman has more than one. That usually has to do with an alliance of families. Like Astor and Torrin have the same father, but they have a different one from Dreama. Together, they were quite a force to be reckoned with."

He pressed the marking down on me, and my mind drifted away. Pain did this to me. I'd had so many years being poked and prodded. It was easier to simply travel in my mind, even when there weren't vids to watch.

"What was your life? In the stars?" Mattis caught my

attention, and I forced my eyes to focus on his handsome face.

"Lonely." I would never have given that answer to someone back home, but I might as well be honest here. Really, what did I have to lose?

He nodded. "It is easy to be lonely, even in a crowd."

Finished with the brand, he set it aside. I stared down at the wound again. Funny, it looked remarkably like a prison brand. I'd seen them on the men who my brother helped rehabilitate by coming back to the fold after they served their time. By that, he meant they got to work in jobs serving others the rest of their lives while everyone judged them.

I was getting downright controversial in my thinking.

"Thank you."

Mattis nodded. "I am to help take care of you. That is what Torrin said. I've been trying to figure out how to do that. I never thought to have a woman who would need my help."

"Why not? You own your own business. You have a close relationship with Torrin. Or maybe everyone does?" He shook his head, meaning I was right, not everyone did. "I'd think you were a catch."

Mattis linked his hands together. "I am fortunate, but my father and mother were not highly thought of. They gave in to the madness. Tried to kill others. In the end, they had to be killed. I am not sought after for family life." His smile was fast. "The madness tends to breed out."

"But that's terrible. Partnerships, marriages, are about more than creating offspring, they're also..." His expression was so shocked, I had to trail off. Back up. Rethink. This world and its customs were turning everything I understood upside down. "So wait, if you claimed a woman or became one of her, um, husbands, you would be required to produce children with her?"

"Where you are from, males and females don't do this? They don't have sex?" That was real horror in his voice.

It was everything I could manage not to burst out laughing. "No, we do. Or rather, married people do. And yes, sometimes they have kids, when the timing is right. But if both partners aren't ready or they have genetic concerns, they can delay conception or alter the fetal DNA or... You don't do any of that."

It wasn't really a question, but Mattis shook his head anyway. No reliable contraception here and no genetic engineering. Well then. Nothing like a lack of technology to throw all my natural defects into stark relief.

"It's better for people like me, with madness in our line, to avoid having children," he said.

"Probably same for me," I said without thinking.

"Why? You said your parents died. Were they also put down for the safety of your clan?"

I wished I could go back and tell five-moments-ago me to keep her mouth shut. This wasn't the kind of place where I could feel safe talking about my medical fragility. If Torrin thought I wasn't good for claiming or breeding or whatever, I could find myself down the street and working on my back for a living.

Carefully, I avoided his question. "My mother and father died when rebels blew up their starship, their, err, sky transport. To my knowledge, there wasn't anything wrong with my parents' minds."

Except, maybe, that they'd supported and possibly engineered the subjugation of those rebels' world. I hadn't been raised to believe conquering and converting planets and bringing their ignorant populations into civilization and Union was madness, but some people out there certainly considered it as such. The rebels who killed my parents almost certainly did.

"Are you tired?" Mattis asked, out of nowhere.

"What?"

"You yawned."

I did? "I guess I probably am. And if I'm not, I should be. I've been running on adrenaline since I woke up from the crash. How long ago was that? Ack, time is a thing here, right?"

Mattis raised an eyebrow to indicate that I was acting a little strange, and then I raised one right back, and suddenly we were laughing together, for no reason at all. It felt a little like I was losing my mind, but this particular descent into madness felt...nice? Yeah. I wasn't getting home soon, that much was becoming obvious, but also, there were kind people here who had sworn to help me and take care of me, and that was something. Maybe I could rest and reset and let some of this terror go. Maybe...

"Mattis? Are we opening tonight? And who's back there with you?" called a voice from the front of the bar. All that laughter and relief froze in my mouth.

He squeezed my leg. "It's okay. He's as safe as they come. You will see. Actually, he is Nox's grandfather." He turned his head to shout behind him. "Cannon, I am opening. Just delayed. And here with me is Torrin's woman, Bianca."

A man rushed into the room. He was old, gray-haired, with weathered skin, and he wore an eyepatch over his left eye. For a long moment, he stared at us.

"Bianca, this is Nox's grandfather, Cannon. Sir, your grandson saved our leader's woman's life today. I think you can expect many rewards for his doing so."

As I rose to my feet, I tried to remember the last time I'd seen anyone's grandfather. Or grandmother for that matter. We didn't put much stock in the elderly playing a role in our lives. For the most part, we sent the old or infirm to live in colonies alone, and if they were really sick, we euthanized them. It was a small miracle and only my brother's intervention that had kept me alive this long.

He bowed his head. "Forgive me, highness. I didn't know, and we are informal with Mattis. I should watch that."

Mattis waved his hand. "Don't you dare start worrying about things like rank. Help me get the chairs down?" He spoke to Cannon and then winked at me. "Be careful, Bianca, Cannon has great stories. If you talk too much to him, you will lose track of the night."

The old man blushed. "I will help with the chairs after I find the broom. I can't locate it anywhere."

Mattis nodded. "You might try the closet in the back."

He waited until Cannon disappeared before he turned to me. "The Reamers captured him ten years ago. Tortured him. Took his left eye. And when he did manage to escape and come back, his mind was gone as well. Simple now. He's a huge help to me." He took my hand, leading me toward the direction Cannon had walked. "If you go upstairs you will find three rooms. One is a washroom. We have running water right now. Take advantage. It comes and goes with the seasonal floods. And two bedrooms. Make yourself comfortable. Sleep, if you can. It will be noisy. But maybe you can anyway, if you are tired enough."

I nodded at him. "Thank you. For everything."

"Does your arm hurt badly? I can give you a cream."

I'd already forgotten it. "No, I'm fine."

His smile was huge. "You're like something from a dream. Falling from the sky. So beautiful. Smart. Interesting. I don't believe in signs. Or prophecy. But maybe you are an indication that things are going to get better."

No one had ever thought I was that, ever. I'd been a curse for my parents, being born sick. Brent loved me. We were twins. There was a bond there, even if every year it strained more and more, but even he had never referred to me as a good omen. "Thank you for your kind words. Your hospitality. And being sort of a miracle to me. All of you. Sounds like I could have fallen into the hands of the Reamers."

"The Reamers." Cannon came up behind us and grabbed his head. "No. Never that. Not the Reamers. Never. Ever. No."

He rocked back and forth.

Mattis moved fast, immediately by his side. "You're right. Never them. You're safe here. I promise you. So is she. Torrin does all that he does to keep us all that way. Here, we're all safe."

See, I knew the lie here; I knew that safety was actually only a fantasy. Wisdom in the Church of the Ancients and Holies invited devotees to embrace today and make the best of it, because tomorrow was never certain. Only the ever-after, the possible and unknowable existence after death, could release us from the constant cycle of exhausting change. In other words, a good life is necessary drudgery, so find the joy in it where you can. Still, despite all my knowledge of these things, when I saw Mattis embrace this fragile, inexplicably beautiful old gentleman, Nox's granddad, I realized a fundamental truth about myself—I was willing to entertain the fantasy of safety.

I was—maybe, possibly, terrifyingly—willing to believe in a lot of blasphemy.

Also, Mattis wasn't wrong. I was exhausted. And no one was paying attention to me for once. My arm was still throbbing from the brands, but it was a good pain. I could absolutely sleep through it. I slipped out of the back room and up the stairs. As Mattis said, there were three narrow doors. I picked one, which turned out to be a tiny, cramped bedroom not unlike a starship cabin. The second door led to another bedroom, this one strewn with man-things and almost certainly Mattis' personal living space. The third was the washroom, and I did take advantage of the running water. It was delicious in every way, not to mention cool against the branding wounds.

The burns on my hands and legs had all but disappeared. How amazing was that? Astor really did have skills.

When I rolled into the pallet-like bed in Mattis' spare room, I thought my brain would recount the whirlwind of events I'd just endured or worry about the ones I was sure to face tomorrow. Instead, I thought about hands, of all things. My hands on fire, Nox's hands examining me at the crash sight, Mattis' hands gentle on the old man's bent form. The images soothed me completely, and at last, I dipped into a deep and dreamless sleep.

CHAPTER FIVE

The next few days were, as I'd expected, a flurry of activity. The war party marched out before I woke that first morning, and it pretty much drained the camp of men. Mattis, Cannon, and Astor stayed behind, and I saw Dreama a few times looking very official. Apparently, she had charge of the women, children, and elderly while the war party was away. She took her responsibilities seriously. We were all under curfew and had to be alert at all times, which Mattis complained was terrible for his pub business. Well, of course it would be.

But that didn't mean folks didn't sneak in to grab a drink whenever they thought Dreama and her guards weren't looking. Mattis was happy to help them indulge, but I noticed he watched them closely and never let them get too intoxicated to respond quickly if bad news from the battle came in.

Of interest to me was how people reacted to the brands on my arm, the first thing they tended to notice about me. Questions in their faces turned to deference and lots of muttered "highnesses." I didn't think their questions ever went away, of course, but no one dared to interrogate Torrin's claimed woman.

Which felt like a lie, because I did not consider myself Torrin's thing at all. If anything, I fit into Mattis' world, with Astor as a frequent visitor, a lot better.

And then one midday, three days after the war party marched out, a woman slipped into the bar's back room, and I could tell right away that she neither deferred to me nor came for a beverage.

I'd been wiping down ceramic mugs for Mattis but paused when she slipped into the room.

"Mattis went out to check the lists. He'll be back shortly. Drink?" I asked, though I had no idea how to mix up one of the elaborate concoctions that were Mattis' specialty.

She pointed at me. "So it's true. He's picked you. A stranger. Thrown all of it away. For you." The still unnamed woman spit on the ground in front of me.

I stared at her, my mouth falling open. In the last three days, I'd done many things I'd never imagined doing before. I'd washed dishes. Served drinks. Helped sweep the kitchen. Ate foods I'd never known existed. But being spit at now ranked among the strangest I'd ever experienced.

Where I was from, people didn't do that to me. I was Brent's sister, and he was intimidating on a good day to those who followed him, and terrifying to those who didn't. No one would have dared spit at me.

I stared at her for a long second. Amazingly, only calmness moved me now. "Sorry. Who are you?"

She narrowed her eyes. "I am Sorcha. I am Torrin's intended."

Now, it made sense. Torrin had a fiancée and, despite the fact that I'd spoken to the man exactly once, I'd taken her spot.

Pity moved me to speak. The pain she was in? It had to be

awful. "I'm so sorry this has happened to you. Please, let me try to explain. I—"

"Not another word." Astor leaned in the doorway, and Sorcha's eyes widened as she realized his presence.

He strode toward us until he stood behind me, his hand coming to the small of my back. "Bianca, Sorcha is not Torrin's intended. She has never been and never will be that. The same way that Nox will never be Dreama's. In that case, neither one of them want a relationship, and in this case, Torrin has flat out rejected the idea every time it is brought up. Seems he preferred a life of solitude and a childless, loveless existence to dealing with her."

She stomped her foot once, then twice. "How dare you speak to me like that? My father is Baron the Great. He is—"

"Overrated." Astor yawned. "Out with you, girl. Baron the so-called Great would be horrified that you came in here, yelled at Her Highness, and spoke to Torrin's brother like this. If I tell him, I imagine you'll be sent to clean out the stables for a week, and boy, after the warring party comes back, will that place stink to high heaven." He nodded toward the door. "Out."

She paled as he spoke before turning to flee from the room.

My chest tightened, and I ignored the pain. I had no medicine to take here, nothing that could help, and Astor was the closest thing they had to a doctor. For the first time in my life, if I were to have an attack, I would die. There was nothing anyone would be able to do.

I turned my attention to Astor. "Thank you. I think. I'm not sure what would have happened if you hadn't shown up."

He tilted his head. "That depends. How well do you fight?"

"Never."

"Ah, then that might have gone badly for you." He held

out his hand. "You're pale. Mattis is keeping you in this place too long. Come. I have something to show you."

He linked our hands together, and I let him lead me out the backdoor of the kitchen to the street. I hadn't been out here since I'd come to the pub. Cooler weather had swept in, blowing some of the dust from the air.

"Don't be worried," he said. "Although I choose to play a different role than a soldier, I assure you that should I be called upon to do it, I could defend us quite well."

"I hadn't thought about that at all. But...great."

His smile answered my declaration. Did Astor worry that I thought it was a problem he wasn't battling? I needed to continue learning how they did things here. They fought. They worried. They farmed. They spied. They sat on bones and hung heads from the ceiling. They drank. A lot.

We reached Torrin's quarters, and Astor took me around past the throne of bones to a back room. It had more books piled on the side. "My brother discovered you can read the old language and then didn't have you do it." He picked up a book and handed it to me. "Would you? Read it? And then maybe some time teach me to do so? I know numbers, yes. And I can make electronics bend to my will. I experiment on nature. But none of us can read. A few generations ago, the decision was made to stop doing so. I would like to know how, though. It eats at me."

I took the book he handed to me and looked at the title. *Winter Plants*. Actually, this one would be perfect for Astor.

"Yes, I can do that. I teach people to read. It's one of the few things in my life I do really well." I smiled at the book. "This one is about plants."

His eyes lit up. "You do many things really well. I can't imagine anyone adjusting as you have. And really? Plants?"

The old book's spine creaked when I opened it, and the pages were so brittle, I worried they'd come apart in my hands. This wasn't an expensive bound book, just a run-of-the-mill library antiquity. We'd had dozens like this, restored of course, in the archives of the school where I'd taught. Our everyday, working manuscripts had been all digital, but I had always loved the feel of a book in my hands, the smell of old paper and binding glue.

My heart had been stuttering on and off ever since Sorcha had come into the pub, but it settled now. On a planet full of strange things, here finally was something familiar and comfortable.

"This book is old, but the language is modern enough, post-universal lexicon at least. The whole writing system is phonetic." I pointed to the first character in the title. "The common tongue we all use now is a mish-mash of a bunch of ancient languages, but one called English used this sound, a voiced labialized velar approximant, to begin its word for *winter*. So every time you see this symbol, you read it as *w*."

Astor touched the title page almost reverently. How long his fingers were. Something fluttered inside me, and it definitely wasn't my heart. I knew what palpitations and reduced oxygen flow felt like, and this was very different. For one thing, it wasn't cold. It was warm. Very warm.

"Can you record all the characters and teach me their sounds?" he asked, not looking up.

"Of course. I'd be happy to. And in the meantime, I can read this book aloud. I think it will interest y—"

A banging on the metal door out beyond the gruesome throne room interrupted us. I couldn't discern a pattern to the knock, but somehow, Astor knew who it was. He practically ran over to the door to unlatch it. Mattis stood beyond, out in the tunnel. He was breathing hard, like he'd run the whole way here.

"Oh good, you have Bianca. We have to go. Right now."

"The lists?" Astor asked, and Mattis nodded.

Oh no. I knew what those were. Casualty lists. Mattis checked them every morning. Battles were games of numbers, he said, and we should all do the calculations to determine how the overall conflict was playing out. That sounded metaphorical, but I thought really he was just looking for names of people he cared about.

"Dead?" Astor asked in a clipped, anguished voice.

"Missing."

I closed the book but held it with me. "Who is missing?"

"Torrin and Nox."

Astor nodded, his gaze a distance away as he considered what he'd just heard. This was his brother, and yet, he didn't seem at all frantic. "That's good news actually."

I swallowed, looking between them. "How so?"

Mattis widened his eyes, lifting his forehead until it wrinkled. "Beats me. How is this good?"

"Nox will never let anything happen to Torrin and vice versa. Whatever has changed in the last years since my brother took the throne, that hasn't. We're still four kids that used to sneak into the Old Lampassess Caverns. Come on. Let me look at what happened and figure out where they've either been taken or hidden."

I followed after them. Why was it important I came?

I didn't ask, but as Mattis grabbed my arm, more of a support than a pull, he answered it anyway. "If we're about to be attacked, I want you with me, not exposed with no one around to help you."

He was so sweet. I shoved away the thought. This was very bad news, and I needed to keep whatever growing fascination I had for him and Astor under control right now. We didn't have to go far. On the other side of Torrin's quarters was a room that had maps. No writing on the maps but pictures of landscapes drawn in. Took me a minute to digest what I looked at. Water was blue. Trees were squiggly lines. Numbers were all over it.

"Who brings the reports?"

Mattis answered without looking at me, his gaze firmly on the map in front of him. "Adolescent boys training to be soldiers. They're called runners. It's actually a dangerous job. We all have to do it for a while."

Well, the men did. As far as I could tell, the women around here really did cook, clean, and fuck for money. Never in my life could I have imagined how easily I'd have thought that last phrase.

"There," Astor said, pointing. "The battle took place where we expected it. And then Torrin, according to the graph, disappeared here." He pointed to another spot. Numbers matched numbers like a children's game. It really was amazing how they'd adapted to having no literacy. They read numbers, sort of, but it was more like picture games. "So that means if Torrin isn't taken to the Reamer camp, then they are in the hidden caves below by the rivers. If he's hurt, Nox stashed him there until we bring help."

Mattis let go of my back, and I missed his comfort immediately. "Stay with Astor, Bianca. I'm going to go save the king."

He ran from the room before I could say a word.

"By himself?" I managed to ask too late.

"No, he'll grab some soldiers and go. He's only not battling because he and I are designated to protect the City-State." Astor sunk into a chair. The first visible sign this had affected him at all. My heart, figuratively and fortunately not literally at the moment, bled for him.

I walked over to him, meaning to place my hand on his back, but he pulled me onto his lap instead. His arms came around me, and he held on as though he might never let go. "If the Reamers have my brother, it's very bad news."

I stayed very still, letting him hold on. I knew this feeling, when you had to be this close to someone else, not separate, because if you did, then everything was simply too real.

"You are so different, Bianca, than anyone here. Your skin is unmarred." Well...he hadn't seen my chest and all my scars, but I wasn't going to bring that up right this second. Although the doctors swore they weren't as obvious as I thought they were. "You read. You write. You use language I've never heard. You're beautiful. Smart."

I shook my head. "Stop. I'm...fine."

He leaned back on the chair. "Stay with me tonight. With Mattis heading to battle, I don't want you in that bar alone."

The deep flutter I'd felt a minute ago spread, and my hands flexed of their own accord, as if they were about to grab him or stroke him or something, all beyond my will. I scrunched them to fists.

He probably hadn't meant that the way it sounded—the way it felt—but I still didn't want to move from his lap. Maybe for a long time. "You shouldn't be alone either."

A strand of his silken black hair had fallen over his face, and my horrible, willful hand reached up to brush it back. He caught my wrist and brought it to his mouth. For a wild and delicious moment, I thought he meant to kiss it. To kiss me. To make *stay with me* mean all the things I secretly desired it to be.

Instead he threaded his fingers with mine and exhaled a long, shuddery breath. "My brother's number is on your skin right now, but it won't always be so. Someday, you will bear my number, and then...things will change."

His gaze met mine, and every sordid, gorgeous, secret thought I'd had about him was reflected there, like a promise.

"I can read to you," I said in a voice that was far from steady.

He closed his eyes and leaned his head back against the chair. "That's a very wise idea."

It felt like surgical separation to remove myself from his embrace, but I did it. I was aware of each touch in the process, my bottom to his thighs, my hand sliding from his, my hair brushing his chest when I leaned forward. Those phantom touches were like tiny brands themselves.

I stood and looked at the pile of books, trying to get control of myself. All ancients and holies. My heart thump-thumped in a deep, steady rhythm. At least *it* was perfectly acclimated to this planet, this man.

I started with the titles. "*Winter Plants*," I said. "*Native Materials in Construction, Mineral Survey*...and some numbers after that. I don't know what they mean. A date, maybe?"

"They are numbers like on our maps," he said.

I could feel his gaze on my back.

"*Procedure and Processes for Judges and Wardens*. Oh, here's a good one. *Medicinal Properties of Native Flora*."

"All of it is informational, not poetry," said Astor. "That's probably good."

I turned and flashed him a grin. "You say that like you'd hoped for poetry."

"I only feared what hearing poetry from your lips would feel like," he replied with an intensity that wiped the grin off my face instantly. "Medicinal Properties. Let's give that one a go."

I wasn't done with this topic. "How do you know poetry? If no one reads, I mean. I used to teach poetry."

Until I'd gotten into trouble for veering off the list of approved poetry. Brent had 'suggested' at that point that I was done with my job. I was willful.

Maybe it was something internally wrong with me that went along with my heart.

CHAPTER SIX

I supposed my internal wrongness, whether it be my heart or my propensity for trouble, didn't matter now.

"We have poets." Astor smiled at me as he answered my earlier question. "They go around reciting poetry all the time while they do their other jobs, and once a year, Torrin lets them perform. They just have to remember it. And some other time, a much different time, I would like to hear some of the poetry you know."

He was such a conundrum. Nox had felt he was different enough I might stare at him. I still didn't understand why. He understood technology, although he had no ability to read. And he could decipher a map from afar to hopefully find his missing brother. And yet he was insecure. I might think he wasn't a good soldier. He was kind to me, said I was beautiful, and made me warm in places that were unusual for me.

I looked back at the book, flipping through it to the end. I might need there to be some kind of index that explained some words. Plants were not something I understood particularly well. I'd killed any ever given to me, and if Astor wanted explanation I wouldn't...

I stopped flipping. Right at the back of the book was a sticker affixed to the very back page. *Property of Longergan Prison.*

I stared at the words for a long moment. Longergan. I knew that name. I wasn't a historian, and most of what we knew altered anyway, depending on who was in charge and their version of the past. When my brother was supreme leader, the great holy ones will probably have walked among us to anoint him. That was neither here nor there. Longergan was a famous story. The prison ships that went missing...

"Bianca?" Astor drew me back to the here and now. "What is it?"

I held up the book. "Nothing. Sorry. I'm easily distracted."

I could have told him right then what I thought, but something stilled my mouth. What did these people know of their ancestors' pasts, and was it possible? Was it even something that could be considered, that the vanished prison ships had somehow crashed here and these people were the descendants of the prisoners? Did they know that they came from people who had been designated enemies of the state and were bound to spend their lives on prison ships? And if they didn't, did I want to tell them? No, absolutely not.

"I am, too." He rubbed a hand down my back. "Please tell me about plants. As they told you the other day, plants are a bit of a study of mine. That is how I made the cream that helps with burns."

I opened my mouth and read. It was easy to do, and it took my mind off everything else. I'd made it three chapters when he stopped me.

"I could listen to you read all day. But I'm hungry, and you must be, too."

I hadn't thought about food in a while, but almost as if it heard his words, my belly rumbled. Honestly, my lack of hunger these last few hours said something about Astor's ability to distract me. The food here was amazing. I mean, generally it was tubers, long yellow grasses, and something called zelbeast that was savory and salty and made my mouth water. But out of those three staples, the people of the City-State—women, chiefly, because they were the cooks—could make a seemingly infinite array of delicacies. A lifetime of monitoring everything that went into my mouth, out of fear that it could negatively affect my health, had made eating a source of anxiety. This arid, dusty planet seemed likely to change that. It was giving me an appetite for lots of things I hadn't considered much before.

"I didn't bring any food from the bar," I said. "Sorry, but I bet we can find a comisaria. It must be about time for them to start making the midday rounds."

Comisarias were the women who brought food around in baskets. Because I'd been living with Mattis so far, I'd never seen actual food preparation. The comisarias who came by were friendly enough, but they didn't really want to talk. Maybe they were intimidated by my brand, my... What was Torrin to me? Not a husband, not an owner. Protector?

Astor peered at me keenly, cocked his head to one side, and said mildly, "I think I can handle this." He stood and proffered a hand, helping me up from the soft pile of blankets I'd been sitting on. "Come."

I took his hand, internally mocking my instant and electric response to the touch. Seriously, I could not keep lighting up every time one of these men touched me. It was ridiculous.

We went back out through the grotesque throne room— someday, I was going to have to ask what was with all the skulls—and I didn't even notice the noise until we opened the metal door to the corridor beyond.

The tunnel was alive with people—people pulling carts,

carrying baskets, holding babies, leading domestic animals. The scuffling of dozens, maybe hundreds of feet on the hard-packed dirt floor was like an angry hiss, illuminating the fact that none of these people were talking. They were all moving swiftly, efficiently, serious.

Almost all of them were women or very aged folks.

"What's going on?" I asked before I could stop myself.

Astor grabbed my hand and threaded us through the throng. The flow of people was moving deeper into the underground warrens, but we went against the tide, headed toward Astor's rooms.

"Mattis would have told Dreama what he read on the lists," Astor said in a low voice. "She has ordered everyone underground, where we are better fortified, just in case."

In case? In case of what? I voiced that question, and he winced.

"You have heard what Reamers do to people, yes? You've met Cannon. Women have even more cause for concern, so the panic is not unwarranted. Look, I understand the instinct and their fear, but I don't hide in times like these."

He led us through the crowd, grabbing things from baskets as he did. I tried to keep up. So far, I'd been moving faster on this planet than I ever had anywhere else. Other than the rare times I was allowed to exercise, I was basically forced to stroll.

"Why not?" I raised my voice above the sound of so many people moving.

"If the Reamers overrun us, I'd rather they kill me fast. And do not worry, I won't let them have you."

Well...that was dark.

I couldn't even process it before Dreama stood in his way, blocking his exit. "Brother, where do you think you're going?"

He came to an abrupt stop, a scowl covering his face. "Sister. Move."

"Everyone is going to the hiding tunnels." She lifted a brow. "Including you."

Astor laughed. "You know I will do no such thing."

"If you wish to play cards with your life, then so be it. But you are responsible for Torrin's woman. You can't endanger her."

He looked over at me and squeezed my hand. "Dreama, she will be perfectly safe with me. If anything, I will be better able to get her away should the Reamers arrive."

"It isn't just the Reamers and you know it." They looked each other eye-to-eye. She was the tallest woman I'd seen here. While most of the women around wore long skirts and kept their heads down, Dreama was definitely treated differently. Was it her rank or just Dreama? "Any number of other groups could make a play for us with Torrin missing and half our troops with him. We could be attacked by the Corchrins. The Dowals. The Marching Men."

Astor nodded. "They could. Or nothing could happen at all. I am taking our brother's woman to eat something. When it is over, I will consider bringing her down below with the others. It isn't possible that any of them, not a single other City-State or raging barbarian tribe could overrun our borders and hurt Bianca in the amount of time that will take. Even you, alarmist that you are, can't deny that."

Her face fell. "Astor, why must you defy me every time something like this happens?"

If I hadn't been holding his hand, I'd not have felt how his body vibrated when she asked that question of him. "It isn't just you, Dreama. Ask Torrin sometime how well I follow his directions. I am a problem. Even to myself. Thank you for...trying."

Dreama looked at me a long second. "Take care of my brother, Bianca. I still can't make sense of you. But I'd like to, seeing as one way or another, we are soon to be family."

I opened my mouth. "Thank you, I'll...try." I didn't know how I would do that, exactly, considering I was the most lost person on this planet. How many groups were there on this planet or this region? And...raging barbarians? Sweat broke out on the back of my neck. Were they all as bad as the Reamers? And had all of these people descended from prisoners who crashed here?

I couldn't even remember who had been on those ships. Murderers. Rapists. Political prisoners. Had they all been together? I should have paid better attention in history class.

But I didn't voice any of these other questions, just followed Astor to his rooms. I did notice the people in the tunnels didn't brush past me or bump into me. They didn't touch me at all, and definitely didn't look at me. It was as if I were invisible, or else they were so interested they had to look away so they wouldn't stare.

Astor's quarters were near the opening of the tunnel system, near the surface. Dreama was right—this wasn't the most secure place to wait out an invasion, if one came. Plus, Astor had more or less told me he wasn't a fighter, and I certainly had no skills in personal defense. So why wasn't I worried?

But I wasn't. It was almost like I could feel this would end up okay. Maybe it was the organized, focused way the others in this clan reacted, like they'd done this process a million times and were used to it. I mean, if they'd lived through it before, by definition, losing to the Reamers or other barbarians must be survivable.

Still, I thought about Cannon and wondered what survival even meant.

Inside the sanctum of his quarters, Astor secured the door and ran a hand through his long hair. "Food. Right."

He went over to one of his tables with bubbling beakers and lab-looking equipment, and deposited an armload of things he'd been nicking from baskets as people had passed us. I didn't recognize any of them, but even as I watched, being at first too confused and then too ignorant to help, Astor started washing, sorting, and cutting the items. He pulled tiny vials from a shelf, sniffed a few, sprinkled some into a cauldron-looking thing, and started adding the chopped bits. After a while, a rich, savory smell suffused the air. My mouth flooded, and my stomach constricted in hunger.

Cooking. Astor was cooking. "You're cooking," I said, sort of awkwardly stating the obvious.

He glanced up but then ducked his face again, as if he were deeply interested in his work. But I caught that look, that vulnerability in his expression, and it squeezed my heart.

"I like to cook," he said in a low, almost defiant voice. "I also like to treat sick people and speak poetry, all of which are things that men do not do. What I do not enjoy is hurting others, claiming rights to land or people, killing, or fucking women who only want payment. My family and close friends know my peculiarities and indulge me, but others..."

Doing this in front of me, *for* me, was an act of trust. I wanted to be very, very careful not to betray that trust. "Have people always been cruel to you because you are so amazing?"

He looked up at me sharply. His sure, steady, long-fingered hand dropped a slice of tuber.

"Does that word mean to you what it means to me?"

I walked toward him. "I'm pretty sure it does. Astor, in the brief time I've been here, I've watched you take an interest in technology, science, strategy, reading, plants, poetry, cooking, taking care of the ill, and who knows what else. Where I am from, you would be highly sought after for those things."

"Your men are...not only valued for their fighting skills and the war trophies they bring home?"

I shook my head. "No. I mean, some are. But some men are gentler, with more intellectual interests. And yet some people can be interested in both. It's what makes us individuals."

I picked up the knife next to him and proceeded to cut with him. Was this why Nox had told me not to stare? Because Astor might very well be cooking something? Or because Astor embodied a lot of characteristics considered feminine?

We stood like that for long seconds, before he lifted a piece of the vegetable he chopped and offered it to me. I could have taken it with my hand. In fact, that would've been the absolutely right thing to do. But instead, I opened my mouth. It was a daring, improper move. But these men touched me all the time, they didn't seem to have the same boundaries.

He placed the food on the tip of my lips, watching as I brought it in with my tongue and chewed. His eyes widened, and he adjusted his stance, turning toward the table to grasp another piece. He did the same thing.

That warm feeling that kept coming and going in me returned. Neither of us said a word as he fed me again and again.

His hand came out finally to cup my cheek. He brought his head down, our lips close to each other. "You wear his brand, but you will wear mine."

His mouth met mine. His lips were gentle, and he kissed me softly. I pressed against him, deepening the kiss. Seconds passed before he opened his mouth, inviting my tongue inside. I was no expert at this, and we seemed to be figuring it out together. Astor spread his legs, and I walked between them. His arms came around me.

"Bianca," he finally said, his forehead pressing down on my shoulder. I held him close and tried to breathe. My heart raced like I'd been running. If I perished in this moment, it might be an okay way to go. I'd just been kissed...and kissed. The holy ones frowned on this, and I didn't care, not a hoot, for their opinion. This was as sacred as anything I'd ever done. "How did you exist in the universe and I not know you?"

I smiled against his chest. "I could ask you the same question. This place? It's not somewhere I even knew existed."

He stared down at me. "Did you leave someone behind? A man that you belonged to?"

"No." I stroked my hand over his heart, feeling the strong, steady beat. His was made correctly. "If I had someone like that, I wouldn't be kissing you. I'm loyal. And I am not sought after where I'm from. There are things about me that are considered...less than desirable."

He raised a finger and traced my lip. Had it trembled? Could he see? What did he imagine when he looked at my face? He'd called me beautiful, desirable, but was that all he saw? Did he understand what I was trying to say, that we were both hurt because we were odd, different? I saw the damage in him and met it with my own experience. I *understood*.

"Where you are from seems a profoundly uninformed place," he murmured, staring at his finger and its agonizing trek across my mouth. "For I find you infinitely desirable. Problematically so."

I had the wildest want to stretch my tongue out and taste the pad of his finger. Just entertaining the thought sent flurries of heat down the core of me and machine-gun stutters in my pulse. I parted my lips, letting him feel the heat of my breath and the quiver I could not contain. "Problematic? Because of Torrin?"

His brows dipped together and then flared. He smiled. "Oh, definitely not."

"But isn't he all those things you described, a man who

likes to claim things and go to war and hurt others? Would he hurt you if he saw us like this?"

"He could try."

"Astor, he's—" I'd been about to say Torrin was bigger, more temperamental, more capable of cruelty. But the insecurity was gone from Astor's face and voice, and I didn't want it back. What I wanted, honestly, was more kisses. More touches. More him. "—your king. Or chief. Or whatever."

"Well, of course he is, which is why he wants the happiness and security of his people more than anything. Especially the people he loves, and although we might annoy each other constantly, he does love me. He would not fly into a rage because I kissed you. Is that really what you fear?"

I sucked my bottom lip in between my teeth, pulling it away from his touch. And here I had been congratulating myself on seeing through all his layers to the damage beneath. But I had forgotten that he was also perceptive. And that he had listened to me. Who even did that?

"Because I believe that you fear the way your body reacts to my touch. You fear the way you feel, the way you want. This is what is problematic for me, Bianca."

"You're right. About all of it. I want a lot right now at this moment, but I can't stop thinking. The thing that makes me undesirable is this stupid, broken body. I mean, yes, my body lights up like a sunrise when you kiss me—even when you touch my face. But also, my heart can't endure it. And I don't mean that metaphorically...err, like a figure of speech? I mean it literally. My heart is weak. Astor. I can't even...even...run a track without—" I was panting now, and dark edges were closing in my peripheral vision. *Don't get yourself worked up, Bianca. You're letting it happen. Get control. Don't do this to yourself. Calm down.* I could almost hear my brother's voice.

Which of course was the last thing in the universe I wanted to hear right now.

I took a deep breath and forced myself to steady. It was easier said than done. "I'm messing this up. Let me explain." I cleared my throat as a means of covering that I was out of breath. "I was born with a heart defect. Where I am from, babies born with what I have are euthanized. Put to death at birth, to spare them a life of being improperly made. But that didn't happen to me because my family is rich. I suppose they thought I could be fixed. Everyone tried for a long time. I'm not fixable. I was on my way to meet my brother, where doctors were finally going to replace my heart with a mechanical one."

He stared at me, not saying a word. Part of me wished I'd said nothing at all. Astor was bound to lose interest in me. I would forever be the woman with the malformed heart now. I knew this because I'd faced it forever.

With a swift move, he cupped the side of my cheek. "Are you okay right now?"

"I'm never entirely okay. But yes, I'm fine. I think...I think I'm a little panicked telling you. It makes it worse. I have to work on controlling how I react to things, and that sometimes helps, sometimes doesn't."

He kissed my lips, which couldn't have surprised me more than if he'd sprouted wings and taken off. "I'm sorry you've had to go through all of this. They can take out your heart and replace it?"

I nodded, but stupid tears leaked from my eyes. "I hate the idea so much. I...I don't want to die, obviously, but they're going to have to periodically go back in and straighten it out. Or it could break, and then I'm dead anyway. I feel like if it's going to malfunction, they should just leave me with my bad one and call it a day."

He wiped the tears with his broad thumb. "You're frightened. I understand. The good news...maybe bad news...is that we can't do anything like that here. You will keep your heart."

I laughed, the sound surprising me as much as the emotion that brought it on. "That is true."

"May I?" He motioned toward my heart, and I nodded. Gently, he brought his ear to my chest and listened. "It beats fast but sounds strong to me. I am not an expert. We have no way of being. Why didn't you want to tell me?"

Astor lifted his head, and I chewed on my lip as I regarded him. He reached out with his thumb and stopped me, smoothing the places I'd been chewing on.

"I hate being locked up and watched every second like I'm about to expire."

He gave me a quick nod. "I won't do that to you. If there is nothing we can do...and I fear there is nothing...then we will continue as if all is well. I am not a person who likes to lock people away in preparation for the worst-case scenario. To a certain extent, we can only control such small matters in our lives that constantly being upset in worry makes no sense. As illustrated by the fact that we are not currently hiding in tunnels."

"My life has been a series of tunnels I've been hidden in."

He brought my hand to his mouth before he kissed my palm. "Bianca, you fell from the sky and lived. I think you are strong. We don't need to hide you away. What we do need is to eat a full meal and go to bed for the night. Tomorrow will bring all sorts of new problems. That seems almost guaranteed."

CHAPTER SEVEN

S o we ate. And we talked. And we...I don't know, bonded? Became friends? I was used to people keeping their distance, seeing me either as a medical curiosity or Brent's sister and, for either reason, unapproachable. And I guess my interactions with people overall here weren't very different. But these particular men, my protectors? I felt like they saw me, and that they liked me anyway. It was all so new and weird.

The culinary concoction Astor had been chopping and spicing required about an hour to cook through—tubers, apparently, were tough little things and took their time releasing the starches—but Astor had a stash of some "medic-inal" beverage that smelled like the stuff surgeons cleansed my skin with before an operation. In terms of taste, it wasn't as good as some of the drinks Mattis had mixed, but I liked it.

Astor cracked open a jar of it, and we consumed it along with the stew. Amazingly, despite the fact that people just outside this room were preparing for imminent military defeat and invasion, I had never been less anxious.

After a very satisfying meal, much better than the dishes the comisarias brought around, we lounged on cushions in Astor's bedroom and sipped the last of his brew.

Separate cushions, but close enough that either of us could reach. Touch. We just hadn't.

"You said when we met that your parents died, but then later that your new heart was allowed because of family connections," he said. "How does that work?"

"My brother. Brent. He is... Important doesn't begin to describe it. He's not a king, but he does have a lot of power over other people, how they live, what they are allowed to do, what they have access to in terms of work and education and healthcare."

"And your father previously filled the role? So you are sister to a current king and daughter to the last?"

"No, Brent was elected," I said.

Astor frowned. "He was not trained and educated to lead people?"

"Well, I guess maybe he was. He was a legal scholar for a while before he ran for office, and he's smart."

"Smart is not leadership," Astor said.

I nodded. "That is true." Outside, the world was getting darker. It was quiet. In Mattis' bar, it was never quiet, and that almost made the darkness seem brighter, in a weird nonsensical way. As though day became night. Here, it actually felt like nighttime.

He hadn't said anything, watching me as though he meant for me to keep speaking. I yawned. "The thing is...where I'm from...it tends to be the same families that lead over and over again. Even though people vote my brother into his office, it isn't like they have much of a choice. Most of the time, he runs unopposed. Every once in a while, there's an outlier who serves for a while, but mostly it's the same crew. So it's elections, but maybe they're more like masked kings."

"Interesting." He took my hand in his. "It will get cold at night."

I found myself quickly dozing off, my lids heavy like I couldn't quite keep them open. "Sorry," I laughed. "I don't think I've been sleeping well at Mattis' place."

"It's noisy," he nodded. "I need it peaceful to sleep. Others are the opposite. They'd hate it out here and need to be in the center of things to get any rest. Go to sleep. I will, too."

As though his words gave me permission, I let my lids shut and drifted in a gentle sleep. I didn't dream, not that I usually remembered them. Jerking awake, I gasped for breath, grasping on to my chest, but it wasn't my heart that had awakened me.

Astor sat up, looking around. It was dark now. He must have turned the lighting off and the temperature had dropped significantly. There was a noise in the distance, not one I knew. Wailing, screeching. What was happening?

His hand came onto my back. "It's okay. That is just the Howlers. You wouldn't have been able to hear them in the center of the City-State. And they haven't been out since you've been here anyway. They are creatures of this planet, animals. Wild beasts. We don't hunt or feed from them. We've never managed to domesticate them. They're fearsome, and you don't want to meet one in the dark, but they won't come here."

I pictured huge monsters like from the stuff of horror stories. His words did nothing to dissuade that image.

"They howl because the weather is changing." He got off his pad, and I shivered. It was much, much cooler in here. The temperature had significantly altered just since I'd fallen asleep.

Astor came back with a blanket. This planet had incredible shifts in temperature. There was nothing gradual about it.

He lay down next to me on my pad. "I hope this is okay."

I smiled. I'd place bets he had more than one blanket he could use, but I wasn't going to say no. The sound—that howling—I hated it. Was it some kind of primal, anthropological response to a predator I didn't know I had?

He covered us both in the blanket, wrapping me against him like we were in a cocoon. I finally found my voice. "I thought it was the Reamers."

"No, you are safe. I am a light sleeper, and there are alarms and people on watch. You're fine." His breath was on the back of my neck, a warm sensation to go with the blanket and his body, all of it shutting out the night.

"Will everyone be okay out there? With this weather shift? Your brother? Nox? The soldiers?"

He paused before he answered me with a laugh. "Torrin will be grumpy. That is for sure."

"Why do you guys have your battles during this cold season?"

He kissed the back of my neck. "This weather will not last. It will come and go before it finally sets in to stay during the winter. And it is preferable to the heaviness of the long summer. We can warm up easier than we can cool off."

He wasn't wrong. Inside the blanket, with him, I no longer felt the cold. Instead I felt, in exquisite detail, the entire shape of him, molded to the shape of me. When I inhaled, my shoulder blades pressed back into his chest, and I slowed the exhale, lingering against the shift in his muscles, the band of his arm encircling me, protecting me. It was everything I could manage not to writhe, just to feel more. Or maybe to provoke him. His heart thrummed against my back, and I realized that even though I had drawn breath, he had not. He was holding it, holding still. Waiting for something?

"You can do that again," I said.

"Talk about the weather?" There was laughter in his voice, but his body was so still, so rigid.

"Kiss me."

He sucked in a breath, but it was ragged, uneven, cool at first as it eddied beneath my hair. His mouth pressed against my neck, and I could not resist a groan of pure pleasure.

The wild things were still howling outside. The soldiers were still fighting, probably still dying. Winter was coming, and I was lost here—completely lost and hopeless—yet I could think of nothing but this.

He had bent his arm and had been nestling his hand to mine, but now he moved it, fanned his palm against my stomach, pulling me closer. There was no space for movement, but I turned anyway, to face him. I wiggled, bringing my mouth level with his. There were no lights in here, and underground like this, it was completely black, but I knew what his face looked like.

Maybe it was the darkness that made me so bold, but I couldn't help myself. "Now, again."

He obeyed, not moving his hand, which in all my turning and wiggling had ended up cupping my rear. This was the most intimate moment I had ever experienced, and sins be damned, I reveled in it, the thick, languid curl of desire that licked its way through my body.

He kissed me again. Or did I kiss him this time? It wasn't awkward like before, filled with unshed secrets and fear and dismay. We had talked through all that and were free of it, of inhibition, I guess. This was a man who admitted he desired me, who wasn't even ashamed of it.

Greedy for more, I nipped his bottom lip with my teeth, pulling his mouth open, and slid my tongue inside. He tasted delicious, like home-brewed wine and mint, and I had a sudden and blazing desire to taste all of him.

Oh, if the holy ones and their inquisitors could see me

now, they'd all keel over. But I put all thoughts of them aside, them and their rules and their shaming. This place had different rules, and though I was just learning them, I suspected they might just suit me better than the ones I'd lived under all my life.

"Bianca..." He said my name—growled it really—and rolled to his back, bringing me over the top of his body.

On top of him, I could feel all his hard muscles. Astor might have been the least interested in battle out of all the men I'd met thus far, but he was strong, like he worked out, or in his case, dealt with a hard world that built muscles in all who lived on it.

I studied him as best I could this close and in the dark. It was more about touch than it was anything else. As though I was sightless and needed to memorize him with my fingertips. I'd read people used to do that.

The long scope of his nose, the broadness of his shoulders, the dusting of hair on his chest. He shuddered beneath my exploration. For his part, he kept still, touching me only occasionally on my back, a long stroke of his fingertips from the top of my spine to the place where my hips met my rear —but never further.

Finally, he kissed my chin. Astor was impossibly hard. If I gave into the urges driving me and ground my hips against him, I'd feel the length of him even more acutely. Would he like that? Would that be taking this too far?

The howls in the air sounded like they were in the room with us. I forced myself to tune out the noise, giving into the forbidden urge and pressing my hips down until my most sensitive parts were flush against his.

He moaned. "You might be trying to kill me."

I smiled. My body seemed to be vibrating. I'd never had a sensation like it before. "This is all new to me."

He quieted for a second. "Feels like it is new to me, as

well, which is...remarkable. Let's stop. And not because I don't wish to continue, but because I wish to have my numbers on you when we officially join."

That was a big deal here. Ownership. Those numbers... Prison markings that they'd passed down? I didn't know yet, and I wasn't going to spoil this moment with those kinds of questions.

Instead, I let him pull me down until I lay next to him, his leg strewn over my body, the blankets over us. The howls were still there, but I cared less.

No way was I going to be able to sleep now.

He kissed the end of my nose, both of my eyes.

I closed them.

M orning came slowly. A pelting noise roused me, and I quickly identified it as rain. It was raining. That was...so normal. Everywhere had rain. I smiled. Next to me Astor slept, deep breaths telling me that he was still plenty out of it.

I'd never been a person who could entirely sleep through the night. I was always up and down, anxiety about the next day or worrying about my health, warring sometimes with wanting to argue with Brent and knowing that wasn't allowed. Here, things weren't entirely different. I'd been up a lot, this time because of the Howlers.

I did like how it felt to be smushed up against Astor. I kissed his arm, and he stirred. I was going to have to wake him. He'd pinned me down with his body, and I needed to pee.

He rolled over, muttering something, which freed me to get up and use his facilities. Shivering, I hurried through the motions. It was cold in here. Ridiculously so. The fires he had burning were entirely out, and I didn't know if it was okay to relight them or if I'd even know how.

Could I figure it out?

Coming out of the bathroom, I found Astor leaning up on his elbows, rubbing his eyes. "Bianca. I see I didn't make you up in my head. You do exist, and you are just as beautiful as yesterday."

I must have been bright red.

Sounds of vehicles caught my attention, and we both looked toward the outside door. He jumped to his feet. "They're back, and they'll need me. If there are injured, I'll be very busy. Come. Let's see what's happened. Oh, the clothes you were given to change into are at Mattis'. We'll collect those later."

When we'd gone to bed, he'd said today would bring new troubles, it always did. I could see he was right. But I saw the world with new eyes this morning, with... I don't know. Confidence maybe. I could help, by reading the books and doing women's work, and maybe... A plan was forming in my mind to see if I could teach not just Astor to read, but maybe some of the women, too, so they could have other services to offer in trade. I was beginning to see myself as part of this society and how I might fit into it.

It didn't even feel so strange anymore.

Okay, the skull throne? That was still strange. That would never stop being strange.

Astor had thrown on a fresh shirt over the leggings he'd worn to bed and was swiftly gathering materials, including a jar of the stuff that we'd drunk last night. This one had a red-wax stopper and some numbers etched into the ceramic. He caught my stare and grinned. "I told you it was medicinal."

"Aha," I said, finger-combing my hair and dragging it back into a tie. "You drugged me into behaving the way I did." Not that I felt even the slightest bit of embarrassment or shame.

As a devotee of the ancients and holies, I had certainly turned into a failure. Not that I was so concerned with that right now.

"Oh no, lovely girl," Astor said, dropping a quick kiss on my forehead, "that was all you in the dark. And I shall carry the memory of it constantly, until we can replace it with another."

"Or we could just do it all over again tonight. Every night. Until your brother returns," I suggested, and felt a delicious thrill just at saying the words. What was wrong with me? I was never this bold. But it felt so freeing. There was a power in knowing that he found me attractive and desirable. And Brent was right about one thing—power felt amazing.

We were just about to leave Astor's quarters when he thought of something. "We didn't bring that medicinal plants book, did we? Damn. You read a list of roots that could be boiled to counter infection. Don't happen to remember which ones, do you?"

"No, but I remember the way to Torrin's rooms. I can go get the book and meet you out in that hangar-looking area."

I didn't really think Astor would let me out of his sight, but he must have been really distracted, more than he was letting on.

"Be safe. And hurry." Another kiss, this time on top of my head. It was like he couldn't help himself.

I'd expected the corridor outside to be crammed with people, the way it had been the day before when the City-State's women had gone underground for safety. But today it was empty. Was everybody still down here, or had they gone up to the surface to tend their returning warriors? It seemed like if the warriors had returned victorious, there would be some noisy celebration going on, but then, if they had lost the battle, shouldn't invaders or Reamers or some other horrible people be slaughtering all of us right now?

I shuddered and hurried down to Torrin's throne room. The door wasn't locked, which I hadn't expected, but the room was also empty, which I also hadn't expected. Down here, I couldn't hear the vehicle sounds anymore, but I didn't want to linger a second longer than necessary in the skull room.

The pile of books was precisely where we'd left them, with the medicinal plants volume on top, marked where we'd stopped reading. I grabbed it and turned back to the corridor.

Dreama stood just inside the doorway. Her face looked strained.

She closed the door behind her.

"We have our victory," she said, but she didn't look happy. At all. "Torrin and Nox are still missing, and now Mattis, too. Baron the Great has assumed regency—you have no reason to know him, but he is utter slime. I...I don't know what to do, but Torrin would maim me if I let them get you."

"Why Baron? Isn't Astor a better fit?" This place and its politics were so complicated, but the politics had a way of devolving to that.

"Of course," Dreama snapped, "which is exactly why that keistered fungus Baron has taken him prisoner."

CHAPTER EIGHT

I gaped at her. "I just left him. How can he have been taken prisoner?"

"It took seconds." She sighed. "They dragged him away the second he stepped outside. It was minutes ago. He managed to call out to me to come and save you."

I shuddered, running hands over the goosebumps on my arms. "What happens now?"

Vehicles sounded outside and above us, and Dreama rushed to the door. "We hope that is my brother and that he is in some kind of position to lead."

I ran after her, my chest tightening when I did. Running was always a problem, even though I craved doing it. Astor had been taken prisoner? Was he okay? We'd only hours ago been wrapped up in each other's arms. How had this happened?

In the big hangar, Mattis jumped out of the transport first, followed by Torrin, who held his arm in an awkward position. It was moments still before two others I didn't recognize came out holding a stretcher.

Dreama winced. "Nox is hurt, badly."

I rushed out of the tunnel, nearly colliding with Torrin, who held me still in lieu of saying a word to me. He called over his shoulder. "Where is my brother? Get him here."

"I can't." Dreama wrung her hands together. "Baron the Great has taken him prisoner."

Torrin narrowed his eyes for a long second before he spun around to face Mattis. "You tell Baron the Great that he will release my brother instantly or he will find himself Baron the Mutilated. And I will cut up his daughter's face until no man will look at, let alone bond with her. You tell him he has ten fucking seconds."

Mattis met my gaze for a second, and heat seemed to move through me. He turned his attention to Torrin. "On it."

"Good." He strode further into the room, practically dragging me with him as he did. Trading his hold on my arm with a hold on my hand, he pointed at Dreama. "Get our people out of the tunnels. See to it that Nox is secured in one of the bedrooms here. He is this hurt because he saved my life. And you, Bianca, I require your assistance. Now."

He'd no sooner made that proclamation than he dragged me to the back room with the books. One of the men I didn't know followed us, dropping a bag on the floor with a thud before he exited in a hurry.

Torrin let me go. "You are unharmed?"

"Yes." I'd never been alone with Torrin before. It was like he took up all the space in the room with his presence alone.

"That is good news. The Reamers have much of your technology. The only good news is that they don't yet seem to know how to use it. They stumbled upon making one of them work, and Nox is hurt because of it." He bent over and, with his good arm, opened the bag. "What are those?"

I stared at the contents for a long second. "Weapons."

He took a long breath. "Forgive me, I was not clear. What kind of weapons are they?"

"They..." I swallowed, forced myself to think. I'd only seen these things on transport security checks and the odd military parade, and I'd never been close to one. I had to remind myself that sitting there, without a delivery system, these couldn't hurt me. Wouldn't. My mouth was bone dry when I replied, and I couldn't stop looking at the bag full of horror. "In space, you can't use projectile weapons, like guns or crossbows, right? If a bullet punctured a spacecraft, the whole ship could depressurize. The Union security forces had a whole string of botched boardings where they inadvertently killed a bunch of rebels instead of arresting them, so Union scientists came up with this technology. They're called burrs, and if one gets shot at you, it attaches itself first to your suit or clothing, then secretes a sort of acid, burrows through to your skin, secretes a different chemical, and burrows through that, and on."

I looked up at Torrin, surprised by the look of agony on his face. "So they're inside him right now? Eating him alive?"

"All ancients and holies," I breathed. "No. Not Nox."

"Do you know how to stop them? Is there a way to stop them?"

"No, they react automatically on impact..." But right at that moment, it was almost like time reversed. Paused. We were here in this room, Astor and me, flirting in and out of that peculiar tension that had developed between us, him staring at me in the most disconcerting way, and me reading aloud, frustratingly unable to pay attention to any of the words. Except, now I heard the words, clear as anything. I handed Torrin the book. "Find the page that says two twenty-one."

He looked at me like I was insane, but he did as I said. He opened the book, found the page.

"Your world has, or used to have, acid lakes near here, near the mountains, and apparently there are islands within those lakes that produce some kind of protein-rich delicacy called felanthes. They were sources of frustration for many years, and many gatherers died trying to get to the islands. But then the people figured out a way to harvest the felanthes safely. The author of this book describes a concoction that, when smeared all over a boat's keel, would neutralize the acid and enable a person to reach the islands. He gives a recipe right there, on that page. I don't know what any of those plants are, but Astor does. You free him from Baron the Great Asshole, we can help Nox."

He might not have recognized my expletive, but he appreciated the sentiment. The tight, vicious smile he flashed when I said it carved its way through my belly. This man was danger personified, terrifying and at the height of his power. Given all I knew of authoritarian control, that mixture absolutely should not have been thrilling. But it was.

Torrin closed the book, handed it back to me, and folded my hand around its spine. His hand on mine was so electric, it should have thrown sparks. "I expect Mattis to arrive momentarily with my brother in tow. Nox is being moved to a room here within my quarters. What can we do to prepare?"

I blinked. He needed information, and it was in the book. Beakers. And bowls. Things to heat something up. And the plants.

He nodded. "Come, Bianca from the sky. Mattis will retrieve my brother, and he will get things set up. You and I with your book will go get those plants."

"I don't know them."

Torrin scowled. "I do."

Seconds later, I found myself alone with Torrin in a transport, me carrying the book on plants that was proving extremely useful and he maneuvering the craft at breakneck speeds.

I had to say something. "Your arm?"

"I dislocated it for the first time when I was twelve. Now it does it rather regularly in certain kinds of fights. I'll be fine, thanks to Nox, who took the hit for me."

I thought of my brother and his secret guard, paid to take a hit for him. I'd never been exactly sure that they would, even for the bonus in their paychecks. Nox did it for Torrin, and now Torrin frantically tried to fix him. That was what loyalty looked like. I wasn't sure I'd ever seen it before, not like this.

"You know the plants?"

He shook his head. "Astor and I were raised together until we were separated at twelve, shortly after I dislocated my arm, actually. Coincidence, not because of it. We are not so different in our interests. But I had to lead, so I was trained to do so, and he was left to sort himself out."

Or be ostracized. "He's amazing."

Torrin side-eyed me. "Yes, Bianca, he is." The vessel abruptly stopped. "We're here."

I jumped out, following after him.

The landscape was different here, it was actually green. There was water, a small lake, a pond sort of. Did they get more rain here? It had been pounding this morning. Where was it now? "I don't think I really understand the weather here."

"Do people understand the weather anywhere?" Torrin replied. As I'd been looking around, he was now waist deep in the pond pulling up greenery. "Bianca, a little help. What does the book that you can magically read tell me to pull up? What do they look like?"

I scanned through the page. "First one has five leaves and a vein through the center of the stem. Pink flowers in summer."

"Got it." He tugged one up and discarded it onto the side of the pond. "Next?"

I described five plants listed in the recipe, and he found all of them, wading out of the pond at one point and then right back in for the next item. Finally, I said, "I, um, think that's it. There are some steps for distilling and infusing, but we can do all of that back at the town, or, err, settlement. City-state."

He waded out of the water for the second time, his clothes clinging to the topography of his body, which, I admitted to myself, was not unimpressive. This backwater planet sure did produce specimens of male beauty.

Or else I just didn't get out much. Could've been both, honestly.

We climbed back into the transport and careened toward the settlement, and I thought of the careful, gentle swaying ride I'd experienced when Nox brought me back from the crash. He must have been making extra effort not to jostle me. What a sweet soul was Nox. Torrin had no such patience, though, and it was lucky for me I found a handle above the window to hold on to, else I might have been flung around, or out of, the vehicle.

Both men were all about protecting, but their methods couldn't have been more different.

I shot a glance at Torrin's profile. Five days ago, I would not have had the courage to quiz a king, even a barbarian like Torrin. But today? I had changed.

"Dreama said our City-State had victory," I called over the noise of the transport engine. "Does that mean the war is over?"

He kept his attention on the roadless terrain but replied, "For today, yes. We hold the Eden fields and will likely keep them until after the next harvest."

"So what happens now?"

"We heal our wounded." His tone implied a *duh*, and he didn't look at me.

"And then?"

"We split into work details and go tend what we have won."

"So if you abandon the settlement—the tunnels and the stables and Mattis' pub and everything—while you go off and farm, what keeps rival groups from coming in here and taking over all these things you've built?" The question sounded sterner because I had to shout it over the engine.

He didn't answer, not for a long time. I'd pretty much given up on him ever speaking to me again. He seemed to have a very mercurial appreciation for my intellect—I could read these books, great, but I couldn't question his illogical social planning? He was no better than the Union and the inquisitors—just swallow anything we tell you, little girl, and don't bother questioning. Clearly, that was the sort of woman Torrin was used to.

Well, he was going to get an education, courtesy of me.

Righteous fury boiled in the back of my mouth the whole rest of the ride back, and by the time he shut down the engine, swung out his side, and then came over to me, I was ready to spew a lot of criticism in his general direction.

He opened the door and reached out a hand. To help me out.

He was big and intimidating, but also—how did I not notice this before—he looked really, really tired, and he still carried his hurt arm gingerly. The weight of his responsibilities clearly rode him hard.

The stinging critique I'd prepared smothered itself, and I took his hand, letting him help me down to the ground. He reached in behind me to retrieve the bundle of green-cloth-wrapped plant cuttings.

"We divide our forces," he said, walking only a half step ahead of me, but he did slow his stride so I didn't have to run to keep up. "A work detail and its guards farm for fourteen days, and then they return, and the next detail goes out. We never abandon this place. It is ours. We have been here, right here, for more than a hundred years. The bones of my forebears for eight generations make up the scion throne, which I have noticed you staring at as if you would mock it. For a woman who has been treated with nothing but respect and care, you make many assumptions about us."

CHAPTER NINE

Torrin's words took up space in my head, but I had no chance to really digest them. Astor had been returned, seemingly unharmed, and we got to work preparing the remedy for Nox. As the only one who could read to him exactly what was needed, my attention had to stay on the task at hand.

The time came to administer the medicine, which meant getting Nox to drink it. It was a two-pronged cure. First, he had to drink it, and then we had to seal up the wound with the remaining batch.

I chewed on my lip. "I am suddenly nervous," I spoke to the room, which included Torrin, Astor, and Mattis. Everyone else had been told to leave. When it came down to it, it really seemed like the four of them formed a unit separate from the rest of the world. "We don't know the validity of this book. I mean, there were once books claiming that the universe had floating monsters by the suns."

Mattis blinked. "There aren't?"

I opened my mouth, and he held out his hand. "I'm kidding."

"He is going to die and soon from his injuries, this can't make it worse."

I supposed that was true. I sat on the edge of the bed. "Nox?" I rubbed his arm gently and then more firmly when he didn't rouse.

His eyes fluttered open. "Bianca?"

"We have medicine for you. I need you to try to drink it down."

I wasn't sure he was really hearing me, but Torrin stepped forward, looking down at Nox over my shoulder. "Open your mouth, and let her help you drink this."

Nox nodded. In slow pours, I helped Nox drink down what I hoped would fix him and not kill him in a more painful way. Finally, he was finished.

Torrin squeezed my shoulder. "Good. Apply it to his leg and we shall see."

I did as instructed, turning to look at Astor as I did. Shouldn't he have been doing this? I was sure he'd be vastly more appropriate. For the most part, he'd been quiet since his return.

"Are you okay?" I asked him.

He nodded. "Yes. If he lives, it's thanks to you." He visibly swallowed. "Torrin, I..."

His brother waved his hand. "You helped Mattis find us. If once again your head was somewhere else and you managed to get captured, I suppose it's just a standard day. I'll have to punish Baron, again. Someone wake me when Nox rouses. Bianca, you're with me."

I was?

As if it were a live thing, I could feel the almost-healed scar on my arm, reminding me that, yes, yes, I was with him. Officially and until whatever such time he released me. The thought made panic oscillate inside my chest. Or maybe not panic, not fear. Curiosity? Adrenaline? It was weird, and I wasn't fond of it. Except that I sort of was.

I followed Torrin—still with his shortened strides for my benefit, though I'm sure he would never admit to adjusting his pace for me—back out to the hangar. I'd never seen it more crammed with vehicles, but there were at least ten in here, and the air was thick with fumes from all those combustion engines. Metal flaps had been pulled back on a few, and people were bent over the machine innards. Mechanics, I realized. One of the teachers I used to work with was married to a mechanic on Jooron Five, though she fixed starships.

Someone approached Torrin and asked a question, and he answered. Then someone else came up with a different information bit to share. He didn't intimidate these people, and he responded effortlessly, encouraging more questions and gently nudging others to realize answers that were staring them in the face. He didn't always behave like a tyrant, then. Maybe he saved that for me?

After talking to at least five different people, he reached toward me, and... Maybe all the time I'd spent with handsy men like Mattis and Astor and even Nox had changed my own need for touch. Whatever the reason, I reached back and clasped his hand, as if it was the most natural thing.

He stopped, looked down at me with a quizzical brow-twitch, and then, I swear, he smiled.

"I require something urgently," he said, "and I suspect you do as well."

Where I came from, that statement, especially accompanied by a handclasp and a look from eyes that burned like stars, was absolutely a double entendre.

And what if it was? I had been claimed by him, belonged to him. In this society, that meant he could do anything he wanted with me. I bit my bottom lip between my teeth, hard, and let him lead me out of the wide cavern and into daylight.

The air was still dusty up here, even with the cooler shift in weather, and though it made breathing less than easy, I didn't want to search for my scarf. Or to be more honest with myself, I didn't want to let loose of Torrin's hand. People stared when we walked past. Some greeted him, and some even called him "highness" and nodded to me, but everyone was warm and congratulatory. Walking beside him, with his number on my skin, made me feel...proud? Was that the right word for it?

I didn't know my way around the tiny town all that well, so I wasn't sure where we were heading until we got there, and then relief flooded me. Mattis' bar.

We ducked inside, and to my surprise, the place was empty. Only Mattis was there, tucked into his private room in back, where he had done my brand. He looked up when we arrived, and the question on his face almost broke my heart before he spoke.

"Any update?"

Torrin released my hand and flopped down in a chair. It was the most casual, normal thing I'd ever seen him do, very un-kingly, but also very, very human.

"He's been treated still, and now we wait. Bianca and I need drinks. You, too."

"On it," said Mattis, moving into action, already gathering bottles and these little mineral pods that made liquids fizzy and cool.

Torrin tipped his head back against the chair and closed his eyes. "You will forgive me if I don't thank you properly. But thank you."

"You're welcome," I said. With Mattis off mixing cocktails, Torrin almost had to be talking to me.

"Not just for saving Nox, but also for taking care of Astor and letting Dreama feel important and... You have done much."

I blinked. "Anything I've done has just been accidental. I don't think you should be thanking me."

He shook his head. "Sometimes, people are naturally helpful." He opened his eyes. "I am glad you are one of those people. Those books you can read? Could you teach me to do so?"

"I was hoping I could be of use that way. I was a teacher of reading, of books. Before most of them were banned as inappropriate. I'd like to teach whoever would like to learn."

He nodded, and his gaze could best be called haunted. I wondered what had put that look there. "The Reamers still have weapons, but once you show us how to use the ones we have, I will endeavor to take the rest of them from them. I'm sending the farmers out tomorrow to start tilling the land. And I have to do something about Baron the Pain in my Ass."

I snorted, and Mattis, who arrived with our drinks, jumping up to sit on a chair at the table, too, grinned. "One of these days, you will get enough of him."

"I reached that point long ago, but one does not simply eliminate a rival's family simply because one does not like them."

"Well..." Mattis sipped his drink, and I picked up mine to do the same. The taste was sweet, easy to go down. "You don't. You kill plenty of other people who deserve it maybe less."

Our leader seemed to ignore that comment, staring at his drink. Finally, he spoke. "Mattis." Torrin placed his good hand on the table. The other was still at a weird angle, reminding me the amount of pain Torrin must be in. "First, I would ask you to please fix my arm. Yank it back."

The other man rose. "Sure."

In a swift move, Mattis yanked Torrin's arm back, and with a snap, his shoulder went back into place. Torrin winced but made no sound as he fisted his hand once, then twice. "Thanks."

"Second thing?" Mattis walked back to his seat.

"You saved all of us. You, Nox, Astor. You save my life. Save our City-State. All the damn time. You do it all without comment, without fanfare. This time, I would like to reward you. Ask me for something, and it's yours."

Mattis stared at Torrin. "I do what I do for our home, and for you because you are my friend."

"Ask me for something." Torrin sipped his drink, taking deeper swigs of it than either Mattis or I had done.

"All right." Mattis sat forward.

Torrin's smile made me do the same. He was easy to watch, enchanting to listen to, and I could see how he'd be deadly if he chose to be. This was why they followed him. His charisma. I'd fallen straight into the Torrin hole with the rest of them. Yes, I'd listen to him, and I didn't want him to yell at me again.

"I knew there was something you wanted," he said. "Everyone has something they want."

Mattis lifted his eyebrows slowly. "I want my brand with yours on Bianca. I want to share her."

My mouth fell open. What? He could have anything, and that was what he wanted? Me?

Torrin shifted in his seat. "That's what you want? To share Bianca? With me? I've already promised her back to Astor and plan to make Nox the same offer I've made you. It would be with all of us."

"I see no problem with this," Mattis said. "We've shared most everything since we were all kids."

I noticed that at no time did either of them turn to ask me. They wouldn't either. That wasn't how it worked where I was from, and it wasn't that way here either.

A muscle ticked in Torrin's jaw. "Your boon is granted. But

she is mine tonight. Go ahead and brand her. And you're right. I have to...speak to my brother."

I should have felt overwhelmed, upset even, that they both bartered with my life like this. Only, I wasn't. These were two of the most powerful men in the City-State. If they wanted me, that only meant that I'd continue to find safety here. Also, for a woman who had never dared hope for one lover, the idea of four of my very own, committed to caring for me as well as each other, was like finding a life-changing treasure in an old coat pocket. The fact that all of these men were insanely attractive only made the treasure sparkle more.

Still, there were things to say, and I needed to say them now. "You both should know something I've told Astor. I have a bad heart. I was born with it. I won't get better. It has made me less than desirable in the past. Likely, it will kill me."

They both stopped to regard me. Finally, it was Torrin who spoke. "Well, we will mourn your death. But don't misunderstand. The likelihood is that you will still bury me. None of us are going to live to be old."

"But it's not just a short life span," I said, speaking slowly. How could he not understand what I was trying to say? "It's me, all of me. I'm...not normal. Not whole. I can't run or fight or climb or travel in space frequently or live on high-gravity worlds or bear children. I'm not worth—"

"Stop." He didn't yell, but Torrin's voice was the keen edge of a knife, slashing my words into silence. "You will not complete that sentence. And as for your litany of lack, have I or anyone here asked you to do any of those things?"

I thought about it, and I felt my face heating. "No."

"What qualities I have desired of you—to wit, your reading skills, your patience and empathy, your logic and consideration for others, your obedience and," something in his face shifted, gentled, and he went on, "your disturbingly soothing voice when the whole rest of the world seems in chaos—you have offered unquestioningly and generously, to the benefit of us all. Are you unable or unwilling to do any of these things in the future?"

His words formed a funnel, a storm in my mind, and I tried to sort them out, but they moved too fast, were possibly too much. "No," I whispered.

Torrin leaned forward. "Then, Bianca, please know you are enough. More than, in fact. You are enough for me, which is no small thing, and I respect you tremendously in a way that has little to do with your physical attributes."

My expression must have looked tragic, because Torrin reached forward with his good hand and brushed my cheek. Touch, again. It was becoming a thing I anticipated, sometimes longed for. The pad of his finger was warm and dry and a little rough against my skin.

"That's..." I didn't know what I was going to say, possibly that he was kind or that I couldn't quite believe or that I didn't deserve all this attention and fuss, but Mattis chose this moment to rejoin the conversation.

"Well, it's horse shit, is what it is," he said, setting his half-consumed drink on a table. Then he turned to me, and I swear his eyes twinkled. "I find your physical attributes insanely desirable, and if Torrin doesn't see that, he's had his brain baked out on the battlefield."

"I was keeping this on a respectful level," sighed the leader of our people, leaning into that dangerous-sounding voice.

"Yeah, and I was lowering the level," replied Mattis.

They stared at each other for a long, bleak moment, and I was reminded of the tension between Astor and Torrin the first day I was here, before the battle and injuries and, um, kisses. Oh dear, I really had inserted myself right into the center of these friendships, this brotherhood, and I'd done so completely innocently, with no intention to break anything. But what if that was exactly what I'd done? What if I'd caused this deep and life-long friendship between these men to fracture?

But then, I don't know who cracked first, but suddenly they both burst out in laughter and were performing some complicated handshake-backslap thing. It was all very alien and male and, well, confusing. I waited until they were done.

"I'm flattered, really," I said, hoping it was acceptable for me to add my opinion to this arrangement they were making on my behalf. "But it feels really awful to have this conversation without Astor and Nox."

"Well, it would," Mattis replied. "Didn't Torrin just call you out for excessive empathy and consideration?"

"Excessive?" I repeated. Back where I was from, *excessive* often meant *wrong*.

"What he means is we could all stand to be a little more considerate of each other. You are right to say so." Torrin stood. "Come, let us discuss our future with Nox and my brother."

So yay, that he had listened to me. Eek, that his tone when he said "my brother" sounded a thousand kinds of ominous. And of course, when I recalled the night I'd spent with his brother, I wasn't at all certain how we were going to explain it.

CHAPTER TEN

"Yeah, where is Astor anyway?" said Mattis. "When I brought him back from Barron Dink's, he seemed shaken up, but then he went off somewhere and I couldn't find him. I figured he needed some time alone, so I didn't push, but when he's like that it's, you know, worrisome."

They exchanged a look, but I interjected.

"I know where he is," I said. I hadn't known Astor long, but everything I knew about him pointed to one place. "He's watching over Nox. Came and went, so to speak."

They both stared at me, so I spoke again. "He's a caregiver, a healer. That's what he prefers to do to all other things. You're not dissimilar, Torrin. I mean, you also take care of everyone. Astor just does it on a smaller scale, more intimate."

Torrin rapidly blinked. "That's an interesting perspective. Come. Since my bed is in the same place as where Nox and Astor are, that is where we are heading. Mattis, you can spend the night in one of the extra rooms." He abruptly stopped and looked up at the ceiling. "Wait. What am I going to tell Dreama?"

"About what? My sleeping in your rooms or the brands or...?" Mattis ran a hand through his hair. He seemed sort of nervous and distracted, which honestly wasn't such a strange reaction. Their just-ended battle had resulted in casualties, and they'd just decided to share a wife, like forever. All that had to mess with a person.

Torrin shot Mattis a side-eye look. "No. About your bonding with Bianca. Instead of her."

Mattis gaped at Torrin. "Dreama? I was never going to..."

Torrin grinned before he cracked up. "I know, man. I'm just fucking with you."

Mattis dropped his head for a long second. "That's not funny."

"It is, actually."

A week ago, I would have agreed with Mattis whole-heartedly—not funny. But in this ultra-tense, battle-ready mood that hung around the City-State all the time, these men really needed to take the edge off sometimes. I could see the sense in Torrin's joke, even if it hadn't landed perfectly. It had been superficially crass but deeply kind, which I was starting to suspect described his entire leadership style.

Torrin took my hand in his. We'd walked all this way to have one drink and apparently for Mattis to ask to bond with me.

He stopped to lock up the bar, but Torrin didn't halt his stride. I easily walked next to him, which meant that he'd either slowed to accommodate my bad heart or because he really was dragging.

"I don't imagine that you ask questions you don't know the answers to very often. What did you think he was going to ask you for?"

He lifted his eyebrows. "Oh, I knew he was going to ask for you, Bianca."

"You did?"

"Yes, of course." He squeezed my hand.

Well...I hadn't seen that coming.

"Torrin, I stare at the skull chair because it scares me. And I tend to hide from what scares me. Every time I walk in that room, I want to run out of it."

"Then it's doing exactly what it was designed to do. Intimidate. But those aren't the skulls of people I've executed or anything. They're former leaders, my ancestors. And I sit on them as my father did before me, as his father did before him, to remind us of what we've lost and what we've gained."

Now would be the perfect time for me to tell him what I knew of his ancestors. Only I didn't. He was a king here. He sat on a throne. I didn't want to disclose what I'd learned. Someone had thought his people, all the departed who lived here before him, had been so undesirable, so dangerous, so scary, they'd been locked away, never to return.

And yet...they lived by a code that didn't seem any more nefarious than where I'd come from. Better in some ways.

Life was complicated.

A stor rose when we walked in the bedroom, putting a finger to his mouth to shush us when we would have talked. He nodded toward the throne room, and I was soon back to staring at the skulls once again. How did they not disintegrate over time?

"I was just going to send for you," Astor said. "He roused enough to know he's back, and he's healing. Now he's sleeping again. I think the restorative powers of sleep are what's called for now."

He wasn't looking at me, which was weird. Astor being avoidant? When had that ever happened? This was the man who usually couldn't hold himself back from touching and joking and insinuating and making me crazy. I mean, it was a mix of adorable and aggravating—especially when he led us up to a brink of some point and then backed away—but now that it was gone, I missed it. He didn't seem at all like himself. Had Baron done something to him? Something...Reamerish?

Or was this because his brother was back and throwing his weight around and running things? And also holding my hand in a very possessive way.

I disentangled my hand from Torrin's and felt a blush flame across my cheeks. Astor wasn't going to like the deal Torrin and Mattis had just made. My problem was that I... did. Like it. Sort of, I mean? All of these men were good people, kind people, brave people. And okay, yes, scorchingly attractive people. I wouldn't have thought up such a life for myself on this planet, and every cosmic power knew I hadn't expected it, but now that it was laid right out in front of me like a done deal, I figured I could do worse. I *liked* them. All of them.

However, getting Astor on board with the sharing thing was not going to be fun. I was so glad I didn't have to do it.

"Excellent," Torrin said. He shifted his weight slightly, to let me know he felt the distance I'd put between us. Of course, being Torrin, that didn't disturb him. "We have things to discuss. First, though, I thank you for looking after Bianca while I was away."

See what I meant? Right out with it. Torrin shied away from nothing, which, to someone who had been sheltered and held back all her life, looked exhilarating. I would have loved to have been so brave.

Though courage didn't necessarily require a lack of cruelty, did it? Mattis arrived at that moment, carrying a bundle that almost certainly had to be his branding equipment. Torrin had told him to add his numbers to my arm tonight. He didn't say anything, just looked from brother to brother.

Astor, for his part, got very, very still. His eyes narrowed to slits, and he tilted his head, a smile sliding across his mouth. It wasn't a friendly smile. It was more like a challenge. I remembered that smile from when I first met him, when I sincerely believed Nox's joke that he might eat me. He might not have been a war leader or a fighter, but he was definitely a dangerous man.

"Did she tell you how *very* well I took care of her?" he drawled.

Tension sparked between the two of them. But didn't it always? Astor said his brother loved him, but their relationship didn't look particularly loving. And the last thing either of these exhausted, anxiety-laden men needed was to engage in a pissing contest over an alien female. So this alien female interrupted them before they could even get started.

My cheeks still flaming, I stepped between them and smiled brightly. "I'm just going to peek in on Nox, okay? Astor, we're all here for the night, Mattis too, so we might as well get comfortable. If you brought any food, maybe you all can figure out some lunch, because I'm starving."

And I ducked into Nox's room before any of them could say a single word.

I put my back against the wall and pressed a hand to my chest. My heart was unexpectedly just fine. In fact, I felt amazing, like I'd just spoken truth to power or something. Like I'd been even the slightest bit...brave? But they made it easy. I knew that none of them would hurt me if I behaved like a brat.

Because it was the thing I'd said I was coming in here for, I glanced toward Nox's bed. And sucked in a breath. He was shaking. Oh no, that couldn't be good. I scanned through all I knew about drug interactions as I sped over to him, my mouth already open and loading in words to call for help.

Then I noticed his face. His eyes were open, he was looking straight at me. Smiling. And he was shaking from...laughter.

I almost punched him.

"What's going on? Are you okay?" I whispered furiously. "I thought you were seizing."

"No, I am so much better. Thank you. It's just that you..." He struggled to keep his laughter quiet. "I can't believe you just did that, ordering them around. Torrin is going to be so furious. You truly are unexpected. And perfect for us."

Us, he'd said. I sank onto the side of his bed and swallowed my fears, after a few moments, even sharing some of his humor, but I couldn't quite get that *us* out of my mind. Nox, easy-going as he was, would be fine, but Astor? Sparks could fly, and I really didn't want to be at the center of that blaze.

The curtain swung away, and all three of them followed me in.

"Nox." Torrin stepped toward him. "You are awake, my brave friend. What you did? Stepping in front of the blast meant for me, I would not have you do for anything in the world. If it's my day to die, it's my day."

Nox shook his head. "That's not going to happen on my watch."

"In repayment for what you did, as is our tradition, I offer you whatever you'd like that I can provide. What would you have of me?"

The two men stared at each other a long time before Nox spoke. "I would like to share your brand with Bianca."

Torrin turned to look at me, a smirk on his face. He'd known this was going to happen, too. He nodded. "Well then, it is settled. Mattis, you have the tools to brand her now? Proceed."

"Now hold on," Astor interjected, raising both hands to indicate a time-out. "When I gave you my jewel, it was in expectation of you having your numbers removed and replaced with mine. Only mine. I wanted to be responsible for her safety."

Torrin eyed his brother. "And you will be...with us. Or would you deny us the happiness we would never hold back from you?"

Astor's mouth fell open. "You know what? Fine. It probably makes sense, since I can't even be counted on to take care of myself in the face of Baron the Idiot and his horde of bandits. How could I possibly take care of Bianca?"

Was that what this was about? I looked between all of them, noticing Nox as he tried to sit up in the bed. He struggled but managed. Mattis turned his back, pretending to be interested in branding equipment.

"You want to do something about that?" Torrin's voice was low. "You want them to stop bothering you?"

A muscle ticked in Astor's jaw. "I want to be worthy of the woman who fell from the sky. To be an equal among brothers."

"Fair enough." Torrin nodded. From his back pocket, he pulled out a knife. The longest blade I'd ever seen. "Go do something about it. Go let him know that you are the king's brother and you aren't to be trifled with. Kill him if you want. Anyone gets in your way, they'll deal with me. Go do it, and when you've finally claimed the honor that should always have been yours, come back and claim Bianca with the rest of us."

Astor stared at the knife but didn't reach for it right away. His face looked blank, like he was hiding a lot of emotion, and I could guess at all the things he wasn't saying. *Why am I not worthy already? Will this one thing, the murder of an evil man, truly change that? If I do not perform this task, will I lose her affection?*

No. No he wouldn't.

Maybe this was my day for crashing everybody's party, because I was not going to let Astor go down that path. It would break everything beautiful about him. I shoved myself between the two brothers and snatched the knife away from Torrin.

"This is ridiculous," I said. "I comprehend that your ways are different from what I'm used to, and yes, I realize that this isn't done here, but holies-curse-it, I get a say. I get to say who owns me, who cares for me, and who I care for right back. I'm not a thing to be traded and stuck in a hermetically sealed room and poked at and discussed in hushed voices as if I don't have a perfectly good voice of my own. You will listen to me! And if I can't get all of your agreement on this, this *one point*, I swear to everything sacred in the universe that I will take this knife and...a-and..."

I had no clue how to finish that threat. I wasn't going to go kill Baron Whatsit, even as satisfying as that sounded. I definitely wasn't going to kill me, not after going through all I had over the years just to keep this body alive. And I wasn't going to kill any of them, my beautiful men.

But I needed them to listen, to hear, to accept me. And also to accept Astor just as he was. Because he was already worthy. And maybe I was, too.

I was breathing hard and more furious than I could remember ever being—Torrin did have a way of waking my rage, didn't he?—and then Mattis did exactly the wrong thing. The wrongest thing any man had ever done in the history of male wrongness.

He laughed.

At me.

A low, indulgent chuckle, really, the kind of laugh that stroked its way down my throat and deep, deep into my belly, and it wasn't fair on any level. But even as I turned the laser of my fury upon him, he set his bundle of branding tools on the ground beside his feet, calmly walked over to me, took the knife from my nerveless fingers, pushed one big hand up the back of my head, deep into my hair, and kissed me.

Smack on the mouth.

In front of everybody.

CHAPTER ELEVEN

That kiss was bold. It was infuriating. It was...delicious. I didn't want to be the woman who melted in the face of opposition. I *wanted* to be more like Dreama, tough and respected and living a meaningful life, and for a while there, it had seemed I had a shot at that through my reading and teaching. But right then, with Mattis' mouth on mine, with my brain telling me this was the absolute wrong reaction in every way, I—oh all gods help me—I kissed him right back.

I didn't do it by half, either. It was like I was out of my skin, a totally different person, wild and powerful and staking my own damn claim. I reached up between us, put my hands on either side of his face, and pulled him into the kiss, sealing him to me as if I were going to consume him. I licked the seam of his lips, forcing his mouth open, and poured all my fury and desire and fear and need and hopes—*my voice* —into him.

He took it. He accepted all of it willingly and never flinched or hesitated. His hand in my hair gentled, cupping my head as I tipped it back. And none of the others said a thing. Neither did they pull me off Mattis or mock us or laugh or anything. They just stood there, patiently, accepting.

See what I meant? Good men.

I swallowed as I stepped back. Okay. I had to get my head on straight. Somehow. I had to think. "Astor, you aren't killing anyone. You're a healer. Don't concern yourself with what happened. Seems to me the problem is not you but Baron the Great. With the Reamers and whatever else coming after all of you, shouldn't you be able to walk down your own territory unmolested?"

"I think so," Nox responded. "I'll get rid of him if you want me to, Torrin. I really don't mind."

"We can't, or at least I can't order you to do it." Torrin sighed. "It's complicated. I made a promise to my father not to kill him. Dad had a...soft spot for Baron. To do so—and I'm not saying there isn't a threshold over which I could be pushed to do it—would be a betrayal of that promise. I won't do it until I have to. And Astor is not hurt. He's just...bothered."

His brother pointed at him. "That's why you told me to do it. You can't. Dad didn't make me promise."

Torrin grinned. "True. Now who needs to eat? Bianca? Hungry?"

"Brother," Dreama interrupted, stepping into the room. To a one, the men jumped like they'd been startled, but Dreama seemed to take the whole tableau in stride. These four had probably done enough wild things in their lives that she was immune to shock. "Perhaps I could take Bianca out to eat with me. You could all use a little time to settle in."

"After she's marked." Torrin plopped down on a chair. "Mark her up, Mattis. Then she can go out with you, sister. By all means."

Dreama rolled her eyes, but it seemed like all the men

were looking elsewhere, and I was the only one who saw her. I smiled to myself. I could grow to like this woman.

Which was probably good, right? Since I was basically getting hitched to all of her male relatives, not to mention her friends. In my world, that wouldn't alter our relationship much—kids tended to leave their birth families when they formed their own households, mostly because travel between planets consumed a lot of time and resources, and you couldn't very well haul an extended family around. Plus, with enforced euthanasia at a certain age and health markers, we tended not to have a lot of living relatives. Only special cases stayed close with their siblings well into adulthood. Like me.

I'd never had a sister. What did you even do with a sister? Not that Brent and I did much together other than check in on each other. A lot. Dreama didn't seem suffocating like that.

Mattis was unrolling his cloth-bound set of tools, and Torrin stoked a fire in the hearth. This room had a little fireplace at the base of one of its ventilation shafts, and the shaft itself was cased in a material that looked...familiar. Like starship insulation? Could some of these tunnels have been dug early on, right after the prison ships landed or crashed here?

My secret knowledge weighed on me, and I wished I could share it, talk about it, but I had no idea how that would change any of these relationships. Truthfully, I was too scared to try.

While Mattis heated his branding tool, I looked around for a place to sit, but this room wasn't Mattis' bar. There weren't tables and chairs and nice, comfy places to rest my arm while he mutilated it. I perched myself on the edge of Nox's bed, down by his feet so the smell from the branding wouldn't bother him too much.

I glanced up to find Torrin looking at me, though not with his usual scowl. This time, he had laughter in his eyes.

"You may use the throne in the anteroom if you require a more suitable chair."

"Yikes, no," I replied before even thinking. "Also, how did you know what I was thinking?"

He exchanged a look with Astor, and both men cracked up. Laughter looked wrong on Torrin, but it was also comforting on a deep level. Which I didn't want to think about right now.

"You have what the elders call a speaking face," Mattis explained, testing the heat on his branding tool.

This time, Dreama didn't bother to hide her eye-roll. "Can we just get on with this? I'm starving, and I'll wager she is, too."

"Don't rush the artist," Mattis said, letting a droplet of water fall on the tool and judging the instant steam.

"It's not art," Dreama said. "It's inhumane."

"Oh, why don't you tell us what you really think?" Astor said, but I had been watching Torrin, and the laughter was gone from his expression. Instantly. The black clouds had drifted back into his eyes.

"Dreama, this is our custom. Be silent, and do not harass Mattis," he said.

Astor shook his head. "Not to mention you would kill for this to happen for you if you could find someone who fit all your requirements."

Now that was interesting. I regarded Dreama. She was very pretty and would probably look feminine under all that armor. But maybe femininity held different meaning here? "What are your requirements?"

"I need to not have known the person since I was born."

Mattis pressed the brand down on my skin. I winced, but it wasn't bad. "Whose numbers are those?"

"Mine," Nox supplied, clearly proud, even though he looked like he was about to fall over asleep.

"We will affix the marks in the order in which we met you," Mattis said. "That's the custom when a woman takes more than one husband. Granted, it's unusual to mark all the claims at the same time. Usually families take months or years to arrange themselves. Just another way you're special, B."

"Except for my mark," Torrin said, "since it was already there, mine will be first. And I also claim first night."

Astor made a strangled sound and looked like he was about to protest, but then he must have caught the humor in Torrin's eyes, and he just shrugged. They did that a lot, I was beginning to realize, the back-and-forth arguing underpinned by love. Maybe that was just how brothers behaved. Brent and I certainly snipped at each other, though I couldn't say there was a lot of love beneath it.

I looked back at Dreama, wresting the subject back to her future plans. "There are other City-States. Surely you could..."

She winced. "Hard to fall in love with someone that my brother might kill any second. And believe it or not, I think our City-State might be the best of the bunch. Women don't fare so well in other places. And I know I said I just wanted someone I didn't know, but it's more than that. I want someone who challenges me. Who I don't always agree with but that's okay. Who I can argue with and sometimes lose."

So maybe the arguing itself was a way people expressed affection around here. Odd, but also kind of sweet. It sure took the edge off of the seemingly constant state of conflict.

On the bed, Nox had started snoring lightly. I looked over. He'd passed out, as if he'd been keeping himself awake just long enough to watch me become his.

"We should leave him be," Astor said. "He is still healing and needs rest."

"Almost done." Mattis laid in the next number as gently as he could. It did hurt, but the pain wasn't bad. If these were going on in the order in which I'd met them, this would be Astor's number. I peered down at it and then glanced at him. When our eyes met, a charge zapped through the room.

I wished I could read his mind. I really didn't know what he was thinking.

He stalked across the room, and a second later, his mouth was inches from mine. "I never wanted to share anything with Torrin, but you're worth it." His lips took mine in what could only be called possession. "Don't forget me. You're mine in three days."

With that, he left the room. My lips were bruised, and my head spun. Where had he gone?

Torrin laughed, throwing his head back. "He's always been so dramatic."

Mattis pressed down the last brand. "Mine." He winked at me, and that actually did take some of the sting out.

It was official. I belonged to all of them.

Dreama grabbed my hand. "Lunch. Now."

Happily, she'd grabbed the hand that wasn't attached to a freshly scarred arm, but she didn't yank right away. She paused to let Mattis clean the brand site first, and, although the branding itself hadn't hurt so much—like before—the cleansing part was a little more thorough. A sharp spike of pain pushed tears into my eyes, and I clenched my teeth and held my breath.

I couldn't help myself gripping Dreama's hand hard, though. She would have bruises, probably. But also, she didn't react, so maybe she knew how it would hurt. Hadn't Mattis said something about little kids getting brands to mark them as members of the City-State? So even without receiving a husband's brand, Dreama likely remembered something of this pain. She let me squeeze pretty hard.

When Mattis applied the cleansing solution, it cooled and numbed the wound, and then, like with my burned hands after the crash, I just instantly felt better. I wished I could thank Astor for concocting such amazing medicine.

And then I realized I would get my chance to thank him. *You're mine in three days*, he'd said. Well then. My mouth went a bit dry.

I could feel the others looking at me, especially Torrin, drat him. He always saw my secrets and would probably fling this one back at me at an uncomfortable moment, just like the others. I deliberately turned my face away from him and flashed Mattis a quick smile. "Thank you, it's good now."

"It'll look prettier in a couple of days, like the first one," said Mattis, setting his tools aside. "We just need to keep it clean."

"What we need is to get her fed," Dreama grumbled.

"Agreed," said Torrin. "Go on, already, and when you finish up bonding with my branded lady, bring her back to me."

Mattis stood and held the curtain aside gallantly. "I'll watch over Nox while you're gone."

I met his gaze and remembered his mouth, and a strange feeling shivered through me—hot, slinky, scary, and exhilarating. I felt it at the base of my spine, the back of my throat, and—alarmingly—between my legs.

I had met Mattis last, so his brand was last. Which meant...four days. His eyes promised it would be worth the wait.

I stood, and Dreama let loose of my hand. When she turned and made for the door, I followed, hoping no one noticed the heat in my face.

We didn't go right back to the surface or the hangar, and the only other part of the tunnel system I knew was Astor's rooms, which were so near the surface they had vents that let in light and air—and Howler sounds. But where we would have turned left to go there, we turned right, and the corridor widened and something else changed, something subtle.

The smell. The throne room suite, Astor's lab when he wasn't cooking something delicious, and Mattis' bar all smelled like human-filled extensions of the dusty, bitter planet itself, just overlaid with the not unpleasant scent that I secretly thought of as "men doing things." It wasn't as pungent as full-on sweat, and it didn't smell like all the busy people I'd known in space, but it was distinctly male, or at least common to *my* males.

Mine. That word was surfacing fairly often now, and it no longer scared me. If I was theirs, so also were they mine. I would have to remind them of this. One by one and over and over. That interior, slinky, secret feeling stroked its way through me.

Ahem. Right. I gathered my wayward thoughts, which I was sure had only deepened my blush.

The place where Dreama brought me smelled different, like water. Clean, organic, cool, and about as unlike the surface of this planet as it was possible to get. We passed under a wide, curved doorway into a cavern that was easily as big as a starship. The ceiling and floor reached for each other in a series of spikes, and lanterns glittered off of slick rock surfaces and languid, still pools. A group of women sat on cushions near one of the pools, and a basket had been unburdened of its contents between them. They looked up when we arrived, but seeing Dreama, they made space for us.

"This is Bianca," Dreama introduced me, and most of the women nodded like they already knew who I was. "She just took four brands—including both of my brothers—and has no idea what's coming. Figured you all could give her some idea what to expect."

I blanched. "What?"

Were things...different here?

The woman all the way to the left, with brown hair and

sharp green eyes, leaned forward. "Did you really fall from the sky?"

"I did." I sat in an empty space among them. If I was going to be here, I should be comfortable. "My ship crashed."

She nodded. "My bonded says that there are all kinds of new weapons, too. But it makes me a little nutty to think that there are ships flying around up there over our heads that we can't see."

"Okay," Dreama interrupted, and they all shifted. They definitely deferred to her. "I didn't bring her here to talk about the ship. That's not something we can control. What we do about that is up to Torrin." She passed me a loaf of bread and some kind of meat. I still wasn't sure what I was eating half the time. It all tasted good, and so far, it hadn't made me sick. I was just grateful that everyone was feeding me, since so far, I had provided nothing to the City-State. Well, maybe my reading skills had saved Nox, but other than that, not much.

"What are joinings like where you are from?" This question came from a blonde in the corner. She sewed while she asked me. "That might help us know how to tell you what to expect."

"I've never been married, ah bonded, or whatever you want to call it." I sighed. "My brother isn't wed either, and not many of the people I worked with were married. It's one of those situations where most people marry for politics or for money. Clout. All kinds of reasons. With the breeding restrictions, there's little point in doing that if you're not going to get to have children anyway. My parents seemed happy enough, although they spent almost no time together when they weren't having to be political. She lived her life, he lived his."

They all stared at me. Did they suddenly think I had two heads? I rubbed the back of my neck. Yes, I was feeling a little bit alien at that moment. We were all human, but I was not like them. The blonde rose from the floor and walked over to hug me. I startled. What was she doing? Oh, we were touching. Yes, I'd gotten used to the men doing it, but now it looked like the women did, too.

"Sounds lonely. I can promise you that you'll never be alone like that here. If you're not with them—and in plural bonding, you're with them a lot—you'll be with us. Probably exactly us. We do tend to be sort of...caste like here. The prostitutes stay together, the wives together, the single women together. Except for Dreama. She's with everyone."

Dreama shook her head. "Bianca will be with everyone, too. This is Torrin's bonded. The wife of the leader takes care of everyone."

I'd never had friends outside of my work when I'd been teaching. But we'd mostly talked about work. As I digested all the information I'd been given, the blonde woman walked away. I needed names to call them since they all knew me.

"I'm afraid I don't know what to call all of you."

The green-eyed woman smiled, and it was so friendly and open and *easy*, I was taken aback. My first instinctive thought was, what's her angle? But that wasn't fair. These people had been nothing but kind to me.

"I'm Farrin, Gaetens bonded, and she," she gestured to the blonde, who had stopped near a larger basket crammed with textiles, "is Birdie, bonded to Ivors *and* Orlis."

Dreama rolled her eyes at this, and I was sure there was a story, probably an amusing one, but Farrin didn't tell it. I'd have to ask Birdie about it later.

A third woman, who hadn't spoken yet, offered a shy smile.

"You can call me Nina," she said. "I'm bonded thrice, similar to your four, and reciting all their names every time I meet someone would be exhausting. That's one thing to know, I suppose—your role in our City-State and to some extent your social status are dictated by tradition, but although our men use words like 'claim' and mark you with their numbers, they do not own you as they own cattle. Neither do they make claims for the purpose of politics or power."

"Tell Sorcha that," Dreama muttered.

Nina smiled and went on, "When a woman is claimed by one or many, she becomes his responsibility and purpose. His heart." She flattened one palm over the center of her chest. "To some extent, your bondeds serve you. It is their goal to see you content and safe."

"That isn't exactly how they've presented the situation," I said.

Nina laughed, and it was the sweetest, most musical sound. I wondered if she was a poetry-singer like Astor. "We are talking about Torrin and Astor, are we not? I can imagine how *those* two have described your situation."

Dreama joined in the laughter. "That's why Torrin wanted you marked right away," she explained. "To protect you. He knew that he was essentially committing the rest of his life to your comfort and security. He always leads with his heart, poor brother."

"But he offered all that, right off, to an alien who fell from the sky?" I said before I could stop myself. "That's insane. He knew—he *knows*—nothing about me, not even whether we will get along." So far, we weren't doing just fantastic at that, Torrin and me.

Nina and Dreama exchanged a look.

"What?" I asked.

Dreama shook her head, but Nina responded carefully, "When our men engage in battle for the right to farm Eden, many of the rules are put aside. Raiders, Reamers... The dangers are everywhere. A pair bonding, the marks on your arm, is sometimes the only thing that keeps women from being kidnapped or sold or worse."

I didn't want to hear about the worse. I shuddered. "I should thank him, I guess."

Dreama let out a scoffing laugh. "If you want to surprise the hell out of him, do just that."

"If what you're saying is true, he just—they *all* just committed their entire lives to keeping me safe, even though they had no guarantee I wasn't a spy or a biological weapon. That's a lot."

Nina raised her brows and nibbled a corner of the sweet bread. Took her time. Swallowed. "I don't know, if a potentially game-changing weapon fell from the sky into my lap, I'd want to put my numbers all over it right away, before somebody could steal it."

She probably didn't mean that to be as deflating as it sounded.

"But all of them?" Dreama said. "I could see your point if just Torrin had put his numbers on her, but there was no reason for Astor and Mattis and Nox to do so, too."

Nina's eyes widened, and her mouth formed an O, but before she could say anything, Birdie flitted back to our group and plopped down in her seat with a whole new armful of cloth pieces for her quilt. She made a thin woo sound and giggled. "*Those* are your four? Girl, you weren't claimed because of your mysterious flying transport or weapons. If those particular men all put their numbers on you, this is something else, something much funner. You're gonna... So who's got first night?"

I was going to what? "Torrin. But I spent last night with Astor."

Farrin sat forward. "Before you wore his marks and while you were just marked by Torrin?"

"Yes." I made eye contact with Dreama, who winked at

me. Why did she do that? "But I guess technically tonight is the first night."

Nina smiled. "Have fun with that. I hear Torrin commands attention, not just on his throne. Hearts are breaking in the City-State tonight. And as for what they think versus what will happen... Give it a little time, Bianca. They've never had a woman bonded to them before. Nox will get it correct right away. He's sweet. Good to his family. Loyal. Mattis may not trust it, and Dreama's royal brothers will stumble around for a while. That is my prediction."

Dreama shook her head. "I don't want to hear anything about any of them in bed, ever. The four of them used to be together so much that Mattis and Nox might as well have been my brothers when we were young. Nothing. I mean it. Otherwise, it's quite nice to have a sister, Bianca. And maybe someday, you'll feel more settled and you'll tell us about your life before. We can share secrets."

Secrets were always something I'd kept to myself. There was always too much at risk to share anything that could land anyone in trouble. Including myself.

Still, I'd never had friends before.

"Tell me about your families."

I sat back to listen. I'd always been really, really good at that.

CHAPTER TWELVE

Dreama dropped me off back at Torrin's place with the promise to return the next day. If I was going to teach people to read, then I had to go through the books and see what we were dealing with. I had planned to spend the next day doing that, but she wanted me to stop after lunch and come with her to view the farms. Since I was one of them, I needed to see what we were fighting for.

That made sense. Maybe someday, this would all feel normal. I wasn't there yet.

Nox slept in the same guest bed, with Mattis out cold in the chair next to him. I looked around until I found a blanket, and I covered him in it. He stirred but didn't wake. The room was chilled. If he wasn't careful, he was going to get sick.

I walked back through the throne room and ducked past another curtain, toward where I thought Torrin's bedroom might be. It was quiet in here. I could almost hear my own heartbeat in my ears. Light in the room was low, but I could make out a shape in the center of this room. A bed. Like heat on my skin, Torrin's gaze burned from across the room. He lay on top of that bed, dressed in pajama pants and nothing else.

Without a word, he extended his hand, and I walked toward him. "Did you have a nice day?"

The closer I got, the more I could see that his eyes were red-rimmed. He had clearly not slept, and maybe he hadn't slept in a while.

"I did. The women were all very nice to me."

"There are a lot of underlying politics that get played around here all the time. I imagine if Dreama brought you to a group, then they're all on our side. Tomorrow, I will deal with those that aren't. You seem very smart to me. I imagine you'll figure things out."

He rose, my hand still in his, and drew me toward a closet and a dresser. "These are filled with clothes for you. I think they'll work. Including pajamas. I don't want you to get cold at night."

I stared at the selection. "Thank you. That's so nice of you to think of me."

"I want you to be comfortable here." He drew me toward the bathroom. "We have running water right now. That usually stops in the winter. Take advantage of it. Every year we have to fix the mess of it...and I'm never sure how long that's going to take."

Maybe if they didn't have to constantly fight the Reamers, they could work some of that out. Seemed like it was an endless cycle of fighting and survival. He let go of my hand. "I'll let you get yourself ready for bed."

"Thanks." I was repeating myself with the gratitude, but he was proving to be more considerate than I'd have thought he would be. I took a long shower. The pressure wasn't great, but it was there. Exactly how gross was I going to be with all the dust in the air when we didn't have running water? I dried my hair as best I could and slipped on the pajamas he'd left for me. When I came out, it was to find Torrin sitting up on the bed, staring at a wide paper covered with a series of numbers in front of him.

He didn't look up but sensed my unasked question. "They're crops we expect to have before the cold season. I'm doing brief calculations. Current number of citizens, how many babies will be born, how many mouths to feed. We always have to reduce a certain amount of the population that will die in accidents, illness, murder, or war. Rough estimates."

All of that with no written language. It really was remarkable. I sat down next to him, tucking my feet beneath me. "You're worried about food supplies."

He smoothed down the paper. "Always. War and food. But they're not new problems. Ongoing. Are you tired?"

I wasn't, but he clearly was, and I'd bet he wasn't going to sleep unless I did. I moved the paper to a side table and pulled the blanket up, taking a moment to admire his naked chest. He was strong, sculpted, and beautiful, even covered in scars. "Won't you get cold?"

He'd given me warm shirts and pants to wear to bed.

Torrin shook his head. "I like the cold at night. Harder to get cooler than it is to get warm. If I get chilled, I'll cover up." He paused. "Does it bother you?"

"No." I smiled at him.

This Torrin, soft spoken, slow moving, caring, he wasn't nearly as intimidating as the version I'd met on that throne of bones. He extinguished the light and climbed in next to me.

"I understand I have a lot to thank you for," I said. "Marking me made me safe. Thank you."

Beneath the blanket, he took my hand in his. There was no light in the room, and his gentle squeeze anchored me when I might have felt lost in the darkness. "You're welcome, but I admit that wasn't the only reason I did it."

"To secure me if I was a weapon or threat of some kind, then."

His laugh surprised me. "I never thought you were that. I'm pretty good at reading people. I saw who you were right away. A lost, beautiful woman. Not a weapon to be used or something like that. Although, I admit I love that you can read and that you knew about the burrs and how to heal Nox from them. Smart and beautiful."

"Then what was your other reason?" Talking in the dark was easier than in the light. It was like we were cocooned away from the rest of the world.

"Maybe Dreama isn't the only one who didn't want to bond with someone so familiar they were practically relatives." His lips met mine, and I blinked in surprise. Torrin didn't push, didn't try for anything else. Just held me like that for a long moment before he kissed the end of my nose. "I probably won't sleep much. I never do. But stay right here with me, I will take care of your heart. I take care of everything."

He did. He took care of everything for everybody. "Does anybody ever take care of you?"

I asked the question before I thought about it, and for a minute, I wondered if he even heard me. His breathing didn't change, he didn't move, and his reply was a long time coming. Finally, he said, "How do you mean?"

In the brightness of day, those words and the voice that made them would have been absolutely innocent. They could have referred to the people who cleaned his clothes or fueled his transport or cooked his food. Here, though, I allowed myself to believe in a deeper, more intimate meaning.

"Turn on to your stomach," I told him.

Torrin obeyed. And the universe did not even stop its motion. Stars didn't fall out of the sky. Wonders.

"Your subjects behave as if you have a shell of invulnerability around you. You cannot be touched by harm. But also, you cannot be touched." Sighing into the dark, I rolled toward him, giving into the yearning and pressing the heels of my hands into his hard-muscled back. "And touch, I've learned, is kind of a big deal around here. So who touches *you*, the untouchable leader? Who cares for the man who cares for everyone else?"

The bedclothes muffled his voice when he said, "See what I mean about you being smart? You see too much, girl from the sky."

I chuckled low and continued my kneading, working up his spine and digging deep into the knots in his shoulders near his neck. "It's dark. I see only what is in my mind, my memory. I've had thoughts."

His body moved beneath my hands, but I couldn't tell if he answered my laughter or groaned. Was it possible to do both? Despite my core disbelief that I could make a man like him groan in pleasure—the feeling of exclusion and lack of worth went deep—I realized that I wanted to believe. I wanted to comfort him.

"You are too good at this," he said, his voice a rumble that I felt as much as heard.

My mouth was dry. I had to moisten my lips when I leaned over him, putting my weight into my hands. "Where I am from, I wouldn't be allowed to be with a man like this. I would not be allowed a husband."

"What?"

"Because of the medical condition, my heart, right?" I feathered my words close over him, letting my breath bathe him. So close. My hands traced the shape of him—strong arms, sculpted back, his spine dipping down at the band of his pajama bottoms. I lifted the waistband, testing the warm skin beneath. "It never occurred to me that there were whole levels of interactions I was missing. Not just the big things, like pride at being chosen by another person or satisfaction in providing safety or security for someone I care about, but also the little, immediate things. Like touch. Like working the knots out of muscles in the dark. Like..."

I put my mouth against his shoulder blade, and there was no mistaking his groan this time.

"Like kissing someone's skin, just because you want to."

He flipped me over fast, his body hovering over mine. Even in the darkness, I could see the flash of his eyes as they held my gaze. "Then they are foolish up there in the sky where you're from, and I'll be glad that we're rid of them down here. Women can't be so different in place to place. You are stunningly beautiful, sharp-mouthed, smart, and intuitive. If they did not value you, then their loss is my gain."

He kissed me. I never could have imagined what Torrin's kiss would feel like, how it would consume me from the outside and press into the very cells of my body, until I no longer needed air, I just needed him. I wrapped my arms around his neck and drew him closer.

He sighed against me, kissing me again and again. The markings hadn't told me what his embrace did—that this was forever. That Torrin was a man who was willing to share but not to give up what was his. Right then and for always, that was going to be me.

He kissed me with all of his attention, all of his restrained aggression, all of his focus consuming me. His lips were full, strong, and beautiful. I smiled at that last thought, and he pulled back to kiss my face. "And I make you smile. I'll take that as a good thing."

Torrin had no sooner uttered those words than he rolled us over so that I was on top of him. What did he want? I wasn't sure why he'd done that. But maybe it had to do with what we'd been doing earlier. Maybe he liked me touching him, letting me be in control for a moment. Even if he'd demonstrated that in half a second and without warning, he could take that back.

I had so little experience with this, and yet I pressed my lips down onto him as though I'd done this a million times. He wrapped his arms around me but let me lead in this exchange. The minutes passed, and soon I couldn't breathe from the want forming inside of me and didn't care that I couldn't. Torrin grew impossibly harder.

With a soft moan, he slipped his hand inside my pajama top, feeling my breast. My nipples immediately pebbled, hardening to the point of pain, and yet it was the most delicious discomfort. I sucked in a breath, stopping what I was doing just to feel that moment.

"I think you like that."

"I...do." I liked it a *lot*, but speaking right then had become difficult. Between our bodies and under the thin slip of pajamas, his hands cradled both of my breasts, squeezing, even as he stroked the nipples. With his thumbs? Probably. Felt like thumbs. But whatever he was doing, the tactile sensation was rough and warm and winding itself through my body, pooling between my legs.

Which was exactly where I wanted his touch most.

"There's something else wrong with me," I managed. He needed to know this, but deep in the haze of desire, I hated myself for bringing it up. Why couldn't I just enjoy the moment, the act?

"There is nothing wrong with you." He shifted somehow beneath me—maybe sitting up?—and one of his hands slid to my hip, steadying me atop him. "And you've nothing to be ashamed of."

Oh holies, he was right—I was ashamed. That was the word. "I've never done this before."

I just blurted the confession. He stilled, and I thought, oh no, now I've gone and done it. I've turned him off for real this time. But then both his hands dropped to my waist, and before I realized what was happening, he had the pajama top up and over my head. He flung it out into the room, and cool night air met my skin.

"That's why you're on top," he said. "Your pace, Bianca, your first night. Show me what you want."

Torrin's thoughtfulness caught me off guard, but in retrospect, it probably shouldn't have. He was a tactician, always thinking several steps ahead of everybody else. And clearly, *he* had done this before, so I relaxed and sank into the yearning, pulling sensation.

I drew my knees in close to his hips and knelt, moving his hands until they were at the band of my pajama bottoms. "Here," I said. "Touch me here."

He pushed the trousers down until they rode low on my hips and stroked long fingers beneath, delving through thatch and folds to find the slick, superheated point of my arousal. Oh holies. All holies. This was the ecstasy the priests sang of, ten thousand times better than a prayer. I tried to pinch my eyes shut and bite my lip to keep from crying out, but a mewl escaped. His finger paused.

"There?"

I was beyond words and could only emit something vaguely mmm-hmm-ish.

He circled the spot, slow and torturous, pausing intermittently to press, and each time he did, my body convulsed. I was shaking, moaning, wanting to writhe. And beneath my pajamas, I could feel the shape of him growing longer, harder as I rode him. The pajamas themselves were too much. I needed them gone. His too. I needed to feel him, just Torrin, skin to skin, against me and inside me, but as much as I wanted all of this, I couldn't pull away. The connection between us, his fingers on my clitoris—pinching now, *all ancients and holies yes*—was inexorable, untenable. I was breaking and loving every second of it.

And then he withdrew his touch. Pulled his hand away. Abruptly. I almost wept.

"Pajamas," Torrin rasped in a voice completely lacking his usual control. "Off. Now."

Ha! He might have said he was following my lead, my pace, but he just couldn't abandon command entirely, could he?

That was fine by me. Right then, I wanted nothing more than for him to tell me what to do, to dictate how we would make this ache riding through me stop. I needed...I needed him to do something.

Both of us finally naked, he flipped me onto my back and moved until his head was positioned right by my most private spots.

"It is my pleasure to teach you things tonight. I have a feeling before very long, you'll be instructing me, and I'll gladly beg you for it."

He'd beg me? I didn't know what I'd say, because he quickly distracted me by placing a kiss on one of my thighs. I sucked in my breath. Was this allowed? Was this something that people...did?

Torrin kissed my other thigh, and I shuddered.

"Is this...is this...normal?" I managed to voice my question.

He nuzzled my thigh as he answered me. "There's no such thing as normal. There is only the pleasure that two people can give each other in the heat of the night. And sometimes the heat of the day, too. And sometimes, it's more than just one-to-one. Whatever people consent to, that is what is."

I'd have to dwell on that later. For now, I couldn't think as he pushed my legs apart. Why had he done that? What was he...?

His mouth pressed down, kissing me *there*. I gasped and might have closed my legs, except that his hand on my knee stopped me from doing so. Slowly, ever so slowly, he licked me. I moaned, the sensations surprising me. What was happening?

Sometimes in the middle of the night, I woke up throbbing. A bundle of nerves always seemed to be the cause, and the only relief, particularly when I was young, was to rub against my pillow until it stopped. This felt like that, only so much more intense. What was I going to do? Could I rub against his tongue?

And then...oh by the holies...he found that bundle of nerves. I gasped and couldn't have controlled what I did next if I'd tried, which I absolutely didn't try to do. Why? Well, because Torrin really seemed to like it.

He moaned, and the noise spurred me forward. I rode his tongue, the more he licked, the more I writhed. I was wet, more than I'd believed possible. I practically gushed. He'd told me not to be ashamed, and so I wouldn't be.

But soon I was panting. Was this normal? Should I ask, or should I just...

I exploded. Stars crossed in front of my eyes. I gasped, sucking in air, but this had nothing to do with my heart or my lungs. This wasn't physical malfunction. It was the opposite—perfect physical function.

Pleasure.

Holies, yes.

It came in waves, like gravity or sound or water, pressure after pressure after pressure of delicious sensation. I didn't tell my hands to grip Torrin's head, to fist in his lush, thick hair, but suddenly, I was holding his face against me, holding the moment. Holding the stars.

The crashing subsided, like an orchestral denouement, leaving me with a deep, intense, and glorious exhaustion. I loosened my grip on his hair and exhaled one long, unsteady breath.

"Ancient and holy ones, log my plea, wrap me in the mesh of your grace, ere I descend to rapture." The old prayer, the first prayer, slipped out of my mouth without pauses between words, as a reflex. It was any devout person's reaction to certainty that the end approached.

I wasn't devout, but I felt like I had just survived the most brilliant death, the perfect end, and I'd come through it.

The rumble of Torrin's chuckle brought me out of the fugue. He pressed a kiss against the ridge of my pelvis. "I've been called a lot of things," he said, "but never ancient, and never, ever holy."

"And yet, you deliver rapture like a god."

"Hmm." Another kiss, near my navel. "You do know how to make a man feel like one."

He moved up to lie beside me, sharing his warmth with me, and I turned into him, ready for whatever came next. I knew, academically and biologically, what happened during coitus. But I'd long decided it wasn't going to happen for me —to me. And I had no idea what the immediate next step was here. The thing he'd done with his mouth, should I also do with mine? How would that work?

For all those years in medical isolation, reading and learning, you'd think I'd know a little bit about the most important things. These things. How to return the gift of physical pleasure. And yet here I was, with one of the most attractive men I'd ever encountered, my body still humming with the skill he'd lavished on it, and I had no idea how to proceed.

Disappointment in myself—in my body and my lived experience—formed an obstruction in my throat that tasted like tears, but I forced myself to swallow it.

CHAPTER THIRTEEN

"Where you are from," Torrin said, his voice a rumble deep in his chest, beneath my cheek, "do people ever run long distances, as a contest or sport?"

"Well, not me personally," I said. "Bad heart."

"Right. But others do this?"

"Yeah." I tried not to let the word sound wistful, but it hurt a little, him bringing up something else prohibited to me, some other very human activity that I'd been made to believe was not possible. Was he now going to tell me that I couldn't actually go through the rest of the mating? That I'd done something wrong? Please no, don't stop. I'm fine. I'm better than fine.

"Here, we call this a long-haul. It is a test of stamina, but also a chance to be alone with the land, to learn her shape and to accept and endure her challenges. To prove oneself to her."

Okay. I said nothing, but surely, he could feel my tension.

Torrin dropped a kiss atop my hair and enveloped me in his strong, warm arms. "Please think of tonight as your long-haul with me. Take time. Find the hills and the valleys. This is not a fast run. Explore. We have all night."

We had all night? This could go on all night? I opened and closed my mouth. He shifted slightly, rolling more toward me and tugging on the end of my hair. "Do you need anything? Water?"

I'm not sure what spurred me forward. I wasn't the aggressive type. But he'd just had his mouth on my most private spots. I loved it. I wanted more. And I really didn't want to wait.

I kissed him, square on the lips. He sucked in his breath. This whole evening had started because I'd wanted to take care of him, something that obviously didn't happen very often. Maybe that was the thing to do.

He thought he was looking after my needs.

I could taste myself on him. That shouldn't be exciting. And yet...it kind of was. I scooted forward. We lay on our sides, facing each other. I reached out and found what I was looking for. I'd heard men call it many things, mostly when they didn't know I was listening. The dirtiest had always seemed to be *cock*. In this moment, that's how I thought of it.

I stroked Torrin's cock. It was warm, thick, hard. I swallowed. Would that eventually fit inside me? It seemed highly unlikely.

He jerked as I stroked the length of him. "Bianca."

The unflappable Torrin, who led men into battle, was moved by this. "I think you like this, Torrin."

"You are why men speak poetry." His voice was low. "I was going to be patient and unhurried. It's not my nature. Yes, touch me, Bianca. Touch me until I tell you to stop, because the truth is that when I lose myself tonight, I want it to be inside your hot pussy."

I widened my eyes. Not that he could see it. Between my thinking *cock* and his saying *pussy*, we were being downright dirty tonight. I grinned. It was kind of fantastic.

"Tell me how you like it. Like this?" I continued to stroke him as I had been.

He grunted before he responded. "Harder."

I tightened my grip. I didn't want to break it or hurt him. But also, he was kind of the most solid thing in the universe. Unbreakable. Dependable. I had never felt this safe or wanted, and with every stroke, I told him so. Thanked him for it. And felt his passion grow. I could feel it in the tension threading through his body, tightening all his muscles, in the way his breathing became more rapid. I leaned toward him and kissed him, even as I stroked his cock.

"I'm not sure harder is possible," I murmured against his mouth. "Feels plenty hard already."

"This is what you do to men, to me," he said.

I could tell him what he did to me. Oh, I could tell him lots. But mostly this... "Torrin, I want you inside me."

His breath caught, and he stilled. There was so much latent energy in the room, so much delicious restraint, that I felt like I was swimming languorously through it. I brushed a thumb over the tip, and he flinched into my hand, slick and hot.

"Do it."

I released my clasp and pushed him slightly, and he rolled to his back. Desire thrummed through my body. Not only did I want him—want to fuck him—but I wanted it rough and dirty and delicious and wild, and at the same time, I was terrified of all my many wants. And he was so in control of himself. Would he think less of me if I just lost it? But could I stand to not lose it? *I mean, really. Bianca, you're overthinking*, I told myself. *He just said to do it*.

So I did.

I mounted him, pressed the tip of him against my opening, and guided that gorgeous, enormous cock exactly where I wanted it.

It didn't fit. He was too big, and I was clearly not doing this right, but he didn't chide or criticize or correct. He didn't move at all. Just like he'd promised, he let me set the pace, let me ease myself onto him, impale myself with the length of him. There wasn't a lot of resistance. Should there have been? But it was like my body knew how this dance went, and it was primed and ready, opening like an iris when it let in light. I took him all the way in, tip to root, and then paused. Waited.

He felt perfect here, like this, in me.

"Are you okay?" he asked.

"Um, better than okay. Possibly better than perfect."

The warmth of his hands bracketed my hips, then moved downward. Big hands, warm. There was kindness in his voice when he said, "It absolutely is. You are."

Between the gentleness of his words and the heat of his body, I felt like a star, too bright for my own eyes. Too happy. I'd never been this happy.

"Bianca?"

"Mmm-hmm?"

"You can move. Or not. If you have ideas you want to try out, things that you think would feel good, feel free. I have loved everything you've done so far. I trust you."

He trusted me with his pleasure, and with my own? I was still hot with desire, but a different warmth suffused me right then. A softer, more painful, too-sweet warmth that pushed up behind the backs of my eyes and made me want to press kisses into his skin forever. It was...ugh. I'd have to find a name for it later.

Because right now, with his urging, I moved.

Slowly at first. Up and then down. He moaned, a delicious sound from the back of his throat. I wished I could bottle that noise and listen to it over and over. But then I couldn't think of that at all because the more I moved over him, the more I let my body do what it was that it seemed to know how to do. I ground against his cock slowly and then sped up.

Oh yes, this was heaven.

He smirked. "I knew you'd be a natural at this. You're so fucking hot."

That kind of language, the coarseness of it, was absolutely perfect for moments like this. I moved even faster. In and out. I loved this. Feelings rushed through me, a pressure and a need for something I reached for, even if I wasn't one hundred percent sure what that was yet.

I knew I could get it if I just kept going. He reached forward, grabbing on to my hips to steady me and change my motion just slightly. Yes, I sighed, throwing my head back.

"Just like that," Torrin said through gritted teeth. "I can touch you better this way."

He was right. I'd figure out why later but for now it was just...

Again, explosions, a series of them, one coming hard on the heels of the last, melting my body into a hot cauldron of pleasure. My first thought was I couldn't breathe. But then I realized, oh yes, I could. Breathing was fine, everything automatic was working great. It was the thinking that was gone, and I was completely okay with that. My muscles clenched. Beneath me, his body jerked, warmth filled me, but I hardly noticed compared to the other heat waves rushing through my body.

This was heaven.

How had I ever done without this?

Sometime later, I lay on his chest, listening to his strong heartbeat. I'd always been jealous of how easily people went through life with their strong, healthy hearts, never thinking of them at all when I'd had to worry about every beat. Yet, I was enormously glad for Torrin's strong beat. Slow. Steady. Doing exactly what it should do.

He squeezed me tighter against him. "I don't sleep very long or very well, but I won't wake you. Or I'll try not to. I've never actually slept with anyone before."

I digested that information. I knew he had a reputation for being good at what we'd just done...and I'd agree with that assessment. Not that I'd ever tell anyone. I was suddenly feeling really protective of that information. That was interesting, and I'd dwell on it later.

I couldn't seem to focus on much of anything. So I let my eyes close.

Morning pressed through the window, light making me open my eyes slowly. Next to me, Torrin breathed deeply. I wasn't nestled against his chest anymore, but he held me close, pressing me to the bed, his arm over me like he was afraid I'd move away while he slept.

I lifted my head, slightly. Torrin shifted with my movement but did rouse. I managed to move his arm and sneak toward his bathroom.

This was a different planet, so much was completely *other* than how I knew things, but the bathroom was pretty much the same, which made things easy. I groaned. They'd warned me the water could stop being warm. I wasn't going to take it for granted.

Finishing up the things I needed to do, including putting on a shirt I found in there that was his, I made my way back out.

Torrin lifted his head, rubbing his eyes. "Fuck. Sorry. I...I really knocked out."

I climbed in next to him, scooting close, and he snuggled down again. "You needed it. You got injured in battle."

He laughed, a warm sound. "I don't think that is what

zapped me. I think it's my new bonded woman who blew my mind."

My cheeks heated up. I was probably bright red. "Torrin..."

He kissed my neck. "You got dressed. Boo." He seemed to realize what I was wearing though, and he drew back, frowning. "That's my shirt. Did none of the clothes I acquired for you fit? It's okay if you don't like them. I can have others sent over."

"Honestly, I didn't go through them yet, but I'm sure they're fine. This morning, I just wanted to wear your shirt. It smells like you." I kissed his chin. "Which I like."

He seemed about ready to say something that I really, really wanted to hear, but an alarm sounded, and instead of picking up from where we left off the night before, Torrin jumped from the bed. My heart raced, and I clutched my neck. Okay. Okay. I was okay. It would calm. What was happening?

"Torrin?"

He threw his shirt on followed by his shorts. "Reamers."

The door flew open, and in rushed a shirtless Nox. He breathed hard but looked better than the last time I'd seen him. "Orders?"

"I don't know yet. Keep her safe, Nox."

Dressed, Torrin ran from the room. Nox put out his hand. "Come."

But I didn't take his hand right away.

"Do you plan to take me deep underground again, like to the cavern with the pools and the stalactites?" I said evenly, like I did this all the time. Like I wasn't seeing Cannon's traumatized face in my memory. Like I wasn't thinking about the Reamer atrocities Nox had hinted at when we first met. None of that. Fear and timidity didn't seem right for a woman with four numbers on her arm.

Which was me. I was that woman. Their woman. For some reason, the knowledge made me instantly strong.

Nox narrowed his eyes, clearly confused, but he nodded and didn't hurry me when I pawed through the dresser drawer and quickly drew out serviceable clothes. Torrin hadn't asked me what I liked in terms of clothing. He'd just guessed, or he'd had someone else do it. Whoever had chosen sure liked green a lot. I thought of the green cloth Nox had put over my face to keep the dust out. Soft, protective. I dressed faster than I ever had, and Nox watched the whole time.

Odd. I wasn't used to being seen, to being so vulnerable and beneath a person's gaze, but he made it seem...I don't know, not awkward. He made it seem like his watch was protective, like as long as one of my men was observing me, no harm could come to me.

And he wasn't wrong. His presence made even the war sounds endurable. Torrin's throne room was close enough to the surface that we could hear everything. Activity out in the tunnels, up on the paths above ground. In the distance, shouting and thuds like giant projectiles skidding through the air and slamming into the ground. In elder times, our planet-bound ancestors had used cannons and guns, and this world wasn't too far off from that level of technology. It sounded horrible, but it was death on a small scale. They didn't have the capacity to scour a city from orbit.

Thank all the holies for that. It meant our enemies hadn't found the worst of what could have been in my ship's wreckage. However, those things were probably even now either in the wreckage or being examined by the Reamers. Eventually they'd figure out how to use everything they'd scavenged.

I disguised a deep shudder by pulling on an extra robe-like garment. Torrin had said the weather would change soon, but this world was already growing colder by the second.

CHAPTER FOURTEEN

"**O**kay," I said to Nox. "Now the books."

Poor Nox, his frown and accompanying confusion just got deeper.

It was hard not to smile. "Torrin has collected a bunch of old books, and they contain secrets that may help us defeat the Reamers and everyone else long term. If I'm going to be taken to a safe place, so are those books. Oh, and Astor. We should bring him, too. I've taught him a little, enough to help." Actually, he probably didn't know enough to read, but he would be relieved to be away from the fighting, putting his clever mind to the task instead of dodging bullets.

The truth was I wanted him with me. I wanted them all with me.

Nox still looked confused, so I stepped close to him and put my hands on either side of his face. He flushed at the intimate contact, but he couldn't look away without shrugging me off.

"How are you, really?" I asked him.

He took a breath, opened his mouth, and appeared to consider his words. "My wounds are much better, if that's what you mean. I feel like I slept forever, yet I am still not fully rested."

"Recovery can take some time." I stroked the pad of my thumb over the sharp line of his jaw. "What else could I have meant?"

"Well, you could have referenced the attack, asking how I am coping with the new threat."

"And?"

"Part of me needs to be beside Torrin," he confessed, staring straight into my eyes. "It's where I have always been, protecting him, even when he claims he needs no protection. Only now, this time, the larger part of me knows that I am doing what both of us—what all of us—need me to do. Protecting you, for you are mine."

I rose up on my toes and pressed a close-mouthed kiss to his lips. "Thank you."

Between the two of us, Nox and I made quick work of the books I'd brought up here. Many were still in Astor's quarters, but we gathered what we could immediately carry, wrapped them in two blankets, and carried them out into the corridor.

Which was chaos.

A howl sounded around us, like an animal...and yet not. People winced, throwing themselves against the walls. A woman rocked back and forth. I held to the bravery I'd felt earlier. Yes, that was terribly scary, but somehow, I was going to be worthy to be their wife, meaning I wasn't going to have a panic attack.

Nox shook his head. "That's close. The Reamers got through the first blockade."

I spun in a circle. Dreama was nowhere to be found right now. What would she be doing were she here? I grabbed on to Nox's arm. "What has to happen now? What would you like to see take place?"

"I'd like it if these people took shelter. I know the tunnels are not going to happen, but if they could all move into rooms and houses, get out of the way."

I waved my hands in the air, shouting to be heard over the sounds of whatever destruction was taking place nearby. "Everyone right this second, get yourselves somewhere else. Inside." I clapped my hands. "Now."

My heart full on raced, and that wasn't good in these circumstances, but I couldn't be thinking about me. I could Bianca-worry later. My focus had to be on others. What was even stranger than this weird shift in me, was that everyone listened. They ran inside, stopped panicking and got out of the way.

"Well done." Nox squeezed my shoulder. "Let's take your own advice and go to—"

I wasn't sure what he'd have said right then, because that was when I got my first full view of a Reamer. Two of them stood staring at us. They were dressed in full body armor that had clearly seen better days. And they were completely intimidating. Skin peeling, eyes bulging, slack mouths drooling. They seemed more animal than man, and yet I was perfectly sure that was what I looked at right now. Men who wanted to kill us.

Nox shoved me behind him. "Back up slowly."

I did just as instructed. "What's wrong with them?"

I'd thought them enemies, bad people who hurt others, but there was so much more to it than that. The one on the left, the taller of the two, flared his nostrils and charged toward us. Nox pulled his sword that was always strapped to his back. They lunged at each other, the sounds of their weapons clinking. Nox darted forward, shouting over his shoulder.

"Run, Bianca. Now."

I turned and did as he instructed. If I had any means to

protect myself, I'd like to think I would have fought with Nox, but I was weaponless and completely untrained. No one was willing to participate in a duel of knowledge of ancient poetry, which was really my only area of expertise. The best thing I could do was to get out of his way. I shot a look over my shoulder. Both of the monsters attacked Nox now, but as I watched, he beheaded one of them. I winced and tried not to cry out. I was certain they'd kill all of us without uttering a word if they could.

There was a niche behind me, probably the door to someone's quarters—or house? Strong hands grabbed me by the shoulders and pulled me in.

"Your Highness," someone said. It took me a full minute to realize that person meant me.

Highness. Wife to the king. Torrin. My men. Oh gods.

"We are committed to your safety."

The person who had pulled me into the hovel, or maybe someone else, pressed something metal into my hand. I didn't have to look down to know it was a blade. What was I supposed to do with this? I didn't know how to fight. I barely even knew how to breathe like a normal person. But their names kept cycling through my mind—Torrin and Mattis and Astor and Nox—and every time I thought of them, they made me stronger. These men were indomitable. They were heroes. And for whatever reason, they all believed in me.

I turned to the other people who huddled in this dugout.

They were all women and children. No Dreama, but I spied Nina in the back, clutching two bundled shapes. Her children. All holies, children.

"We have a cavern that is fortified and safe," I heard myself say. "You all will follow me. I will protect you. Okay?"

I clutched the metal shard in my hand. A sword, short and sharp. Ha. As if such a weapon would do anything against one of those hulking, drooling monsters I'd spied outside.

Who were even now engaging my Nox. *Mine*.

Fury rose in my stomach like I had never known. Fuck them all. They were not harming *my* people. *My* husbands.

I was going to fight back.

I turned and met Nina's eyes over the cowering heads of her children. "I will not let anything happen to you. We are going to that fortified cavern. Follow me."

She nodded, and I pushed open the door.

The corridor was a sort of hell. By which I mean, it was everything evil I had ever imagined. The drooling, grotesque Reamers had invaded a place that I considered sacrosanct, my own home base. With them came the stench of war—firing powder, early necrosis, sweat, blood. Two enemies still engaged Nox, and it took every cell in my body not to throw myself between them and him. He'd dropped the blanket-wrapped bundle of books at his feet when the fighting started, and I considered darting in now to retrieve it. The knowledge those books represented had once been more precious to me than my own life, but now I had more important things to consider. More important people. Something landed on my shoulder when I paused, but I ignored the blow.

"I'm okay," I shouted, and I knew he heard. He fought harder. "Be safe, my husband. Come home to me."

I hoped my words, my *care*, would reinforce his courage, remind him that he was amazing. Because he was. Already, one Reamer lay unmoving at his feet, and he had engaged two more. He was holding his own. He was... I could stand here and admire him all day, honestly. My beautiful, honorable, Nox. But I didn't. I could feel the rush of bodies behind me —could smell the sweet innocence of children, probably Nina's two little ones—and I couldn't let them down. I slanted my sword across the chasm, waited for the frightened innocents to duck into the deep tunnel, and then I turned and followed them, perfectly prepared to commit murder for their safety.

My men had taught me war. I would honor them. However I was going to do that. I had the sword-thing but no idea how to use it. I'd get the people to safety and then... Then what?

"Follow me." I both could and couldn't believe I was doing this.

I only had a general sense of where I was going, but eventually, I found the opening I was looking for. This run had told me two things. The first was that if I was going to run like this in the future, I had to train and build up my strength. I was already out of breath. My heart wasn't ready for this exertion. Still, I was getting these people where they needed to go. Second? Dreama was hugely important. This was the stuff she handled. Where was she? Was she okay?

I skidded to a stop, pulling open the small door, and the women rushed in past me. They all had to know where this was. Why hadn't they done this themselves? I swallowed. We had to figure this out. Maybe they were just used to being told what to do. We had to get the people to where they knew to do it on their own.

I looked over my shoulder. What did the others do? The prostitutes? The people not as socially acceptable as the ones with me? Where did they hide?

Questions I needed answers for.

The last person ran by as Nox appeared, hauling the books with him. My stomach clenched. In the midst of all of this, he'd remembered them.

I threw my arms around him. "You're okay?"

"Not any more injured than I already was. And you?" He felt all over my arms and back like he'd checked me when I first arrived, when I just assumed he had medical training.

I nodded. "I'm okay. You were so brave."

He dropped his gaze to the sword I held. "Where did you get that?"

"Someone handed it to me."

His smile was fast, sardonic. "Guess it's yours now. We'll have to teach you how to wield it. Shut them in. They'll be safe. I'm pretty sure we've pushed the Reamers back. But I need to check on my grandfather. He's probably at Mattis'. He's not...right."

I remembered Cannon, especially his fear of Reamers. "He's sweet and kind. Let's go."

Nox squeezed my hand. "Don't drop your sword. It's a good one."

I might never let it out of my fingers ever again.

The corridor and streets were empty. There were dead bodies strewn about, most of them looking like they were Reamers, but some who were clearly ours. My mind turned to my brother. He sent people to die in wars all the time. Did he ever see this? Did he ever think about what an actual battle looked like? I'd never see the man again, and these were questions I wouldn't have thought of when I'd known him. My twin brother who, just weeks without contact, now felt like a stranger.

I was living in a world where war happened right in front of me.

"Why do they look like that?" I kept my voice down as I questioned Nox. "They don't look like us."

He nodded toward Mattis' bar, and we entered it soundlessly. Maybe he'd answer me in there, maybe he wouldn't. I supposed now wasn't the best time for questions.

The sound of low crying greeted us, and Nox dropped my hand to rush toward the kitchen. I followed on his heels. There, hidden badly in the corner, enough in the open anyone could see him, was his grandfather.

"Hey, Popop." Nox knelt down and squeezed Cannon's shoulder. "It's almost over. I'm sorry you were alone."

I needed to sit, badly. Catching my breath seemed integral, and sitting would serve the double purpose of helping Nox comfort the poor older man. I sank to the ground right next to Popop.

"We're here," I said. I hoped that helped.

Nox met my gaze. "We don't know what the main Reamer settlement is like, but out in the battlefield, the Reamers live in terrible conditions. They are constantly exposed to the elements, and in some seasons, the wind and rain are corrosive. It doesn't make sense to me why they've never built better shelters. Also, their diet is awful. There is much supposition that they eat human flesh when they run out of food. It's not just rumor, unfortunately. We can't prove it because people like my grandfather don't escape in their right mind. But we're pretty sure."

I wanted to puke. They hadn't just come here to attack us, to harm us, to—it was hard to think about—rape and kidnap women. No, they may have been here to consume us.

Nox squeezed my knee with his other hand. "It's awful. I know." He settled down on the floor in front of us. "I may have overdone it."

Yes...he was pale. "I don't see as you had much choice."

He leaned on his knees. "You understand this better than anyone, I think. You're pale."

That wasn't surprising. "I just thought the same thing about you."

"We will rest, then," he decided.

Only, I could hear the hesitation in his voice. Resting out in the open, on the surface, here in Mattis' bar, meant we were exposed. That couldn't be a good idea.

"No," I heard myself saying. "We need to get Popop back into the tunnels. Also, we need to find the others who live up here, the prostitutes and other vulnerable people. We need to bring them to safety, too."

Or else. Or else... I couldn't get the thought out of my mind—cannibal.

Nox closed his eyes and let his head fall back against the scuffed wood paneling. There was blood on his chin. His own blood? Was he wounded?

"Please, Bianca," he said. "Fragile Bianca, so slight, so precious. And wounded now, too, with the branding. Safe. I need to keep you safe."

It occurred to me that he would protect me and Popop no matter what it cost him, no matter what it was already costing him. I had no idea what the recovery time was for those herbs we'd used. The book didn't give that kind of information, just treatment instructions. Nox wasn't recovered enough to be doing this. But the alternative?

"Nox," I said, shoving my sleeve up and pointing to my completely pain-free arm, "look. The brand is healed. I am fine. Better than you, probably."

"You have... Your health is poor," he reminded me, and I almost screamed.

Instead, I bit the fury off at its root. I thought about my brother's words a lifetime ago. *Deep breaths. You're letting it happen*, juxtaposed with Astor's and Torrin's confidence in me. Someone had handed me a sword. Me. Most of all, no one was locking me away. They were letting me fight. Live. The freedom of it energized me, and I realized I wasn't even breathing hard. I might be pale, but my heart was steady.

"Come," I told Nox. I stood, held out a hand. Without a word, Popop took it. He was shaking, and his eyes were wild, but he responded to my instructions. With a heave and muttered protest, so did Nox, though he got up under his own power. "I'm getting us into those tunnels."

CHAPTER FIFTEEN

The next few minutes were a blur. I couldn't describe it in terms other than mystical nonsense. It was like another presence inhabited me—some goddess or woman who was fully confident, in command. As if someone like Dreama just slipped into my body. I called, and people came. I gave them commands, and they followed.

I used the sword, slashing wildly when Reamers came near us. Nox joined in, and I think he killed one. Or we did. Did I actually...kill someone? Some*thing*? It was entirely possible, but I never went back and checked. The air was thick with that horrible dust, and there was nothing to cover my face. Grit caked at the corners of my eyes, and I could feel the tears pushing through, trying to cleanse my sight, carving runnels down my face. My overused and dust-choked voice grew hoarse, but I couldn't stop.

We met up with Dreama sometime in the melee. She was coming up the street with a group of women, probably prostitutes.

"I'm going to put them in Mattis' bar," she said, her voice as hoarse as mine. "He won't mind."

"Are you kidding? Take them to the cavern, the deep one with the stalactites. Nina's down there, and Nox's grandfather."

She frowned. "These aren't respectable folk, highness."

"We're worried about that right now?"

Dreama's eyes met mine, and something passed between us. Understanding, I guess. Camaraderie. Compassion. She pulled her raggedy group toward that yawning hangar entrance where the fortified tunnels started.

Last time there was fighting, I'd been down there, protected. Now I was in a thousand times more danger, but I felt so much more alive. I was doing something. Living.

"Hey, beautiful," a familiar voice rumbled from behind me. I turned to see Mattis, gore-splattered and hulking, grinning at me. "If Nox let you up here and gave you that sword, you know I'ma have to kill him."

I wanted to kiss him. I wanted to wrap all my arms and legs around him and hold on. Nox, beside me and clearly worse for wear, could barely stand but managed some saucy rejoinder.

"Couldn't stop her," he said. "She's impossible."

Impossible. Girl who fell from the sky and lived. Yeah, that was me. "None of my men are dying today," I said. "But I think Nox needs to go in there and fortify the caverns."

Mattis flashed a glance at his friend. "Yeah. Can't leave all those kids with only Dreama to protect them."

"Torrin told me to protect our woman," Nox argued.

As I had before this all began, I put a hand to his face, only this time, the other hand held a blood-soaked sword, so perhaps the gesture was not as sweet. "You have protected me. It would kill me to lose you. And Mattis is here now. Go. I will see you soon."

He pulled my hand to his mouth and pressed a kiss to the

back. His pretty eyes burned through the dust-blown air. "Soon."

My hand throbbed where his mouth had been, but I let him go. I needed him to go, to get out of this fight.

"Now your turn," Mattis said.

"No."

He smiled at me. The disarming one that made me want to kiss him even more. Would he mind? In my battle euphoria, I decided I didn't care, I leaned up and kissed him. Gently at first, and then, as he pulled me to him, I deepened our embrace. I'd never have risked this the day before, never have thought it possible.

Mattis pulled back, staring at me in the eyes. "And tonight you are with Nox." He shook his head. "So unfair. Make no mistake, sweet Bianca, when you come back to me, I intend to show you that you are mine as much as you are theirs. Plus, you have distracted me from forcing you into the tunnels. Okay. You can come with me. The battles are almost over. Just the stragglers left, and it seems you have bloodied your sword. With our young men, we call that first blood. I'm not sure, other than Dreama, that any other women do that here."

He pulled a rag from his pocket. "Cover your mouth and nose. You're not as used to the dust as we are. I don't want you to have a coughing fit night. They're awful."

Tingles still ran up my body as I took the rag from him, but before I covered up my face, I had some questions. "Is everyone okay? Torrin? Astor?"

"We've lost some people. Torrin was fine when I left him minutes ago. He goes stone-cold efficient in battle, and that's what he's doing. But he seems perfectly fine, as unaffected as he ever is. Astor came through with some new devices that blew up just in time. And we're all wondering what triggered the Reamers to do this in the first place."

He took my hand, and I brought the rag to my face as we walked together toward the crowd in the center of a square. I hadn't been here before today when I rushed through and encountered Dreama. I supposed there would have been little reason for me to have been here.

Torrin stood in the center, talking to three other men while dead bodies were being hauled into one pile on the left. Fewer ones were being gently placed on a cart on the other side of the square. Our dead versus their dead.

"What do they do with them?"

Mattis put his arm around me. "They'll be burned. We won't waste space on their dead. Also, they carry a lot of diseases we don't want spreading. Ours will have a warrior's burial later today."

How had all of this come to be? And the rest of the planet, was it like this, too? Factions of people fighting each other for space to grow anything? Resorting to cannibalism? And how much of it had stemmed from their beginnings? And did they even know about them at all?

Tonight, when things were settled, I was going to tell them what I knew. What I'd read. The prison ships that carried their ancestors here.

Were these men the descendants of the political uprisers now used as cautionary tales to suppress upheaval in the government? Or were they murders and other horrible criminals? I didn't suppose it mattered. We weren't responsible for our ancestors, had no say in where we came from, we were what we became.

Someone must have lit the pyre of Reamers, because the too-sweet stench of burning flesh curled over the square. In the center, Torrin's group had grown, and they appeared to be having a serious conversation, right there in the aftermath of murder. Right there with blood still on their clothes. I suspected that the woman I'd been just weeks ago would have cringed at the barbarity of it all, but what I took from that gathering was protection. These people were taking an unthinkably bad situation and doing their best to maintain civilization.

Mattis must have noticed where my attention had drifted, and he tightened his arm around my shoulder.

"Torrin's not even human. He can just switch it on and off, the ability to kill."

"Maybe we all have that ability," I said, thinking of the Reamer who had crumpled after receiving blows from both Nox and me. Had I been the one to deliver a fatal wound?

"Sometimes, warriors can focus tight on the moment, and it's hard to turn it off, to return to thinking like a person instead of a killer," Mattis said. Beside me, wrapped around me, he felt so solid and sounded so wise. "How are you, beautiful?"

"Oh, I'm fi—"

He cut me off by lifting my face-scarf and planting a kiss that effectively wrested my attention. "Don't lie to me. I don't mean your body—not at the moment, anyway. I mean your spirit. I'll ask you again, how are you?"

Why were there tears in my eyes? It didn't make sense. I wasn't sad. I was... "Elated. Proud."

"And you're worried because you don't think you ought to be proud of fighting or killing?"

"How did you—?" I shook my head, clearing the words. "No, not that. I was out there today, with my men, my people, protecting something good. It felt deeply right, when all my life, I've been told that avoiding confrontation is the way to go. Be quiet. Take what you get and don't fuss. Let others make the hard calls. Let them protect me. I never realized how angry I was about all that or how good confrontation could feel. I think..."

"Oh, don't you stop now. I need to hear all of this." I

could hear the grin in his voice, even if he had covered his lower face with a scarf.

"I think I love this place, these people."

"All the people?" he asked.

Something at the base of my throat tingled in alarm, and I swallowed. Some people especially, yes, but I wasn't ready to say that out loud. Maybe not even in the privacy of my own mind. "All of them," I affirmed. "And I love who I am here. Even if someone did come to rescue me, somebody from my world, I don't want to leave."

He turned me in his arms so that I was facing his solid chest. He smelled pungent, like sweat and dust and ever so faintly of beer, but it wasn't at all unpleasant.

"And I thank every power in this universe for that," he said, holding me so tight I couldn't reply.

We stood like that forever, or maybe just a second, until I felt him tense. His massive arms bunched around me.

"What?" I asked, my voice muffled against his chest.

"I've never seen this, I mean ever. What the *hell*?"

"What?" I repeated, detaching myself from Mattis and turning to see.

The huddle in the center of the square had grown and now consisted of maybe twenty men. And one Reamer. Alive. On its knees. Across the dust and stench, he looked straight at me, and fear sank its claws into my spine.

"That one," the Reamer called, his voice rising over the crowd and his grime-encrusted chin gesturing toward...me.

Torrin shot him a look that spoke of death as Astor approached the crowd. It was Torrin who answered him with clenched teeth. "You speak of the woman who belongs to me."

Astor stepped up next to him, staring down at the Reamer. "I might just kill him for you, brother."

Torrin kept his eyes on the Reamer. "Speak."

"We were sent to get her. They want her. The leaders. They have the other female from the sky, and they want this one."

I jolted. Another female from the sky? Mattis squeezed my shoulder. "They aren't getting you."

"Nope." Nox walked up from behind us. Still too pale, but his gaze fierce on the scene in front of us. "Not a chance."

They'd missed the point. I wasn't worried for me. Not even a little bit. "They have someone else. Someone who was on my ship is with the...cannibals."

Mattis winced. "We really hope that's not true."

"You and I both know it's true," Nox countered before he put his hands on his hips. "Torrin may want to go get the person. Now that they've targeted Bianca. In fact, I'd be shocked if he didn't. We have a safety concern now."

My heart raced, and I concentrated on breathing. Someone else had been on the ship, crashed, survived, and was now at the mercy of the monstrous men. The ones who might eat people. I shuddered.

Nox squeezed my fingers. "Bianca, I'm worried about you."

"You're *both* concerning me, and look, you got Astor's attention. Expect to be locked up until you feel better." Mattis kissed my cheek. "And...oh fuck."

Nox groaned. "I don't suppose one of these days the fucker could die."

They couldn't be talking about Astor, so I followed their gaze where they stared daggers at an older man who stormed toward us.

"You." He pointed at me, and Mattis' arm went back around me. "You are why my daughter has been shafted, and now it seems everyone has had to fight and some died because of you."

Heaviness hit me hard. He was right. The Reamers had

come for me... This was in some ways my fault. I hadn't asked for it, hadn't meant to cause it, but there it was. I held on to my neck. Breathing was getting a lot harder. "Sir, I don't believe that we've met."

My voice was low. Fainting wasn't out of the question. If I weren't being attacked, I might take a seat somewhere.

"This is Baron the Great. As he calls himself," Mattis answered.

Nox had gone silent. Maybe it had to do with rank. Mattis' family was scandalous but above Nox's in rank.

"I know you're not talking to my wife like that." Astor stood behind the Baron, which made him jump. "Kidnapping me is one thing, but insulting my wife is something else entirely. In fact, I bet you have Torrin's total attention right now. That's what you want, right?"

Baron pointed at me again, as though Astor hadn't spoken. "I will see you dead. You fall out of the sky and expect to just—"

He was yanked backward, Torrin holding on to his ear. "I think it's time I added to my throne. It's never been enemies, but maybe it's time for a change. What do we think, boys? A new head to the collection? Make your daughter an orphan and your so-called followers leaderless and pathetic? Yep. I think that's just what I'm going to do. After I beat you in a challenge."

Held down by his ear, the man stuttered, "I-I haven't challenged you."

"You insulted and kidnapped my brother. Now you are yelling at my wife and making accusations that are not yours to make. Those amount to challenges. I'll see you at six. As the sun goes down. In the main hall. Let's see you live up to the insults you make." Torrin actually smiled. He couldn't possibly be finding amusement in this? "I've let you get away with being annoying long enough. The City-State is mine.

You all live by my protection. And I'm tired of protecting you."

I shook my head. It was hard to reconcile the barbarian-king Torrin with the husband who had cared for me so thoroughly last night. It was like they were two different men who looked startlingly alike. Here he was, having spent a terrifying day murdering half-monster Reamers, and now he was going to fight some more? Just because he liked it.

I opened my mouth, but Nox squeezed my hand. I was kind of surprised he was still holding it, but there it was. Mattis still had an arm around me, too.

"Wait," Mattis said in a low voice. "He's our leader. Let him lead."

"If you speak against his challenge, you'll lessen its effect," Nox explained, similarly in a near-whisper.

"But he's been fighting all day," I said, keeping my voice in line with theirs, so others wouldn't hear. "Why can't he let someone else deal with this? And didn't his father prohibit him from killing Baron the Great?" I was so confused.

Even more so when Mattis laughed. "He's not going to kill Baron, just humiliate him and make him stand down."

I wasn't so sure. I watched Torrin give an order, and two other men hauled the Reamer prisoner away. Probably I didn't want to know his fate. Cannibals and demi-humans the Reamers might be, but they were still living creatures. One of whom I might have killed today, and at the very least had a hand in killing. That nipped my self-righteousness off at the stem. I still felt the wetness of Reamer blood soaking through my new clothes. Who was I to judge Torrin for his show of force against a slime like Baron the Great?

"Does this happen a lot?"

Mattis replied, "Baron made a play for the throne after their father, the king—after what happened to him. Torrin was really young, just a kid, but he beat the sh—"

"Thoroughly defeated Baron the Great in a challenge very similar to this one," Nox finished. Not primly, though his interruption wasn't lost on me. "And the war party has followed Torrin ever since."

I hid a smile. "So he re-enacts that victory periodically?"

"Well to be fair, Baron the Great does make it real hard not to punch him in the face. Daily," said Mattis. "But yes, victory in battle is one thing, but all the men seeing Torrin pound on Baron some more will just be the end to a beautiful day."

This culture was really messed up. And I was both alarmingly and thrillingly part of it. "Do I have to watch?"

Were wives of leaders supposed to observe the beating? My brother and his government were big on optics, and I'd been rolled out on numerous occasions as a decoration or to prove that well, if Brent's sister is there, the cause must be legitimate. As if he wouldn't lie right in front of me or something. People could be so willfully blind. I'd always hated contributing to Brent's power grabs, even as a silent onlooker.

I wasn't prepared for the charged silence that met my words. Mattis grinned and dropped a scarf-covered kiss on my head, moving away from me. He might have muttered something under his breath.

When I turned to Nox in question, the look on his face arrested me completely, even my breathing.

"You mustn't attend the challenge," he said, "because tonight you will be with me. It's second night."

Oh. Right. I swallowed.

CHAPTER SIXTEEN

Nox brought me into his rooms. He opened the door, and I stepped inside. The books I'd asked him to carry were in the corner. When had he brought them here? That was so sweet of him in the midst of everything to even remember.

My fight elation had fled, and in its place, I was...tired.

"So..." He leaned against the wall. "Here's the truth. My rooms are very small. My guess is that when Torrin misses your presence tonight, he will order all of us to move into the royal residence. Astor will object, he won't want to leave his lab area. Mattis will hate it because it will mean he's running back and forth to the bar. And I will be sorry, even though my rooms are so small, because I have something the others don't have."

His lips twitched, and I knew he was about to say something really amusing. "What is that?"

It was more fun, even in my tired state, to play along than I could have guessed. I was still getting to know these guys. Did Nox laugh a lot? Play these games? I couldn't remember ever really being teased. Was that what was happening right now?

"Because I have permanent hot water. When everyone else loses it, I don't. Has something to do with the layout of the pipes. Sucky rooms. Great water."

I grinned at him. "That is really incredible, considering I keep hearing that it goes away all the time."

He nodded toward the bathroom. "Want to soak?" Nox paused. "With me?"

My smile that crept up my face was huge, and my cheeks were hot. I must have been a tomato. "Yes."

"Great."

I followed him into the bathroom. The bathtub was practically bigger than his bed, which took up most of his bedroom. He turned on the water, and steam rose immediately. Wow. He hadn't been kidding. He really did get hot water.

Nox pulled off his shirt, and before I could talk myself into feeling embarrassed, I did the same. Just because Torrin and I had the night we'd had didn't mean that I was suddenly without my years of background that shaped my feelings of nudity.

I watched him while he took off his clothes, and he did the same for me. He nodded toward the shower in the corner. "Let's get the blood off first. While the tub fills."

He turned on the spray, and I stepped under it, wetting my hair. Nox, who was visibly hard just from watching me undress, got under with me. He handed me a cloth, and a thought dawned on me. Rather than rub the blood off me, maybe I should get it off him first. It would certainly break the ice about touching him.

So I did that. With smooth movements, I rubbed the blood off his body. He stiffened and then closed his eyes, relaxing. My own breath caught in my throat. This was intimate. Private. Just about as close as I could be with him without having him actually inside of me.

He opened his eyes and ran his hand down my arm, stopping my movement when he got to my hand. Nox took the cloth from me, dropping it onto the ground. He grabbed another one from the small shelf and ran it down my body.

"My turn."

His turn? I wasn't entirely sure I could endure *his* turn. But also? I trembled—literally shook—with wanting it.

And exactly as if he knew what sweet torture he inflicted, Nox took his damned time, kneeling there on the wet tile floor and starting with my feet, working his way up with the cloth—a texture rougher than I was used to, making every centimeter of my skin feel touched, abraded, *desired*. Tops of my feet, between my toes, back of one ankle, and then the other, the rough scour of the cloth followed by a slick runnel of water, sluicing. Bit by excruciating bit, uncovering me, unraveling me.

He'd knelt and bent his head to better focus on his task, so I couldn't see his face, and that honestly might have been a mercy. It left me free to not worry what I looked like in response. I might have been standing there with my mouth hanging open, like I'd never had a clear thought in my head, but I absolutely didn't care. At first, I bit my lip to contain a mewl of pleasure, but then he was kneading the tight muscles in my calves, and I let loose. I dropped my forehead against the wall, letting water rush over the back of my head, over my shoulders, blinding me, threading my hair, blanketing me with steam and sensation. It absorbed me as I absorbed the moment.

The pressure on the back of my knee was not a cloth. His mouth? Tongue? But it was gone again as quickly as I registered it, replaced by the steady upward march of his hands as he stood.

It was like he cleansed my body with fire. Delicious, agonizing fire. Upward over the curve of my rear, circling my waist, plunging down again. He had to reach all the way around me to stroke his cloth between my legs, and in so doing, he embraced me. Without thinking, I pushed back against him, bringing our bodies together, trapping the hot water between. I would swear it turned to steam.

Nox was long, lean, hard against my ass. The mewl I'd swallowed before slipped out. "All holies, yes."

He paused, one cloth-wrapped hand cupping my pussy. For a moment, it was just pressure, and then he moved beneath the cloth, stroking. Rough, hot, wet against wet.

My hands curled to fists against the wall, but I couldn't find anything to hold on to.

Nox was tall, too tall to make us fit like this, standing up. I tried to rise up on my toes, but he shushed wordlessly against my shoulder, continuing to methodically wash me, even as he worked one hand between my legs.

That fire he'd bathed me in was building. I needed to move, to writhe, to blow apart and fuse together and let the pleasure take me over, like it had last night. Every cell in my body vibrated with this need.

Skin slipped against skin—his chest against my back, the press of his mouth against my shoulder. He was everywhere on me, except for the place I wanted him most.

Inside. Right now.

"Please."

I turned around and he smiled at me, a warm adoring gaze to his eyes before he dropped to his knees. I gasped. What was he going to do? His mouth pressed against my most sensitive spot, kissing me on the bundle of nerves that begged for attention. I cried out, my head hitting the back of the shower.

"Easy," he spoke against me. "Just feel. I'm going to make you feel so good."

I was sure that he could and would, but it wasn't what I wanted right then. Not entirely. It wouldn't be enough. I needed to be filled with him.

"Nox, not what I want right now."

He met my gaze. "You want me inside of you?"

I nodded fast. "That's what I want, right now. I'm..."

"Coming down off the fight can make everything feel intense. I will always give you what you need. I promise." He stood slowly and kissed me. It was so sweet. Tears rushed to my eyes. I didn't even know why I was crying, just that I needed him, needed this, and the tears were happening. I was powerless to stop them, and for some reason I'd never fathom, Nox didn't seem to mind them. He kissed my cheeks as he pressed a finger inside of me where his mouth had just been.

I almost told him it wasn't enough, but he pulled me up his body. "Wrap your legs around me."

I nodded as I did the best I could to hold on to him and do just that. With a deep, possessive kiss, he pressed inside of me, picking me up and twirling us around until I leaned against the wall again.

"Yes," I cried out. I was so full of him, and that was what I'd needed. I could feel him everywhere. He pulled out and then jerked his hips to enter me again. This wasn't gentle lovemaking in the bed. This was primal. This was life. This was living through hell to get to the other side.

This was Nox and me.

Even my thoughts were muddled. I couldn't think.

"You're so perfect, Bianca. You are mine. My wife. Mine."

"Yes," I think I said. I couldn't find the words, not even to agree, while pleasure hit me hard. There was pleasure. There was pain. There was everything.

"Bianca," Nox cried out as he followed me into the moment.

We both panted. As I caught my breath, Nox depressed the lever, shutting off the shower, and carried me to the tub, pulling out of me as he did. He climbed us both into the tub, sitting down in the hot water, my back against his chest as he pressed my head against his shoulder.

He kissed my neck, my cheek. "Just rest. Let's be warm for a few minutes."

I nodded. "That was...just what I needed. Thank you."

He laughed in my ear. "Don't thank me. I should be thanking you. It's hard to come down from the battles. It's why people party until the early morning hours afterward. But I'd rather lie here with you and just be." He put his hand over my heart. "Listen to your heartbeat. Eat. Laugh. Sleep. Whatever you want."

Lazy and languorous as we were in that moment, a sharp thought snuck in, and I tensed. "Nox? How are you feeling?"

I could feel the rumble of his laughter against my back, his breath puffing against my wet hair. "Ah, there is a crude term for it, but basically, I feel like I have just made love to an incredible woman. Content? Satisfied? Hopeful, maybe."

His words made me glow all over, but he hadn't answered me, not really. "Physically, I mean."

"You mean the injury from the... What did you call them?"

"Burrs."

"Yes. I won't lie, the places where they entered my body, the wounds, still ache. I suppose it will take a while for that to go away, but with the fugue of battle, I didn't think about them until you mentioned it just now. I would imagine it's like your branding scars."

Beneath the water, I touched my forearm. I could feel the raised welts where my men had burned their numbers onto me, but there wasn't any pain. "No, they are all healed."

"Already?" He seemed shocked.

"Yeah. That salve Astor makes for burns, the stuff you used on me when you found me at the crash site, it's kind of magical."

Nox was quiet for a long time, breathing in and out, his chest rising and falling steadily against my back, making the water quiver on its surface. Steam curled up into the air, warming even the exposed parts of us, blanketing us in warmth. This tub was large enough I could stretch my legs out straight and still not touch the far end with my toes, and Nox's arms held me the whole time, as if I were something precious. It was bliss, even without the luxury salts and oils I was used to.

"It really isn't," he said after the longest time.

I'd forgotten what we were talking about, honestly. "Eh?"

"The salve," Nox clarified. "It's effective, yes, but unusually so on you. I've never seen anyone heal the way you do. And that's just the physical part. Mentally and emotionally... I mean, you fell from the sky, almost burned to death, discovered yourself abandoned on an entirely new world, and you've adapted so easily. Bianca, I'm not understating when I say that if anything is magical here, it is you." He paused and then added, "You've certainly ensorcelled me."

Ensorcelled. What a word. This man was adorable. I leaned my head back against his chest and closed my eyes.

He had a point, but the magic wasn't me. Nothing about me was magical or wondrous. "I've ingested a lot of medications over the years because of my heart condition. They boost my regenerative capabilities, I guess. And the emotional stuff. I feel like I lived my whole life before the crash just waiting for something to happen. Every time I'd get excited or hopeful about something—like teaching poetry—

I'd get some bad medical news or politics would shift, and the exciting thing would end and my life would fall back into its rut of being a Cervantes, being my parents' kid, my brother's sister, a piece of someone else's household with no expectation that I'd ever get to go out on my own or be a person myself. And then I get here and the waiting is over. My life started. I'm alive."

"For which I am grateful," he said, dropping a kiss against my hair. "And I still think you're magic."

The aches of the day bled out of my muscles, and the longer we talked, the cooler the water became. When I shivered, Nox suggested we get out and move to the bed, maybe sleep. Honestly, it had been a day. Sleep would be good.

Except then he stood, climbed over the lip of the giant tub, and held a hand out to help me, and I saw him in all his glory.

And sleep was the last thing on my mind.

He met my gaze, his own heating up when he did. Without a word, he wrapped me in a towel, bending over to kiss my neck. "Maybe you would let me take my time with you before we sleep. Maybe you would allow it, my Bianca."

I sucked in a long breath. "I'd love that."

"Good." He picked me up in his arms. He hadn't dried himself. I almost mentioned it before I decided I really didn't care. If he didn't mind, I certainly didn't. He laid me on his bed, coming over me for a second before he ripped the towel away, throwing it on the ground.

My nipples were hard, achingly so. His gaze swept over me, and I almost moaned from that alone. How could I be so ready so quickly after what we'd just done in the shower? He leaned down, kissing me slowly. I opened my lips, and he pressed his tongue inside of my mouth, moaning when he did so. He pressed his weight on top of mine. It was heavy, and I loved the sensation. It shouldn't have made me feel safe to have such a big man so in control of me in that moment; it should have made me nervous, but it was just the opposite.

This was Nox, who had pulled me from the crash wreckage, cherishing me.

I wrapped my legs around his waist. He thrust against me but didn't enter. No, he'd said this was going to be slow, and I took him at his word.

He pulled his mouth from mine to kiss my neck, starting right under my ear and then moving to the spot where my neck met my chest. I giggled. He lifted his head to meet my gaze. "Ticklish?"

"No, I just sort of loved it. I giggled."

His smile was very warm. "I sort of love that you did."

He traveled lower, down my chest to my breast, where he found my nipple and sucked on it. He wasn't gentle. No, he was anything but, and I loved it. His sucking quickly changed to a light bite, and I jerked in response. He held on to my shoulder, keeping me pinned down. I wasn't going anywhere.

Nox let go, looking up at me. "You are so beautiful. I can't believe that I get to touch you, let alone that you are wearing my numbers. I will take care of you, Bianca. Forever. However long that is."

I believed him. Nox was a person who understood that time wasn't guaranteed for anyone. That was so different than where I came from. With the exception of me, everyone believed they'd live to be old. But here he was, promising to take care of me for however long the time was. Warmth flooded me. This man got it. He understood. It might not have been a health issue that took him out, but a day like today could end everything, and they had them in abundance.

We had to find our pleasure when we could and—wow— when he found my other nipple with his mouth, I knew we could have that in abundance. With his patient mouth and teasing nips, he drew a cry from the deepest part of my chest, a guttural half-sob, and I didn't care who heard it.

In my old life, touch was a detached, almost ritualized thing—one hand touching another, a kiss on this cheek and then the other, a cold and sanitized embrace for the media's benefit. Maybe that was why it was so hard for me to experience a moment like this, because there was no part of me that wasn't being touched, laved, stroked, warmed. His mouth on my breast, his hands moving down my arms, braceleting my wrists, then fingers twining with mine. The warmth of his chest on my legs, and the tickle of damp hair painting my collarbone.

Nox usually kept his hair braided back, for convenience maybe, but he'd loosed it for washing, and it felt like cool ribbons on my heated skin.

Sensation was too much, overwhelming, but the last thing in the whole universe I wanted was for him to stop. I curled my fingers around his, locking our hands together, and brought my legs up to encircle him.

"Nox, if you need to..." I didn't even know what I was going to say, but when he pulled his mouth away from my breast, I lost the words.

"This," he replied, putting only as much space between us as he required to meet my gaze, "is everything I need."

I bit my bottom lip, and then let it out slowly. "Rest. I think I was going to suggest rest."

He frowned. "Have I pleasured you incorrectly?"

"Um, no. I am thinking of you here. Or maybe of both of us. Didn't we fight a war today or something?"

His frown dissolved into a beatific smile. A lock of damp hair slipped over his brow, giving him a rakish look. "We did. You were magnificent—have I mentioned that? No running for you, brandishing that sword like a warrior. I was so proud."

I had been warm from his touch before, but his words warmed all the parts of me that weren't even physical. "I was, too. I still am. But, erm, war."

"I wouldn't call what happened today a war," he said, unthreading our hands and moving up to lie beside me. He snagged a blanket and covered us. "More like a skirmish, or a very stupid attempt to kidnap you."

"But I thought the fighting was over—you guys won and get rights to the farm. The fighting was supposed to stop. Or am I reading this all wrong?" I pressed close against him, hooking one leg over his hip and stroking the back of his thigh with my heel. But lazily. No pressure.

"The truth is the fighting never truly stops. True, our big battles are over for the season, but we must remain vigilant, especially now that you're here."

There was a note of desperation in his voice, and it made me feel precious, worthy. Then he dipped his head, and without another word, placed all of that desperate focus right where I hadn't realized I wanted it—my pussy.

I didn't know what to do with my hands as I squirmed, wanting more and somehow less at the same time. More because it felt so good, and less because I couldn't imagine anything being more intimate than this, more invasive in a way. I had no secrets from him right then, no ability to hide anything.

He moaned against me, using that tongue to... Wow. Yes. Did he actually like this? His hips jerked against the bed, and I smiled. Yes, it appeared that he did. Nox was getting as much out of this as I was.

I cried out. No, maybe not. I was probably still getting more. But then I couldn't think at all. My noises must have spurred him forward. He was kissing me everywhere, saying my name again and again. It had never sounded so beautiful on anyone's lips as Nox's.

With a jerk, he lined up on top of me and pressed himself deep within me. I cried out again, this time digging my fingers into his back. He'd have marks. I wore his, and now he'd wear mine, at least temporarily.

In and out, our bodies seemed to dance together. We'd wanted slow, but it wasn't a night for that. Or maybe it wasn't a life for that. I didn't care. I had him with me now, making this happen.

His moans joined my own, and soon the bed slammed against the wall in loud bangs. For all the almost violence of the joining, when I came, it was on the sweetest surrender, an easy pull of pleasure that wasn't hard to reach. His own came like a sigh, my name on his mouth, as we held each other like neither one of us ever wanted to let go.

Nox leaned over, kissing right over my heart. When he spoke, it was in a soft voice, not looking at my face but right into my chest. "Keep beating. Don't ever stop."

I ran my hands through his soft hair that was slowly drying under my fingertips. We might both need another shower. I smiled at the thought.

He lifted himself off of me to settle next to me on the bed, and my gaze fell on the books in the corner. I had to tell them about my prison ship discovery tomorrow. I would. Unless we got attacked again, in which case it could wait. It had lasted this long, and truth was, it might not make any difference at all.

Nox pulled me against him, spooning me from behind. He yanked the covers over us. "When we cool down, it will get cold in here."

I nodded. Maybe I'd lost the ability to speak. I closed my eyes and let him hold me, expecting sleep to come fast. The room was quiet, and soon, Nox's breathing changed to light snores. It wasn't a troublesome noise, easy breaths to listen to. The sounds outside increased, and I opened my eyes. What was happening?

As gently as I could, I disengaged myself from Nox's hold and got on my knees to look out his small window. Tracing my fingers over the glass, I couldn't help but notice that it resembled the cabin window that had shown the darkness of space in the ship I'd been on. How old was this building? Had they assembled it from crashed spaceships?

The scene outside immediately stopped my musing. Being paraded down the street, covered in feathers and jeering yells following him, was Baron the Great. I gasped. What had they done to him? He'd been trying to hurt us, and I knew Torrin was mad... Had they feathered him?

"Bi?" Nox's voice sounded tight. "What's wrong?"

I pointed, not that he could see, but did anyway. "The Baron is covered in feathers."

Nox's smile was fast, even as he closed his eyes and patted the bed next to him. "That's actually kinder than I thought Torrin would be. Little humiliation to go with his humiliation of Astor. They coat him in sweet stuff and then stick the feathers on. Takes hours. It's embarrassing but not fatal. The good Baron has been feathered before."

I lay back down next to Nox, and he tugged me closer, putting us back where we were. "Sleep off the remainder of the day. Let it go. I've got you. I'm not letting go. You can rest."

It was like his statement gave me permission to do so. I closed my eyes.

CHAPTER SEVENTEEN

I n my old life, my circadian rhythms were regulated by my holowatch, which talked to whatever environment I was in and adjusted the lighting accordingly. I didn't sleep long unless I was medically induced to do so, and if I were in a particularly cutting-edge medical facility, I'd even get an injection at key points during my sleep cycle to trigger REM and dreams.

Here, I didn't dream. And although I didn't have a working clock—hello, busted holowatch—I suspected I was sleeping way longer than eight hours. Even so, I woke up thinking of feathers. Also possibly giggling.

Nox must've heard me either moving around or giggling, because he leaned his head into the doorway.

"Breakfast?"

I sniffed. If he had cooked something, I couldn't smell it, which of course wasn't a criticism of his cooking. Most food didn't have an aroma. Or maybe Astor's food and Mattis' brew were spoiling me.

"I'm up," I said, pushing back the cover, shuddering at the chill in the room—they weren't kidding about the weather changing fast around here—and forcing my legs to swing over and my body to sit up. Parts of me wanted to stay in the night just a little longer. I could still feel Nox's body wrapped around mine.

"And happy?" he asked, still not coming into the room.

"Very." I searched his face, but his careful frown hadn't completely gone away. "Did you hear me giggling in my sleep? Or did I talk through all those scorching sex dreams?"

He flushed and ducked back into the other room, which almost made me laugh again. Instead, I started collecting clothes and padded over to the bathroom.

"You did not talk in your sleep," he replied. I was dressed and halfway through scrubbing my teeth when he tapped on the bathroom door. "I invite you to tell me more about the scorching sex dreams, though."

I did laugh that time, and rising up on my toes, I pecked a kiss on his chin. "I made that up. Truth, I slept like the dead. You are a super comfortable bed."

"Good to know."

"So where's breakfast?" I braced for whatever aroma-less kibble was available. Interstellar travel had taught me to choke down anything that was minimally nutritious. Besides, I could hunt down yummy stuff later.

"Astor's lab," Nox said, and I kissed him again, this time pulling his head down so I could meet his mouth.

"Excellent. And then reading lessons?"

He kissed me back, angling our bodies so that my back was against the bathroom wall. It reminded me of the shower wall last night. Hot water. Hotter Nox. And suddenly, I wasn't hungry for food at all.

"Why is the thought of you being a very strict instructress so compelling?"

"Sexy?"

"Gods, yes."

For a few long moments, with his mouth on my throat, hands twined with mine and holding them fast against the wall, it really felt like this day was heading right back to bed. But then Nox pulled away, humor in his eyes. "Breakfast first, and then yes, Bianca, you can play teacher."

"Oh, you bet I can. It used to be my job." I kissed him one more time. "Okay. Give me two seconds, and I'll get ready."

He shook his head. "When we get there...it's your day with Astor. I have to...behave."

I laughed. "We'll see how that goes."

This being with all of them was going to be complicated. The question really was, how was I going to behave when I wanted all of them?

It felt like it had been years since I'd been in Astor's lab, but it had been...days? He looked up with a grin when I walked in, and I saw he wasn't alone.

Torrin sat with his feet up on Astor's table. Mattis next to him, but his feet were on the ground. Mattis rose, a big smile on his face, too. Torrin stayed seated, but as his gaze moved over me, it was akin to him taking off my clothes. I shivered with anticipation.

Astor pulled me to him, his mouth coming down on mine. He tasted like he'd just drunk cool water. I wrapped my arms around him. "Hi there."

"Hi." He pinched my chin. "You okay? You had a long day yesterday."

I nodded. "Right now, I'm not feeling much about yesterday. But last night, Nox took care of me. So I think I'm okay."

He smiled. "I'm going to feed you. I made breakfast."

Astor, still holding my hand, took me over to where he'd prepared a feast of foods. Most of which I'd never seen before. Every day here, I learned something new. As I sat down, Torrin addressed Nox.

"I would have thought you would have brought our wife to the show last night. I made the good Baron wear honey and feathers while he danced in a circle. I was rather...pissed you weren't there."

Nox walked over to grab some food. "You didn't order it, Torrin. I thought it was okay for me to spend time alone with our wife."

Torrin scowled at him. "Point taken. Astor just got finished letting Mattis and me know that our time here this morning is limited. Reading lesson and then we go. I'll just have to see to it that I bring down someone who threatens Bianca on my own frickin' night. Next time, I'll make him wait."

Nox took a bite of something that must have been fruit, so I did the same. I copied really well. It was sweet, and I instantly loved it. But light as the tone was so far, I couldn't stay silent about what I knew forever. And for once, no one was fighting or hurting or yelling, so this was as good a time as any.

"Well, before we get started, I think maybe I should tell you guys something I suspect from labels affixed in the backs of the books. I think...I think it's kind of important."

Astor furrowed his brow. "What does it say?"

I steeled my back. "It says that you guys are all descended from...from a group that was on prison ships that must have crashed here a long time ago. History just calls them lost. The ship carried political refugees, as well as people who had committed huge crimes. Bad ones." Rape, murder, burglary... I just couldn't bring myself to say those words right now.

I guess a part of me had wanted them to laugh it off, to

tell me that either it wasn't a big deal or that they'd always known. Or maybe I expected them to be horrified, possibly defensive. They were obviously honorable people now, so knowing who their ancestors were—what those people had done—should disgust such good men, right? The only thing I wasn't expecting was the reaction I got.

Torrin looked at Astor, who looked at Mattis, who looked at Nox. None of them looked at me.

Mattis recovered first. Clearing his throat, he said, "Um, is that part of the lesson? You wanna show me what the words look like, in the books I mean?"

I was surprised enough that I showed him. Turning to the back endpaper of the top book on the stack—*Interstellar Propulsion Physics for Beginners*—I pointed to and spoke aloud the same words I'd seen on the first book I ever touched here. "Property of Longergan Prison."

Nox leaned over to get a good look at the words. He studied them intently, but Mattis played it all in typical Mattis fashion. "Huh. Takes up a lot of space, dunnit? I mean, if I were to translate our numbers into readable words, plus all our names, you wouldn't have any unmarked skin on either arm."

"She has legs," Astor remarked. "And other body parts. I could humbly be content with one of those."

It was a good thing I knew him well enough to understand his unusual sense of humor. This was, after all, the man who had joked about eating me when we first met. I rolled my eyes in his general direction.

"Lovely as it is to hear you all discussing my dismemberment," I said, "I have to admit I'm surprised you aren't more...surprised at this information."

"Not dismemberment," said Torrin. "Never that, never for you." Ah, my fierce Torrin.

I shot him a reassuring smile. "I know. I was joking, but

only sort of. Can we talk about Longergan and your ancestors?"

Nox chimed in, "I'm not sure what you want us to say. Have your forebears no sins?"

Oh. Well, he did have a point.

Mattis added, "Yeah, it's not like whatever they did or didn't do way back when has anything to do with us now."

"But what if it does?" I said. "What if you all fight—and you might not realize this, but you've been fighting constantly since I got here and probably every other day that ends in y— what if you resort to violence to solve all your problems because the first people on this planet only knew violent methods of conflict resolution?"

"You're making a lot of assumptions," Astor said. "You said yourself there were a lot of different reasons someone might have been on a prison ship."

"Yes, but—"

"Bianca, let this go." That from Torrin, his commanding voice cutting through the conversation. He used that tone he used when he was addressing his soldiers, not when we were alone.

"I think it's important," I heard myself say. And it was true. I had no idea why this truth had eaten at me ever since I'd read those words, but it had. It had to mean something. It had to change something.

Torrin held my gaze with his, and I got smaller and smaller and less and less determined under the weight of his certainty.

"Well, I," said Astor, "think the tragedy of prime importance here is that our breakfast is getting cold. Here, Bianca, try this meat-puff." He gestured to a dish sitting next to one of his bubbling beakers. The mouth-watering aroma that had wafted down the hallway and led us here this morning had probably come from that tray, but I was more in a sweet mood than savory, and all the fruit was gone.

"Go ahead and start the lesson without me," Torrin said. "And then, Bianca, you and Astor need to plan a rescue of the other refugee from your transport, the woman the Reamers claim to have captured."

I didn't want to let the Longergan thing go, but the need for a rescue was sort of more immediate. A thrill shrieked up my throat. Another refugee. A woman. I needed to help her, save her, and the need was urgent. He wasn't wrong about that. "You mean we plan it and you, and your warriors make it happen?"

Torrin stood. "Certainly. Very soon. Today, I'm supposed to visit our planting crew, and I've already delayed too long."

My heart sank. "Wait, you're leaving?"

He had already started for the door, but something in my voice must have snagged him. He slowed beside me and touched my face. He bent and kissed my mouth, and I felt that kiss migrate to every nerve in my body. I was like a string instrument, vibrating to life beneath his mouth. Then he drew back. "Only for a couple of days, and I do not leave you unprotected. Teach, learn, plan, and be kind to my brothers, your new husbands. They are good men."

Technically, only Astor was his biological brother, but I understood how close these four men were. They were all as good as brothers. I put a hand on Torrin's arm, but he kept on toward the door anyhow, and before I could say anything else, he was through it. Gone.

Let this go.

Damn him, I didn't want to let it go. Or him. I didn't want to let anything go. Rather, I wanted to hold on to everything. Fiercely.

I could feel Astor close beside me, and as always, his presence suffused me with a deep sweetness and longing.

"First, meat-puff, then lessons?" he said.

I moistened my lips and blinked. "Uh, yeah."

After we went over the relationship between letters and sounds and ate the meat-puffs—which were never going to be my favorite thing—Mattis and Nox left, both of them staring at me long enough as they did to make my cheeks feel feverish. I forced myself to ignore the sensation. It was strange to go from a time when I couldn't even imagine the kinds of feelings I was having, to experiencing the *lust* of all of this regularly. Not only that, but it was perfectly acceptable for me to feel this way.

But we had things to do, and I couldn't just sit around and have a lot of sex. Could I? I shook my head. No, they'd asked me to teach them to read. And I was going to do that.

Astor and I cuddled up on his couch, and I started a slightly more advanced lesson. Like I would with a child, I started out with the basics, but Astor's mind was sharper than any I'd ever worked with before. Maybe it was because they did essentially "read" numbers here, but he quickly made sense of early phonics and started to remember the alphabet in record time. We went a good three hours before I could tell he'd had enough.

He rose, disentangling himself from me as he did. Leaning over, he kissed my lips. "Best teacher, ever."

I shook my head. "Um...I think it's more about what kind of student you are and less to do with me."

His smile was fast. "I'm smart. I'm troubled in other ways, but my brain was never one of them." He walked over to his workbench and picked up what I quickly recognized was my holowatch. He held it up.

"I think I've come to understand it."

I rose. "There's nothing wrong with you. You're not troubled. People who mess with you are troubled. Not the other way around. That's remarkable if you can figure out that watch. I never could."

"Few more days and maybe... No, I won't even say what I was going to say in case it doesn't work. I don't want to disappoint you."

I wrapped my arms around him. "Thanks for trying to fix it. You could never disappoint me."

He wiped the hair off my forehead. "Do you want to go someplace pretty? There aren't many, but there is one place I would show you."

I nodded. "I'd love to see wherever you wanted me to."

"Grab a scarf. I want you to cover your face. Don't ever take the dust lightly. Even I can be bothered by it, and I grew up here."

Looking around, I spotted one of his scarves. "Can I take this one? I need to get more stuff made for myself or figure out how to become useful enough to do my own."

"We'll get you sorted out. It's now on my list to do." He winked at me. "I always take care of getting the things on my list done."

That was good to know. I was a little bit spacier than that. "Aren't we supposed to be figuring out the rescue of the other girl?"

Astor put out his hand. "We can plot where I'm taking you as well as we can here. Easy enough."

As we left his rooms, I was thinking about all the beautiful stalactites and crystals in the caves below, so I just assumed that was where we'd be heading. The pretty place. But then Astor turned and headed up, to the wide cavern at the surface and the buildings that were out in the open. We paused before stepping out into the wind and dust, and fitted scarves over our faces. I must have been doing it wrong, because Astor took mine off, folded it just so, and put it back on, starting with winding it about my head almost like a turban.

"Covering your face like this is tragic," he said, his voice muffled behind his own scarf, though I could see the laughter in his eyes.

"I'd say, rather, that having my ship blow up in space, crashing on an unknown planet, and catching on fire are bigger tragedies," I said. "But I've found all those things survivable, shockingly enough. Guess I'm more of a comedy girl after all."

"Resilient, I should say," he replied. He smoothed the scarf over my covered lips, and I could feel the warmth of his fingertips. It was a completely nonsexual touch, but also one of the most sensual things I've ever felt. My lips parted, and I puffed a breath through the dark linen.

Astor smiled.

"Have you had a complete tour of the City-State?"

"I fought Reamers in the streets yesterday. Does that count?"

He took my hand to help me over a piece of burnt wooden something, probably left over from yesterday's battle. Even through the scarf, I could smell the smoke. That was how they cleaned up after attacks. They burned away the memory and moved on into the next day, the next fight. The people here fully expected every day to be a struggle.

"Well then, you saw the meeting square where my brother —and our father before him—gave speeches and instructions, and where we divide and distribute the food we cultivate. That's an important place to know."

"And Mattis' bar," I added. "I know how to get there."

"Also good." We navigated past someone reinforcing a wall that had been repaired several times before from the look of it. The man was shoving a thick piece of metal at an angle, to keep the wall standing. So much of the architecture here was slapped together from no design or even consistent materials. Like a shanty town, only it looked old rather than temporary.

"How long have your people lived here?" I asked. Still couldn't remember when the Longergan ships had gone missing, but it was at least a hundred standard years ago. Longer, maybe.

"Don't tell me you failed to count the skulls on Torrin's throne."

I...hadn't. Didn't particularly want to, either. "Ah, no."

"That would give you one number," he said, sort of enigmatically. "And there are other numbers. Taken together, they complete a record of our past. I will teach you how to read them if you want."

He put out a hand again to help me over something, but I grabbed it instead and didn't let loose. He turned. Our eyes met. "I think there are quite a few things you could teach me, and I want to learn every single one."

"Likewise," he said. Again, those eyes smiled, and the warmth from them encased me, even in this chilly, swirling dust storm of a world. "I'm guessing in the chaos of the fight, you didn't notice our one tall building. Our skyscraper." He said the word ironically, as if he was completely aware that nothing here approached a real skyscraper.

I instinctively looked around, blinking through dust. Nope, no sleek glass buildings, no hover cars or towers. Except...no, there *was* a shape marginally taller than the rest of the shanty-like buildings. It cast part of the town in shadow, so it must be pretty tall, though it, like everything else, seemed made of cast-off building material just shoved up into a pile and nailed together. Only this shanty was at least four stories of such slap-dash construction. Care had been

taken to make it fit with the other buildings—to disguise it?
—but it was different. It felt different.

There must have been intense fighting here yesterday,
because three separate piles of detritus burned. One smelled
like it might contain Reamer remains.

There weren't any doors to this building, but as I
watched, Astor went along one wall, the one in shadow,
sliding a metal panel here, moving a piece of wood there,
undoing a latch. Finally—and I wasn't even sure what
happened or how he did it—an opening appeared, as if by
magic.

"It's a...giant puzzle box?" I asked, preceding Astor
through the portal.

He moved in behind me and slid one long hand down a
metal strip. The opening hissed closed, and we were alone in
a place with zero light.

"I mean, pitch black *is* beautiful, but... This is where you
were taking me?" I said after a minute. He was close beside
me, warm and solid, and I wasn't in the least bit afraid.

He unwound the scarf from my head, and I drew in a
deep, clean breath.

"How is your heart?" he asked. I jumped a little. He was
much closer than I'd guessed. I could feel his words against
my temple. Without even thinking, I tipped my head back
and rose on my tiptoes, meeting his mouth with mine.

I must have surprised him, because he didn't kiss me back
right away. He did put his hands on my shoulders, but to
steady me or to steady himself, I had no idea.

I drew back and told him the most truthful thing I could.
"My heart is full."

CHAPTER EIGHTEEN

The hands on my shoulders squeezed. I expected a witty comeback, some sly insinuation, but to my surprise, Astor said nothing. Instead, taking both my hands, he led me toward what might have been...stairs?

The dark building smelled unlike anything on this world. No dust, no underground damp, no wood rot or rusted metal or body odor. It smelled, if anything, like a space station, all acetone, charged ions, and industrial lubricant. Weird, right?

We went up. I wanted to reach out and grab for a handrail, but Astor kept both of my hands firmly in his. He had to be going up backwards.

"I am able to climb stairs, you know," I said after about ten steps.

"These are unusual stairs," he said, "and I know the way. You would not want to take a wrong step."

"Why? What would happen if I did?"

He squeezed my hands. "Nothing I want to think about."

"Why is it so dark in here?" I asked, only sort of meaning to change the subject. "It feels like the tunnels, where you guys live, but it doesn't smell right for that, and we are, unless I'm just completely turned around, going *up*."

"You are correct that we're ascending, and this structure isn't part of our electrical system. It's powered from a different source."

From the outside, the building had seemed about four stories tall, but it felt like we climbed much longer than that. I couldn't shake the feeling that it was a magical place, and also a deeply familiar one. I just kept putting one foot in front of the other, matching my pace to Astor's. He kept our ascent slow, and oddly, my heart never complained. I never struggle with breath. What care my husbands took with me, to keep me safe.

I wasn't sure when I started to notice my feet. Like, notice them visually. Which meant light. I'd climbed maybe for several minutes without realizing I could see what I was climbing—creaky wooden stairs without railings. Old. And walls of sleek, shielded metal. A cool, greenish light peeked out from tiny pinprick lamps set into the walls.

I knew this place. I knew exactly what it was. My mouth went dry, and I couldn't summon words.

At the top step, Astor pushed open what from our angle looked like a trap door and hoisted me up through it. Sunlight poured in from what was essentially the roof, a curved dome of transparisteel encircled by dozens of panels lit in a variety of colors. Buttons. Holographic data maps. Control panels.

"Astor," I said, sitting on the floor, which was really a wall, and gazing up at a space that was both familiar and heartbreaking. "This is a spaceship command bridge."

"I figured as much," he said, kneeling beside me. "Isn't it beautiful?"

"You knew?" I could hardly speak the words. "Do they all know? Everyone?" There I had been with my grand revelation, but it was worthless. They'd known.

He shook his head. "Not really. Most people don't come here, don't think about it. If they came here, they wouldn't know what they were looking at and they'd dismiss it as... magic. But I know. And Torrin knows. From their reactions, I think Mattis and Nox did, too. Or they suspected. We don't discuss this. Our father brought Torrin and me here when we were boys. Explained it. We'd come from the stars, but we could never go back. Our crimes were the crimes of our ancestors. They'd follow us, kill us for things done hundreds and hundreds of years ago."

For a second, I thought about arguing about that. But then I thought of my brother. Truth was, he might do something like make an example of these people to have some sort of scene to support the Republic.

"Do you think anything in here could fix your watch? The one thing I can't do is read what the things say. So I don't actually know what they do. It makes me crazy."

I stared at the equipment. This was like being in a museum. I could read what the things said, but I doubted any of it would work, and if it did, then I didn't think it could connect to my watch. I touched a monitor.

"This one would have shown them if there were any ships in front of them." I moved to the left. "And this one would have helped them communicate." That was about the extent to which I understood any of it. "I don't really know how things work. Just how to call someone to fix them. This is old machinery, meaning I'm not sure that it could still connect to the things we use now."

He nodded. "I wanted you to see it. I sort of hoped that there might be something. I want to fix this for you. To show you that I'll do anything for you."

"I already know that. And I know that I haven't been here very long, but it already sort of feels like my other life is fading away?"

He put his hand over my heart. "Just keep beating because it feels like my other life before you is fading away as well."

I kissed his chin, and he closed his eyes. "Such easy affection. And you never extract a payment for it."

"Maybe I will. Maybe I'll demand your smiles and quiet moments."

He took my cheeks in his hands. "They're yours, always. Now we have to figure out how to save this girl."

I walked to the edge of the window and looked outside. The view really was spectacular. This was a dusty, dirty planet, and yet their ancestors had chosen to come here, had done it deliberately because what came for them in the future was worse than this. And yet, I found it to be the most beautiful sight I'd ever seen.

"I don't suppose we could just ask for her back."

His voice was grim when he said, "If someone goes to Reamer territory to negotiate, if that is ultimately our plan, you can bet that person will not be you. You are too precious."

He seemed to want to weigh the moment down with meaning or import, but I couldn't do that right then. Not up here, in the air, so close to the sky. Instead, I nudged the subject back to our refuge.

"This is a communications station," I said, indicating the com panel. "And I'm guessing by all the lights that you have at least a backup energy source here. I'm not an engineer, but I am a professional communicator"—poetry is absolutely communication—"and I'd be willing to give it a try."

Something approaching panic flitted across his face. He paled, and his mouth drew taut, like he'd sniffed something rancid.

"We are forbidden," he said.

"But sending out a signal would be a way we could ask the Reamers to return the other survivor—and as a bonus, nobody would have to actually go to their territory. Nox told you when I got here that the Reamers had scavenged a lot of high-tech stuff from the wreckage, and if they knew what to take, that means they have some familiarity with technology. They just might have receiver equipment and—"

I didn't know what it was in his face that made me stop talking, made me stop thinking about the Reamer hostage, made me freeze. Certainty settled in my chest, wild and horrible at the same time, like I'd swallowed a hurricane. "Astor, you've used this com panel, haven't you?"

He opened his mouth, closed it. Panic. That's what panic looked like on his face.

"When?" But I knew.

"Not just that panel," he said, his voice dry and cracked. "This one, too."

Red lights, lined up like soldiers. Buttons with safety covers, to keep them from being pressed accidentally. The arrangement screamed weapons control.

Did you blow up my ship? But I couldn't force my mouth to form the words. My heart was beating so hard, it felt like it fought to escape my chest. Guilt was written clearly on his face, and he stood there, his posture slightly curled in on itself, waiting for me to come at him. He was used to being at the center of barbs and attacks. Anger.

But what I felt wasn't fury.

I forced myself to pull in a long breath, fill up my lungs completely, and then count as I exhaled. One, two, three, four.

"Well," I said steadily, turning to the outgoing communications array, "let's use this one to contact the Reamers."

He didn't respond right away. "Bianca, ask me what you didn't ask."

I smiled but felt no warmth in it. "After I did such a good job repressing the need?"

He ran a hand down my back. It wasn't steady. That was when I realized it, he'd picked here, he'd picked now, because he wanted me to know and he wanted me to reject him. To throw him out of my heart.

"Did you do it on purpose?"

His mouth fell open. "No. I didn't even know what I was doing. I'd had another incident with the Baron. The others forget between events how bad it gets. They can put it aside. But I never forget. It adds up, gets to me. Sometimes, it gets to be too much."

Astor's truth was hard, but it was his, and I could practically feel it like my own. "And so you did what?"

"I came in here drunk and stupid. I just pressed and pressed buttons. All of them. I don't even know what I was trying to accomplish. Maybe I thought if I could just make something from space happen, if I could make anything happen, then it had to be better than life was at that moment."

I put my hand in his and squeezed. "And then my ship crashed, and here I am."

He laughed, but it wasn't joyful. "Turned out I was right. Something wonderful did happen. But now that girl is over there, and we have to rescue her. She's my fault, too. And all those dead people. They're my fault."

I kissed his chin. "Astor, listen. You didn't do it on purpose. Banging on machinery shouldn't crash ships. That would be an unreasonable expectation. Also, if we wanted to blame someone, perhaps we could blame the Baron. Or your father for making it impossible for Torrin to do anything about him. Let's do that instead."

He took my cheeks in my hand. "You would make me better than I am. The fault lies with me. And...I don't think we can communicate the way you want to. Many have tried.

The Reamers are nothing but monsters. I'm afraid we're going to have to attack."

"Then let's plan one. Get it over with." I wasn't as quick as he was to reject the idea of using the ancient ship's comms panel, but if he'd pressed every button up here and hadn't gotten a message out, he was probably right about the communications being broken. The system would need to be repaired, and even if I could teach Astor to read some of those paper manuals and figure out wiring and such, we didn't have time.

More specifically, that girl, whoever she was, didn't have time.

"As you know, planning military assaults is not my area of expertise. I have no idea why Torrin wanted us to come up with a plan." His tone was still hesitant, but his face had relaxed. Tentatively, though. He was like a caged animal at a zoo, dangerous but conditioned to fear. People who'd been hurt a lot and didn't have a way to make it stop or fight back could get to this point. I'd had students who had endured bully attacks so cruel, they had no idea how magnificent they were, and leading them out of that place of fear was more than a day's work.

But Astor was worth my effort, even if it took months, years. The rest of my life. I was committed.

"Maybe because he knew we wouldn't just run head-first and screaming at the enemy? Besides, you're the son of the former leader," I told him. "Military operations are so common here that your people fight off an invasion in the morning and feast that same night. So even if you haven't planned out movements of armies, you know how to mount a rescue operation. I am certain you do."

I wanted to shine my faith right into his eyes, blind him with it until he believed. *You can do this. We can do this.*

He stared hard at my chin, at his hands still cradling my

face. When he moved a thumb slightly, the touch sent a shiver through me. I wanted to kiss him again, but if I did that, we'd never get a rescue planned.

On the other hand, this was Astor's and my first day...and night. Part of me wanted to forget about the girl in the Reamers' camp and give myself over to another mind-blowing experience with one of my husbands. However, that part of me was deep id, and I knew I wouldn't indulge it.

"I am fairly good at sneaking," he said, almost musingly.

"Sneaking rather than fighting our way in sounds perfect." I turned my head slightly, brushing my mouth over his thumb in a kiss. "Tell me more."

"If we approach both Mattis and Nox regarding this rescue, they'll want to storm the Reamer camp and get us all killed. Well, except you, and they'll want to leave you behind."

"Not happening."

"I suspected you'd say that." A muscle in his face moved, like a nascent smile. "If we use that transport Nox brought you in with, we can get close to the Reamer camp, but we'll have a short hike still on the far side. I don't like it."

"I'm not a flower."

"But I'd be a fool to endanger you unnecessarily."

I shook my head. "Listen, I need to come. She doesn't know any of you. And not that she'll know me, but I'm another female from somewhere else. I can talk to her, make her feel she can trust us. I don't think you all can get this done without me. Also, you guys have gone and given me a ton of confidence in my abilities these days, so I'm all I-can-handle-anything woman."

He smiled. "Okay. You'll come with us. And despite the fact that I know they're going to object to the way we're going to do it, I need either Mattis or Nox with us. One of them. Together, they're going to want to storm, but individually, they should be fine. Plus, it'll help keep you safe."

I almost argued about that. But I was winning this discussion, and it was time to retreat not push forward. "Then which one do you want?"

He thought about it for a second. "Considering the time of day, I am going to say Mattis. Nox is very righteous. It's probably his best quality. He keeps Torrin on mostly the straight and narrow. He won't like leaving here without telling anybody."

We hadn't actually said that aloud, but it had been implied. If we were doing this without a full-blown assault, we had to do it in secret. "And Mattis is better suited for subterfuge? This time of day?"

"He's usually had a drink. By the time we get where we're going, he'll be committed, even if he doesn't like the hiding aspect of it by then. Come on. We should get going. We're going to be sneaky."

I knew why he was doing this. It was because I didn't want another assault, another big war if I could avoid it. On his own, Astor would have told Torrin he couldn't come up with a plan and stepped out of the way. Except that I'd seen him participate before. Before, he'd helped find Torrin when Torrin and Nox had gone missing. So what was it about my complicated husband? How did his psyche work?

I hoped we'd have lots of time to discover each other.

And that I wouldn't live to regret leading him in this direction.

CHAPTER NINETEEN

"**Y**ou want me to go sneak this woman out of a Reamer camp with you two?" Mattis laughed as he cleaned a glass. "You're kidding right?"

Astor shook his head slowly. "Bianca and I are going now. So you can come or you can stay, but either way, we're going."

"Well, fuck." Mattis set down the glass with a clink. "I could run and tell Torrin."

"You could, but you won't. Because you know that both of us will be gone by then. And I think you know this is the right move that will spare lives and reach the objective."

He wiped a speck from the lip of the glass and pondered it. Deep thoughts looked strange on Mattis' face. I was more used to his cocky, joking expressions. Or his kind, sexy ones. His brows drew together and lips pursed, like this didn't feel right. At last, he sighed, a deep sound of defeat. "Fine. I'll fuel up the transport, and you get some supplies together. Remember this woman fell out of the sky, just like our Bianca. She might need salve or one of your tonics or something. She might be in rough shape."

He didn't say it, but a sickening thought followed on that —the Reamers might have hurt her even more.

"This sounds like a good plan," Astor said. "I was thinking of leaving the transport at oh-eight-forty-four, at the foot of the mountain. Right here, there's a cleft and a cave. We can take that cave's tunnels in and infiltrate their main settlement, only after dark."

"Yeah, I see that working. Plus, it gives us lots of time to get there. All day, in fact." His expression brightened, and I saw the familiar mischief in his eyes. "You know what that means, don't you?"

Astor raised one very supercilious eyebrow. "Don't say it."

"Say what?" I asked, but Mattis just burst out laughing. He was nearly doubled over with it when Astor lightly touched my hand and pointed to the door.

I put the mask back on—today was a bad wind day, apparently—and we went back to the cavern and Astor's lab without talking much. The masks made lengthy conversations too much work.

But I asked him again, as we packed jars and vials, food, a light source, and some blankets into soft knapsacks back at the lab. "Why was Mattis laughing at us right before we left?"

Astor had reached up to fetch something from a top shelf, and I admired the long, lean arc of his body. He didn't even need a stepstool to reach everything in this lab, and it wasn't like the ceilings here were squat.

He didn't turn toward me when he said, "He thinks it's amusing that on our first night, I must share you."

There wasn't any hurt in his tone, but I couldn't see his face to be sure.

"Yeah, I thought of that," I said. "But I wasn't going to complain, even though I have been over here admiring your ass for roughly the last ten minutes and would like nothing better than to lock the door and strip you bare for a closer inspection."

He got very, very still, but kept his back to me.

"Bianca," he said in a deceptively soft voice, "are you propositioning me?"

I bit my lip, released it. My heart thudded. "You said we wouldn't be heading to the Reamer settlement until nightfall, right? We have time, a little anyway."

He set the canister on a table and prowled toward me. There wasn't really any other word for it. He moved like a predator. Eat me, indeed. When he stopped inches from me, touching no part of me, I almost whimpered. *Kiss me, damnit.*

"It pains me to say this, but I must decline," he drawled, tracing my mouth with his gaze. "I'm afraid I will need more than a little time for all I want to do to you, my love."

What did he just call me? And all he wanted to... Oh my. My mouth opened, but no words came out.

And then he was moving again, passing me and fetching something for our knapsacks. I let myself breathe.

"Besides," he said over his shoulder, "we have a girl to rescue, hmm? Focus."

He was right. Someone from my world was out there, potentially hurt and needing us. And I was some kind of sex maniac. How had that happened? I was hardly recognizable, even to myself. My brother would have me locked away if he were here. Yes, we needed to focus.

"What can I do?"

"Go collect us some food." He winked at me. "And don't think that I'm not going to be hard all day, thinking about what you just said."

I blushed, my cheeks so hot I could feel my pulse in them. Everyone was going about their business, totally unaware that we were about to go sneaking off into the wild to rescue a woman. Sure, Torrin had told us to make a plan, but he hadn't meant this. All three of us were aware we were being less than truthful right now.

But I wanted to save lives, and so did Astor. No more unnecessary deaths. If we could do this stealthily, that was the way to do it.

Dreama nodded at me when I walked past her; she was focused on something, and I left her alone. That was easier than the next person it was. Nox.

He smiled and rushed over. "What are you doing out here?"

I'd just grabbed food from Mattis' bar and was heading out for where I thought there were supplies for water when I saw him. I hefted my haul and said, "Running some errands."

Although I'd never been much of a liar, being there with Nox right that second and saying nothing caused a physical ache in my chest. I rubbed the spot. This was different than my physical heart pain, even though I suspected this hurt involved the same part of my body being activated. I'd fallen for Nox, and now I was lying to him.

"Astor must have some kind of experiment going on, and he sent you out for supplies." He laughed. "His brain never stops working. Not even when he has instructions from Torrin and his wife to make love to." Nox narrowed his eyes. "Sure you're okay?"

I swallowed and forced myself to smile, but I could tell he wasn't buying my whole 'I'm fine' line. "I really am. I guess I just have a lot of things on my mind."

He nodded. "A lot has happened lately, that's for sure."

The wind blew, causing dust to hit my eyes. At least I could blame the dust on why my eyes might start tearing up. I set my pile of supplies down, threw my arms around him, and held on. Despite the constant dirt, there was never a time that Nox didn't smell clean. He did like his shower. "Thank you for rescuing me and giving me this life."

His arms came around me. "Thank you for living through that crash and coming here to be with me. With us."

This was the amazing thing about Nox. Sure, he could tell I was too emotional for just doing errands, and he probably guessed that I was up to something important and terrifying, but he didn't try to talk me out of it or take control of my decisions. He trusted me. Holies. He was going to be so hurt when he heard what I was really planning.

I rubbed my forehead against him before I pulled back. "I'll see you soon."

"You'd better. Torrin is bound and determined we're all living in his quarters with him. He's going to get really insistent soon."

"Ha. And then it's so long to your awesome bath," I said, trying again to lighten the mood.

He played along, kissing my forehead as if he couldn't help himself. "Well, it won't be tonight or tomorrow, so we might get a reprieve before we have to give up the hot water."

Not tonight or tomorrow, that would work. It was my hope Torrin—and Nox—didn't realize they couldn't find us until we were already back.

And I hoped I wasn't fooling myself.

The masks we had to wear during very dry, dusty days like this one made it harder to talk, but I was okay with silence while we drove the transport away from the City-State and out into the contested wasteland beyond. Or maybe I was more than okay with silence. I needed to gather my thoughts.

I couldn't be sure without looking at a map or something, but it felt like we went in a different direction from where I'd crashed. I saw a blur of green in the distance, through the haze of dust, and that might have been the pond where Torrin had taken me to fetch the healing herbs. Aha! I was right. We were headed in almost exactly the opposite direction from the crash, which meant the City-State was between the Reamer settlement and the crash site. And yet the Reamers had gotten to the wreckage first, grabbed their captive, and set the rest—me included—on fire. They must have been scouting nearer the City-State that day for other reasons. Had they been planning an attack? That would explain why Nox was out there watching them. And also why the Reamers had been ready to go with their attempted invasion yesterday.

That was the kind of plan—or invasion, whatever—Torrin would have devised. And yet Nox said Astor and I had been set to planning this rescue because we would do it differently. Well, we sure were doing it differently. I couldn't handle an all-out assault with weapons and fire and blood and... The smells of it, the intensity and panic rushed through my mind, and I was glad I was sitting down as our vehicle trundled over the bare, undeveloped land.

Instead of that kind of attack, we were doing this. Sneaking.

And lying.

Yeah, the guilt lingered. I didn't like keeping this excursion from Nox and Torrin and even Dreama. What if something happened to us out here and we made everything worse, even wound up needing rescue ourselves?

The guys, Mattis and Astor, didn't talk a lot either, except for some points of navigation, and with my watch broken and the landscape sort of uniformly obscured by the dust, I had no idea how long we drove. I napped, just for a few minutes, but when Astor squeezed my arm to wake me, the bright blur of day had faded to twilight in the deep shadow of a mountain.

"We're here," he said gently. "Time to stash our transport, grab our packs, and get moving."

"Yeah." My voice was scratchy with sleep, and my eyes felt sticky, but I didn't dare rub them for fear of grinding in the grit. I blinked a lot instead, pulling Astor into focus. Yep, still beautiful. "How long is our route through the tunnel?"

I had other questions—like, was this the same cave Torrin had used when he was wounded and Nox rescued him? Who all knew about these caves and tunnels? Were the Reamers likely to be in there, and would we have to maybe fight our way through? But I didn't voice any of those things. The plan that had seemed perfect this morning now felt tenuous and maybe a little silly. We should have consulted with the other warriors. We should have planned more carefully and then presented that plan to Torrin, for him to enact with other people trained for this sort of thing.

All ancients, was he going to be pissed when he found out what we'd done.

I shivered. An angry Torrin was not a thing I was looking forward to experiencing. Again.

"We'll be hiking most of the night, so it's a good thing you got some rest on the way over," Mattis said, coming around to my side of the transport. He was loaded down with equipment, including several weapons holsters. Full ones. Which probably answered my unspoken question about possible attacks. Terrific.

Astor was holding my pack out for me and frowning. I took it and slipped my arms through the straps, securing the belt around my waist. Heavy, but not impossible. I could do this. *Shut up*, I silently told my overprotective—and pleasantly not here—brother. *I absolutely can. It's my decision, my body*.

But even with my bravado and certainty that, regardless

of the risks, this was the right thing to do, when I pulled my mask off inside the tunnel, breathing didn't get any easier.

Not a good sign. This heart was weakening, and I wasn't ready for it.

Still, I trudged on after them and kept my concerns to myself. There was nothing to do, and I didn't want them worrying. We could go back, but then that poor girl was still going to be in the condition she was already in. How would I live with myself when this feeling passed as nothing and I was able to continue on as I'd done? How would I bear the guilt? What if the unthinkable happened to her while I was making things harder?

"You okay?" Mattis asked me over his shoulder, and I nodded before I realized he really couldn't see me in the tunnel.

"Yep," I called back.

How long was this walk? Truthfully, I didn't want to know. I could keep pretending it was almost over if I didn't know for sure that wasn't true. Yes, I'd always been wonderful at deluding myself. It came from long periods of time in the hospital with people questioning why I hadn't been killed at birth. Psychological games could keep me alive. Or mostly that way. I was quickly learning that there was being alive and there was actually living. Existing wasn't going to cut it for me anymore.

And truly amazing was that these guys seemed to get that. The partying after battles, the way they all seemed to laugh despite their hardships, that was all the way they affirmed that they loved life. Particularly after it sucked.

"This way." Astor's voice was low. He must really not want to be heard right now. I took that as a good sign to keep my mouth shut and trailed after them. When we exited the tunnels, what would we see? Reamerville? Would it be as disgusting and unhygienic as their war camps apparently were? Or did Reamers live more or less like we did as they ate human flesh? I shuddered at the thought. People did what they had to in order to survive, but surely there was a line about just how gross things could get.

Astor popped off a lid above his head, and Mattis shook his head. "Let me go first."

"In case they spot us, so you can get killed instead of me?" Astor put his hands on his hips. "Not okay."

"It is, actually." Mattis didn't wait for permission. "You're royalty. Second-in-line after Torrin. You have to stay alive. I'm awesome and amazing, but I can be killed. You can't. So I go first. End of story."

Funny how in preserving Astor's royalty, Mattis was actually ordering him around. Did they even realize how ridiculous these class divisions were?

I was doing it again. Getting lost in my head, noticing life's ironies instead of participating in the things that were happening around me. Why was I doing that all of a sudden? I was about to have the most dangerous thing I'd ever done happen to me. Well, except for the whole spaceship-crashing portion of my life.

Astor followed Mattis up and then turned to wave me to follow. It must be safe to go. Or safe enough. None of this was without risk. That was life for us. We never had a time when it was totally okay to go about things, so we did the best we could.

Of course, this didn't qualify as doing the best we could. We were definitely taking a big risk.

These days, I was Bianca the risk-taker.

Apparently.

CHAPTER TWENTY

The air had gotten progressively more stifling as we proceeded through the tunnels. At first, I thought it was just stagnant air in an unventilated space, but after a while, I recognized it as a familiar stench. Reamers. We must be getting close.

Mattis led the way, but Astor trailed behind me, so that no one could sneak up. Yes, my guys were over-protective, and yes, I'd always hated being sheltered like a fragile, break-able thing. But also? Somehow, their care wasn't annoying or humiliating. It felt sincere. Like love.

"So how many people were on your ship before it crashed?" Astor asked softly, kind of out of nowhere and still in a tone barely above a whisper.

It took me a little while to gather sufficient breath to reply. "I'm not sure. I was just a passenger, so I didn't get to look at manifests or anything. Probably..." I paused to suck in some air, make sure my balance was steady, and then plowed on, "The captain, plus officers for comms, weapons, helm, and three or four flight attendants for maybe a couple dozen passengers? Something like that? Oh! And a doctor."

"A doctor? Is that common on transports between stars?"

"Well, we were going to a medical station, so my guess is most of the passengers were also patients of some kind."

No, the tunnel really was tilting. I lost my footing, stumbled, and put a hand against the wall. Mattis stopped and turned, and Astor clasped my shoulder to steady me.

"Guess I just can't handle Reamer stench," I said, trying to lighten the mood. They were peering at me way too intently, and no way was I going to let anyone—not even them—tell me I had to turn back or couldn't do this. I was *doing* it.

"Yeah, it can get to you," Mattis said slowly, but his tone and the expression on his face both screamed the truth—he wasn't buying my excuse. He was worried.

My heart clenched. Not in a medical way, more in a it-was-too-full way. Too full from all this care.

"Let's take a break," Astor said. "It doesn't make a difference if we get there right after nightfall or halfway to morning. Dark is the same dark. We have time."

I sat on the rough-hewn floor with my back against the wall. It was cold and damp enough that it wet the back of my shirt. Gross. But rest was rest, and I could complain all I wanted, but they were right. I needed this. We were about to slip into an enemy settlement full of monsters. I wasn't going to skip a chance to pause and gather myself before that.

Astor passed a bottle of water to me—the thermos, my thermos, the one he'd given me in exchange for the holowatch—and I drank from it.

There was a weird undercurrent among the three of us, as if Mattis and Astor could speak telepathically and were having a whole conversation that I couldn't hear. And normally, that kind of thing would infuriate me, but for once, I didn't have the energy to complain. They'd known each other all their lives, so it made sense they'd be able to communicate nonverbally, right?

"I wonder..." Astor mused. "If this girl we're rescuing might also have had an ailment, and we know how the Reamers exist and how they treat their prisoners—"

Mattis made a sound that was almost an agreement, but also almost a growl.

"—I can't imagine she will be in top shape for this long hike back to the transport."

"Point," Mattis said. "We should probably call for reinforcements. You know, in case we have to carry her out."

"My thoughts exactly."

"Hold on," I said. "Ignoring for the moment the question of whether we really want to tell the other guys about our little adventure, how do you call for reinforcements when you don't have long-range communications?"

Mattis smiled widely. "Remember when you asked about our sigil for the City-State, the animal profiles in a circle, protecting the flower?"

I nodded. "You said you were a brotherhood."

"A pack, specifically."

Okay, that still wasn't telling me how we were going to get a message back, and I wasn't at all convinced we should be trying to communicate with our people, given how furious Torrin was likely to be. And how hurt Nox would be when he found out I'd lied and run off without him. Ouch.

"He means we can send messages via Howlers," Astor said. "The profiles in our sigil are Howlers. Like the ones you heard that first night. They can copy some tones and run extremely fast over distances and then repeat those tones."

"I thought you said they were wild, undomesticated," I said. My memory was good, too good sometimes, but it kept me from being lied to, which had come in handy plenty of times in my life.

"We don't keep them *with* us," Mattis said. "The terrors! They'd rip our faces off. But they do like to carry songs around for us, and we leave food out for them when it gets cold. I guess you could say we're allies."

A brotherhood. A pack. With terrors. Okay.

"So assuming we're going to do this—and I think it's a dodgy idea, if that even matters—how do you summon them?"

Astor pulled a device out of his pocket. "Our ancestors discovered long ago that the Howlers both love and hate this sound." He clicked it, and all I could hear was the click. Didn't hurt my ears at all. "They hate it so much that they come to investigate it. Like a moth drawn to a flame."

I liked and understood that metaphor. Seemed some things were the same everywhere. "What happens when they get here?"

Mattis scooted closer to me and put his arm around my shoulder. "I wish we'd thought about the, ah, needs of the girl we're rescuing ahead of time. The Howlers won't come in the tunnels. But they'll be close enough that we can signal them."

Astor raised his mouth toward the ceiling and howled. It was such an odd sound to hear him make, there was something utterly surreal about it. He stopped and started, an almost staccato like sound to it. Then he sat back down. Sure enough, a few seconds later, I heard the noise again in the distance. This time from the howlers themselves.

It was...fascinating.

"There, now they know." Mattis squeezed my shoulder. "And we're all going to be on Torrin's shit list for weeks. But we knew that anyway. It was a good idea. There were just factors we didn't consider."

Enough with this. "Let's just speak the truth, shall we?"

"Bianca," Astor sighed. "Look—"

"You're both right. Something went wrong, okay?" I didn't

let him finish. "I've been strong and fine this whole time, but sometimes, something goes amiss with me. It'll correct. I'm just sorry it happened today." I looked away. "You should know there is nothing I hate more than pity."

Mattis leaned his head against mine. He yawned. "I don't pity you. Neither does he. We're both wishing you had said something earlier, but as I once kept the fact that I'd broken my foot a total secret for two miles in training, I get trying to tough things out. And Astor—"

The aforementioned royal held up his hand. "Nope. Don't tell her."

"Fine. I won't. Point being that we get it. We've done the same. And I'm glad to hear you're going to be okay."

I couldn't guarantee that, but my history told me I'd make it through this mess. I always had. The fact that I was living and breathing was a good indication that I was tough and capable. It had taken us a long time to get here. Presumably, it was going to take us that long to get help and...

That was when I heard it. The sound of running feet approaching.

The guys must have heard it, too. They were on their feet fast. I tried to get up but wasn't moving quite as quickly as they were.

"Stay down," Mattis said to me. "Nothing is getting near you."

Okay. As I had no choice, I remained where I was. Seated in the face of danger.

I was still sitting there when five Reamers roared into our tunnel. Ugly, scary, smelly, and wanting to eat the flesh off our bodies. Or maybe that was just what they wanted from Astor and Mattis. From me, they wanted something else entirely.

Mind over matter, I pulled myself up. If there was going to be an attack, I had to at least be standing. And in less than a second, there was no question about the 'if.' It was happening.

They rushed us.

People talk about moments of crisis happening in slow-motion, but they don't tell you how clear details become. Like, I noted each weapon holster on Mattis' body as he found them and armed himself and Astor. Both of them—weapons at the ready and looking fierce—stood between the Reamers and me. They didn't hesitate at all. And they didn't pass me a weapon. Not a single one.

This was how my guys lived, what they knew, probably like daily showering or meditation used to be for me. Part of me wanted to be right there in the middle, fighting with them, but the other part just sat back and took in the show.

It was beautiful, in a blood-spattery and gory way.

Also sort of hypnotic. As they sliced ribbons of putrid Reamer flesh off their opponents, their movements almost had the quality of dance. In the world I was used to, fighting usually happened at a distance, either with ranged burr-launchers or plasma beams, so death, when it happened, was usually obscured. You didn't have to see it up close. You didn't have to hear it or smell it.

The Reamers screamed when they died. One, two, three of them. My men were efficient in dealing with their enemies.

But also, perhaps they were too focused. And I was, as well.

Because none of us noticed the two Reamers who'd broken off from the others, slinking in the shadows to come up behind me. And by the time I felt their hands on me, their filthy rags covering my face and stripping my consciousness, it was too late to scream.

I didn't wake up on fire this time. I woke up in stages, one blurry layer of confusion at a time. Not on a sleepy interstellar ship. Not on a dusty, barbarian prison planet with kind, amazing, sexy as hell men, who inexplicably wanted to take care of me.

The room was gray, perfectly square, windowless, and antiseptically clean. It smelled of astringent, but with a musky undertone, like someone had disinfected it thoroughly, but a month ago, and the chemicals had hung in the air all that time, getting stale.

The cot beneath me left a lot to be desired, but it wasn't horrible. Compared to, say, sleeping on rocks, this bed would be comfortable.

I wasn't wearing my normal clothes, the soft, flowy garments Torrin had picked out for me. I had been stripped and wrapped in that weird, green cloth that Nox made into facemasks back home.

Home. Torrin. Nox. My men.

I sat up, got slammed with a rush of vertigo, and set my hands, palms flat, against the bed to steady the room as it spun. It took a couple minutes of deliberate breathing to not vomit, but I could feel my pulse in my temples, behind my eyeballs, even in my neck. My heart, poor thing, was doing its best.

But I couldn't coddle it.

I needed to get home, back to the City-State. I needed to make sure Mattis and Astor were okay. Had they been captured, too? Panic rose up in my throat, threatened to choke me.

"You're the senator's sister, aren't you?" came a voice from the shadows of one corner.

A woman's voice. No, a girl's.

She rose, and as she crept closer, I could see my assessment was right. She was a young girl. Had I known there was an adolescent on the trip with us? No I hadn't, but I'd hardly been socializing with anyone. It wasn't like I was looking to make friends with people who were going to cringe away from me like I carried the plague because of the well-known problem with my heart.

The girl in front of me was little more than a child. Her hair was long, blonde, and frizzed everywhere. She wore glasses—which confirmed her age as nine at the most. At ten, she'd be eligible to have her eyes fixed so she never needed glasses again. Eye issues still happened in our society, but everyone repaired or hid them. I stared at her face for a second. Her parents must have been very rich to have the newest synthetic glass on the lenses and the frames, so they survived the crash. Even the spaceships didn't have such synthetics yet. Maybe I'd ask her later, when we got away, who her parents were. Or maybe I'd leave it alone. She'd clearly been through hell.

Her clothes were ripped, and it looked like something from my former life and not this one. She was still dressed as she'd been when we crashed.

"I'm Bianca." I cleared my throat. "We came here looking for you."

She nodded as she knelt down right next to me. Despite the dirty clothes, her hair appeared clean. She was a dichotomy of clean and dirty. It made little sense, but I was probably overthinking it. Maybe she didn't have other clothes so she had to keep re-wearing hers.

It probably was that simple.

She put out her hand. "I'm Rae. Are you going to die?"

"Not this very second." That seemed an honest answer. "We're all going to die, one way or another, eventually. For now, I'm okay." I hoped that was true. "Are you okay?"

She looked down. "I'm too young for breeding. That's their rule. They want you for that."

I didn't know if I should feel terrified for me or relieved for her. Somehow, I was absolutely both.

"I'm sorry, they got you," she added. "I hate them. This planet. They're all savages. And I want all of them to die."

I squeezed her hand. "Not everyone here is that way. There are others here who aren't like that. But yes, I agree. The Reamers are awful. We need to get out of here. Before you get older and they realize I'm awake. Hopefully, the latter and not the former."

"Is that your power? Teleporting or whatever?"

I frowned. "Um, no. I don't know what they told you about me, but I don't have any powers. When we were on the spaceship, I was headed to stay with my brother and to have an operation because I'm sick. So I guess you could say I have the opposite of superpowers."

One side of her mouth pinched up, like she didn't believe me. I knew there were stories about my family floating around the galaxy, but they were all part of the branding my brother had devised for us after our parents died. He and his marketing team had made them into legends, which incidentally, made him into a scion of legends, and that was super helpful for his electability.

It didn't help me now, though. All those fairy tales about my family were only making it harder for me to get Rae moving right now.

I put my feet on the floor and tried to stand. Didn't fall over. That was progress!

"Do you know what they did with my clothes?" I asked.

Rae picked at a thread on her blouse, which looked like it started out expensive, before the crash and the fire and all. All ancients and holies, this child must be traumatized.

But not as much as we both would be if the Reamers got to us before we could make our escape.

"They cleaned you up," she said. "They said people from the sky came a long time ago and brought diseases, which is why the Reamers are so ugly and mean now. They had to detox us, and I have to wash in the smelly green water every day. It's gross."

I shuddered. I didn't want to think about them "detoxing" me when I was unconscious. More than that, I didn't want to think of how long I'd been out. How much time did I have before they came for me? Or rather, for us. I wasn't leaving here without Rae.

Or my husbands.

CHAPTER TWENTY-ONE

"So no idea where my clothes are?" I prodded. This blanket-like wrapping was not going to stay on if I moved around much, so I needed my own things.

"No, I have an idea. Come on." Rae turned, flicked a lever set into the smooth wall, and slipped through a door I hadn't noticed before.

The Reamer camp was nothing like my City-State. A long, straight hallway was dotted with doors at regular intervals, each with a lever latch like the one Rae had just used to open our room. The colors were uniformly gray and white, and it looked like someone cleaned regularly, maybe even compulsively. About fifty meters down, the hallway turned at a right angle.

I'd seen hallways like this one before, even with the same levers. In fact, they were so familiar that I followed Rae for several steps before it hit me—this hallway should not exist on this planet. It was a standard prefab used by almost all colony outposts. The lever latches operated a system inside the walls that could compensate for pressure and atmosphere changes if one of the rooms was breached in a hostile environment.

The Reamers had either once been colonists...or had slaughtered the colonists. Was it horrible that I didn't even care which messed-up past spawned them? I just wanted to go home, and for all its familiar-looking structure and technology, this was not my home. My home no longer looked anything like this.

"In here," she said, pulling a lever in the wall and opening a door.

I started forward and abruptly jumped back. In the room were three Reamers.

She paled and then turned slightly to me. "I'm sorry. They told me if I brought you to them without making a fuss I could eat tonight."

I wanted to be angry, but getting fed was the most primal instinct we had. She had to eat. I swallowed. Would I do the same? I had no idea, and I hoped not to find out. "That's okay. I'm glad you can eat tonight."

She peered at me intently. "You're nicer that I thought you would be. My parents used to call your brother a living nightmare." Then she took off running.

I almost laughed. I mean, that was unexpected enough to be ridiculously funny. Yep, Brent was a nightmare. But I'd give anything to see him right now. Or my husbands.

Anyone but the three Reamers in front of me.

"Female." The tallest one sniffed the air. "You smell fertile. I will put my seed in your belly."

I shuddered. Even though I knew it couldn't happen—and honestly, this might have been the first time I had ever been thankful for my weird physiology—the threat was revolting. He wasn't just threatening my current safety; he was threatening my future, not to mention a theoretical child's. What an asshole.

"I'd be worth a lot to you in trade." I spoke the words as they occurred to me, proud of my ability to think on my feet like this. "More than I would be worth as some kind of breeder. My family has problems. Sometimes we have three legs." I was lying, of course, but they'd never know that.

Two of them, the shorter ones, stared at each other. Yep, I was going down this path. "I'm worth much more to you if you trade me than if you try to have a baby with me. My uncle has three legs, and they say it skips a generation." I held up that many fingers. "Surely the City-State has something you'd want more than a defective breeder."

The tall one scoffed. "We no trade."

I nodded fast. "Okay. First time for anything. I could teach you."

"Female no teach."

I was quickly gathering how this was going to go. Fear was a real thing, and my body never did behave the way I wanted it to. I could feel panic tears behind my eyes, but I was damned if these Reamer monsters would see me cry. They were the kinds of brutes who would equate fear with weakness, and then they'd probably assume they'd won. So instead of just wiping my eyes, like I would if I were crying, I wiped my whole face, as if I could rub the truth of my situation away. My heavy sigh was deliberately annoyed.

I wasn't entirely sure the Reamers were buying my show of bravado, until that sigh ended on a cough. Too much dust inhaled on the trip over, probably, or allergies to a brand-new world and its spores...but clearly, the Reamers weren't thinking along either of those lines.

When I coughed, all three of them flinched away from me. *People from the sky came a long time ago and brought diseases*, Rae had said.

The line between looking fearful-slash-weak and looking virulently ill was thin. Kind of like my chances of getting out of this without being raped. But hey. Whatever worked, right?

Plus, I had tons of experience looking sick.

I coughed again, covering my mouth with my hand, and when I pulled it away, I made a show of wiping my hand on the blanket wrapped around my body. Touch it now, assholes.

"You heard the child," I told them. "My brother is a living nightmare. Do you know what that word means? Nightmare?"

The taller one, the one who'd been speaking most, looked confused.

"It means like ghouls, like he is something that you see in your sleep, and it wakes you up screaming." I put one hand against the doorjamb and sagged, like I was losing strength. "How about this word, then—sick. Do you know sick?"

The big Reamer didn't move, but the other two shuffled a few steps away. They looked at each other. One half-shrugged. Neither looked directly at me.

"Look, here's the deal," I went on, pulling all kinds of fiction out of my brain and just hoping that my pale face and practiced sick posture was selling this malarkey. "My brother is a galactic senator, right? He sent me here to infect the people on this planet with the virus we both suffer from. When they get sick, the Union forces will land their starships here and wipe out everybody. It'll be easy. So I'm not a breeder. I'm a weapon. Check your spies and that kid if you don't believe me. The leader of that other group has had me watched constantly because he suspects I'm dangerous. He just hasn't figured out yet how I'll bring them down."

Now, it was entirely possible that the Reamers weren't sophisticated enough to have spies. They might not have imaginations enough at all to buy this story. But then again, those two slightly smaller Reamers still weren't looking at me.

The big one narrowed his eyes and sniffed again. "Clothes off. Show flesh."

A shudder charged through me. The thought of standing naked in front of these brutes—especially knowing what was on their minds—made me physically ill.

Which...you know, maybe I could work with that.

Slimy Reamer hands on my skin, I thought. I closed my eyes, tried to imagine being impregnated by one of these monsters. My gag reflex responded as expected. If I'd had anything to eat in the last half day or so, I definitely would have puked right there. I kept imagining worse and worse scenarios, and the dry heaves kept coming.

"Off!" he shouted, and I stumbled backward.

I didn't have to pretend to shake when I let the blanket fall to a puddle on the white floor.

The Reamers grunted amongst themselves, and one of the underlings, looking none too happy about it, passed me and headed out into the hall. To check my story? Or to flank me in case I tried to run?

In any case, he didn't touch me as he passed, and that was the first good luck I'd had in a while.

"Touch what is mine, and I'll keep you alive to kill you slowly."

Oh wait. I knew that voice. Something bright and amazing flooded me.

All three Reamers jumped as Torrin's voice filled the room, followed by the man himself, looking furious. They all grabbed for their weapons, but two of them were dead before they had the chance to bring their hands to the halters. One of them had a sword thrown into his eye the other a shotgun-blast hole in his chest the size of my head. I swallowed and took a step back.

Torrin advanced. How had he gotten here?

"Do you hear me, Reamer?" He reached my side, and the intense feeling of safety enveloped me.

Why wasn't he killing the Reamer closer to me? That was

when I saw it. The big Reamer had his hand on his weapon. I hadn't seen it because it was small and unimpressive looking, but it could probably take off my head if I weren't careful. Good thing Torrin noticed it, too. Maybe there was no chance I couldn't be shot in the time before he was taken down.

Behind Torrin, Mattis and Nox stood, having discharged their weapons. I swallowed. Which one of them had thrown the sword? It was impressive. And thinking about that kept me from thinking about how concerned Torrin must be about this guy that he hadn't taken him out.

"Drop it," Torrin spoke in a low voice. "Take a fast death. Surely you know who I am. And what I can do. You've worked your way up to a big man. Don't embarrass your ancestors by begging me for mercy later."

For all that they weren't particularly loquacious people, I swore I could see the thoughts pass through the Reamer leader's mind as he thought them. No, he didn't want to die at Torrin's hand under his direction of torture.

He dropped his weapon, and Torrin shot him right in the head. Just seconds apart, if that long.

I shrieked, letting out the terror I'd tried to hide.

Torrin tugged me against him. "You're okay. I don't think I've ever been so scared, Bianca. For now, it's enough that you're okay. For now."

I nodded. We'd known we'd be in trouble, and this eventuality hadn't featured in it. "Torrin, I..."

"Later."

Okay. Yes, I could wait. I'd do that. Sure. Fine. "There's a girl. She's young. Ran off to eat and..."

"Astor has her. Hurry. He's going to blow up the tunnel. We will exit through the front."

My chest tightened. Now was the time for the truth. No

more deception. It didn't work out well. "I'm not sure I can hurry."

Torrin caught my meaning and, after wrapping me once again in the blanket, swung me into his arms, holding me tightly against him. "Then I'll carry you home."

He strode fast through the endless hallways of the Reamer base as if he knew which way to go. Had they been this way before? I thought no one had ever been to the main Reamer settlement before.

Exiting outside, he stopped long enough for Nox to help me shrug back into my normal clothes—who had been thoughtful enough to retrieve them?—and cover my face with a new scarf. He met my gaze for a long moment. Unlike the Reamer, I couldn't read his thoughts. Was he angry? Hurt?

"Blow it," Torrin called to his brother, who stood to the side, surrounded by others whose names I didn't know yet but who had come for me. So many of them had! People I didn't know, who didn't know me. They must have had unquestioning faith in my men. Or love for them.

Nox helped settle me in the middle of the transport bench, and like Torrin, he didn't address the elephant in the room of how I'd run off on a mission without them. But he didn't seem any less careful or considerate in the way he treated me, either. If I'd hurt him, he didn't show it. I wanted to talk, but it wasn't the time.

Someone set Rae next to me on the bench, and I didn't think about it, just slipped my arm around her. She was shaking, poor kid. I wondered if she'd gotten a chance to eat before she'd been rescued.

As the vehicle lurched forward into the night, taking us all home, I looked down at her. "You don't need to be scared," I told her, squeezing her narrow shoulders. "These men are kind. Also, that one"—I pointed to Astor. He was facing away from me, so he didn't see my gesture, but of course he could probably hear—"is a healer of great skill. He can get you healthy in no time. They all will take care of you. I promise."

She seemed to relax a little, but her voice cracked a little when she replied, "But he couldn't heal you. And none of them could keep you safe."

"Rae, all of those things I was telling the Reamers were just to delay them so my rescuers could get there. I am not diseased. I'm...fine. Just like you're going to be fine. All the bad stuff is over now."

I wasn't sure she believed my lies, but she did eventually fall asleep. I was tired, too, but also maybe too keyed up. Terror will do that to you.

And there was that other thing. The secret thing.

Because no matter how convincing I'd made myself sound, no matter how much I protested, I knew there was plenty more bad stuff coming. And none of us could stop it.

CHAPTER TWENTY-TWO

Torrin and his rescue team had come out in some other conveyance. I didn't know exactly what until we arrived back at the City-State right around dawn. But even if I had known, it still would have been a thrill to watch Torrin and Nox at the head of their company come riding into town on the backs of what I can only assume were Howlers, giant red-furred creatures that looked part bear, part wolf. They were like something out of myth, both the beasts and the men.

All of us were tired, except for maybe Rae, who'd slept most of the way. I guessed we'd all been too tired to talk.

Or, in Torrin's case, too angry? And in Nox's, too hurt? Neither approached me, and that stung a little, but I wasn't deeply afraid. Torrin had been so gentle with me back at the Reamer camp. And Nox.

When we rolled to a stop, Mattis reached for Rae. For such a big man, he was amazingly gentle. She didn't even wake up when he gathered her in his arms.

"I'll get her inside and make sure she's comfortable," he whispered, and I smiled back at him.

"Thank you," I mouthed.

There was activity in the hangar where we parked the transport, but the mood wasn't tense. Most people seemed genuinely happy to see us. *All* of us, which was the weird thing. I could understand why these people would be thrilled to have their leaders and warriors back, but they treated *me* with the same awe and respect. It was so bizarre. No one had ever looked at me like that before. Like I was some kind of hero.

Near Astor's lab, Dreama found us. To my shock, and maybe a little bit of horror, she wrapped me in a fierce hug.

"Good thing they fetched you back safely," she said, "else I'd have to kick their asses."

"Um—" I started, but her low laughter cut me off.

"No, you know I wouldn't really. I love my little brothers. All of them."

That was just a tiny bit startling to hear. Little? These guys? But I guess if Torrin and Astor were twins and their mom had died shortly after they were born, that meant Dreama was their *older* sister. The idea of them as children, as small and defenseless, was both hilarious and endearing. I felt a tug of longing in the center of my chest. I wished I could have known them then, been a part of their world instead of growing up in mine. No one here had ever tried to convince me that my continued existence was some sort of charity that could be withdrawn if they found me unworthy.

"And it's good to have my sister back, too," added Dreama.

It took me a long moment to comprehend what she was saying, but when it finally dawned on me, I had no words.

She didn't seem to need any. She looked over my shoulder and half-smiled at something behind me.

"I'm afraid I have to ask you to relinquish Bianca," said Astor, and I almost melted at the sound of his voice, sliding over my spine like that, licking its way up my neck. Even though he'd been in the transport with me, he hadn't said anything on the ride back, and it hadn't seemed the appropriate setting for me to ask what all had happened after I'd been captured.

He and Mattis must have been frantic.

Astor finally turned to me, regret in his gaze. "I'm so sorry this happened."

"You should be," Torrin answered for me, and I shot him a look.

"This wasn't Astor's fault solely. It fell to all of us." I kept my gaze on Astor as I spoke. "This is not on you."

"No," Mattis answered for him. He was still carrying Rae, but something had stopped him in his tracks. Probably Torrin's tone. "It's on me. I'm the one who lost you in the battle."

I swung around. "How do you figure that?"

"I was around on that venture basically to keep you safe, and I failed at that." He didn't look away or cower, but he also couldn't look Torrin in the eye. His resigned posture fit a man who expected his punishment, maybe even welcomed it.

Torrin cleared his throat. "Yes, it's your fault, too. Absolutely on you."

I couldn't stand this. "If you guys want to be technical it's *my* fault. If my glitchy heart hadn't gone and picked then to act up, we'd have kept with the plan and none of us would have been caught."

Torrin swung around completely. When he spoke, it was to his brother and Mattis. "Did you just not trust me? In all of my years sitting on the throne of bones, have I ever let anyone I care about die? Have I ever not rescued a rescuable person? Did you just decide I was too incompetent to be part of the plan?"

A muscle ticked in Astor's jaw. "Maybe I just thought

there was enough death. That we could do this in a sneaky, subterfuge kind of way and spare any more death of our people."

"You think I take their lives anything but totally seriously? You think I have ever sent someone to death capriciously? That may be the most insulting thing you have said since I picked up the signal you were in trouble to begin with." As he spoke, his voice rose on each word until he was downright shouting. Nox winced but didn't look away. Mattis hadn't been looking at Torrin to begin with and didn't begin to now. "Not to mention that you put our wife in absolute danger. And I can see why she would have wanted to do this. I get her thinking. She's just been exposed to it for the first time, so it makes sense she'd be looking for another way. But you should have known better. Both of you."

Rae shifted in Mattis' arms. Apparently, we'd woken her, and her voice was low and quavered when she said, "Is he going to start hurting people?"

"No," I answered, fast, but realized I didn't really know. That Reamer leader had been terrified of Torrin. Enough that he'd preferred to drop his weapon and die than risk having Torrin torture him. What did my fierce husband do to his people when they disobeyed? I had no idea when it came down to it.

"Maybe that's the problem." Astor seemed not to have heard my quick exchange with Rae. He was entirely focused on his brother. "At what point did we become okay with not looking for any other way?"

Torrin turned around and faced forward away from us. "Ideals of our youth aren't important right now. Not when it comes to survival. We get one good thing. A beautiful woman literally falls from the sky, and you and Mattis nearly get her killed. It's like...you don't want to have anything good in our lives. If you want to go and get yourselves killed, I will mourn you, but why drag her along with you for the fucking suicide?"

"Because we don't hide our women like flowers that might disappear in a dust storm," Nox shot back. "Your sister fights as one of us, and while we don't put them on the front line when called to action, our women fight as well as any of us. You told Astor and Bianca to plan, they planned. They brought Mattis in to help with that planning, even. Just because you don't like how it turned out, doesn't mean that they weren't somewhat right, and you know it, Torrin. I know you do."

Mattis widened his eyes. Shock rocked me that Nox had spoken up like that, and I was obviously not the only one who felt that way. The whole cavern fell immediately silent at his outburst.

Astor put a hand on Nox's shoulder, and the two exchanged speaking looks. Then he turned to his brother.

"You have ruled our City-State by fiat for all our lives, brother, and you are right—you've done well by us," Astor said, siphoning some of his brother's anger, or attention at least, away from Nox. "But taking a wife has changed our family dynamic, and as you are also our leader, it has changed our community dynamic. We need to consider solutions that don't involve war and torture. We need to consider solutions that our wife suggests. We need to, for lack of a better term, grow up."

I could hardly keep my face from expressing my shock and horror at Astor's words, and Nox's before that. If all his closest friends, his brothers, were ganging up on him—in public no less—what was that going to do to Torrin? I knew how personally he took the safety of each person he thought himself responsible for. I knew how much his swagger masked a man who felt deeply, perhaps too much.

He was vulnerable right now, without wanting to be, and he could lash out.

I couldn't let him hurt my men. I couldn't let him hurt himself.

I went straight to Torrin, tipped my head back, and set my hands on either side of his face, in effect forcing him to look at me. He did.

"Thank you," I said in a low voice. "Thank you for coming to our rescue. Thank you for trusting Astor and me to come up with a rescue plan. Thank you for welcoming Rae into our City-State, as you did for me. Thank you for loving all of us so very, very much."

His nostrils flared, and as I stared at him steadily, held him between my hands, the fury drained from his eyes.

"That is my reason," he said at last, his voice gruff.

"I know." I raised up on my tiptoes and kissed him. Pulling back, I let him see a smile. "See you in the morning?"

He grimaced, knowing I was referencing Astor's night, the third of my firsts, but then he dropped a kiss on my forehead. "Sleep well, wife."

And before I could think about it and ponder the wisdom of saying my secret truth aloud, I blurted, "I love you back, you know." I made a turn, looking at each of them, my beautiful, loyal, warrior husbands. "All of you."

I watched this declaration break like dawn over their tired faces. Mattis, still holding a semi-drowsed Rae, looked close to tears. Nox's pleased, content nod was like a benediction. Astor's wing-like eyebrows were still drawn tight to his nose, frowning, but he would melt like ice-candy later, when we got privacy, I knew.

Torrin stood exactly where I'd left him, as if he were rooted to the spot. I had no idea what the expression on his face meant, but I knew what it wasn't. It wasn't anger, not at me, not at his brothers. If I didn't know better, I would say we were all witnessing wisdom descend upon the shoulders of our king. As if he'd never thought before that there was more to life than fighting and struggle.

But now he knew. Or was coming to realize.

A hand took mine, and I knew that was Astor, leading me away. I gave Torrin one more smile, and he didn't stop us from leaving. Neither did Nox or Mattis or Dreama, or any of the rest of the people who'd lingered in the hangar to watch us enact this scene.

I could have sworn some of them sighed, and Nina, a shadow on the edge of the crowd as usual, was smiling and weeping at the same time. When I flashed her a look in question, she just shook her head and kept on grinning. Beside her, Birdie made a sweeping motion with her hand, indicating that I should leave.

I was working on it, and this wasn't easy. None of this was easy.

Breathing especially had become difficult.

Little as I wanted to address it, nothing had changed with me physically since the tunnels. I still couldn't pull in a breath, and from experience, I knew what this meant. Back in my world, it would mean a treatment regimen, a lengthy isolation in a med ward. Here? All ancients and holies... What was I supposed to do here?

And how was I going to give Astor the night he deserved when my medical reality had intruded like this? I couldn't tell him. Them. I couldn't tell any of them.

As it turned out, I didn't have to wait long to find out how I'd handle it.

My chest tightened until I couldn't take another step, couldn't catch my breath. I stopped moving, disentangled my hand from Astor's, and bent over, placing my hands on my knees. I didn't know if that helped or not, but that was what I'd always done when it got that bad.

I didn't know why. I'd never understood it. But it was as though as the cage that constricted my lungs and the pounding of my heartbeat in my ears took over my existence, I had to hold on to my knees. This was a bad one. I didn't know the last time I'd had one this bad.

But they'd warned me... It was why I needed a new heart.

"Bianca?" Astor placed his hand on my back. "Are you okay?"

I shook my head, and he winced.

"What can I do for you?"

There was nothing. Without medical care, there would be no making this better. And suddenly, that didn't matter because there wasn't enough air in the world. I gasped, my knees giving out, and Astor caught me as I fell. There was some kind of commotion, but I couldn't lift my head. Life was just getting enough air. In and out.

Was there a transport parked on my chest?

I was lifted off the ground. Strong hands. I wasn't alone. There was comfort in that. I wasn't alone. Really, for the first time in my life.

In. And out.

Med wards have that certain disinfectant smell, not unlike the Reamer compound, which is sort of the opposite of comforting. They also have certain sound, an arrangement composed of the beeps of monitors, huffs of breathing machines, and the odd clink of mechanical surgeons switching appendages. Sometimes, the whir of a saw or the gurgle of fluid being dispensed will punctuate a beat. No one talked in a med ward. I always thought it would be the loneliest place to die.

The reality of my end, here in this strange and violent and

dirty and beautiful world, was far different. There were voices all around me, warm and worried, the voices of my men, and behind them, my people. Running, calling, murmuring encouragement to me. I wanted to thank them, to reassure them that this was okay, I was okay with dying and had been preparing for it for so long.

But they wouldn't listen. They wouldn't understand.

For them, my death was not inevitable. It was extremely evitable.

More footsteps, running. I couldn't see anymore, even with my eyes open, and I no longer attempted to fill my lungs with each inhalation. They wouldn't fill. I just needed to avoid panicking.

You guys, my guys, you don't have to worry. It's really okay.

But I didn't have air to speak. Everything inside me was slowing, preparing to pack up and move on. I closed my eyes, no longer struggling to see.

I felt weightless and thought it was some new symptom, a transition maybe, but then there were hands on me, lifting. They were moving me. To Astor's lab, probably, but the smells weren't right.

The blur of light through my eyelids became a blur of black.

And the smell changed. Gone was the dust and sweat and food and exotic plants. Now I was in a ship. My spaceship. Heading to Jooron Five to get my new heart. Mechanical heart. Not a lover's heart, a fighter's heart.

Beloved voices wove in and out of existence.

"...the air, when you pressed this one? How'd you..."

"...if you'd just..."

"...is she?"

And often, "Hold on, my love. Just stay with me."

Somehow, that last was in all their voices, all at once, over and over. *I'm sorry*, I wanted to tell them. *So sorry. I didn't mean to make you love me. I didn't mean to make you hurt. I will miss you so, so much.*

And also, *Thank you.*

Something shifted underneath me, as if this plane of existence were falling away. My spaceship gave that high-pitched hum, like when it was coming out of hyperspace and new sublight systems were coming online. They were noisier, the sublight drives. Clean and silver and echoing inside my body, like medical saws.

Warm voices and strong hands surrounded me still and comforted me. How were my husbands on my spaceship? Impossible. So impossible.

But not as unbelievable as the next voice, slicing into my oxygen-deprived fugue and chilling me through and through. "Bianca? You okay? I thought you forgot about me."

My brother's voice. Right here on the edge of the universe, on the stark edge of life, somehow, he'd found me.

My heart skipped a beat, then two. I gasped. The air felt like razors down my throat.

I sat up and Brent pushed me back down. "Easy. You know better than that."

Blinking against the too-bright light, I stared at him. He was there—in the room with me—on a spaceship where a white-wearing doctor scurried around touching the machines. The scene was so strikingly familiar that I almost wondered if I'd dreamed everything. Was my time on the planet some drug-induced dream?

No. It was real. It had all happened.

"How?" I managed to talk, even though my throat hurt like I hadn't spoken in weeks.

Brent attempted to soothe me with one of his patented, concerned half-smiles, the kind he saved for public mourning after tragedies. "I've been looking for you since the signal was lost. Took a little time to find you. The ion clouds in this area are almost impossible to navigate for the equipment. Seems I got there right on time. They'd almost lost you, those savages of yours." He had been sitting in a chair by my bed, and now he leaned back in it and stretched out his legs in front of him. "Amazing they kept you alive at all. The medical team has stabilized you for now, and when we get you to a more advanced planet, they'll replace your heart with a metal one. Then you'll finally be fine."

I stared at Brent. It was like seeing his face had become a foreign sensation for me. As though I'd killed him off in my mind as something from another time, a dead time, and I'd been born again to something else. Now he was like an intrusion on my now.

But my feelings for my brother didn't matter right now. There were too many questions, too many things to address. I was in space. That meant I wasn't on the planet. My guys were... Well, I didn't know what had happened to them. And I had to hide my feelings. If Brent saw a reaction he didn't like, things could be made much harder for me. He was a person who wanted things to be the way he wanted them to be.

Still, he'd come for me. He'd searched. Had he been expecting a body? He'd brought doctors. He must have wanted to find me. Or he was covering all angles.

It didn't matter. I had to repeat that over and over in my head. Brent looked tired; lines I'd never seen before traced outwards from the corners of his eyes.

"I missed you." He spoke words I'd never have expected to hear from him, ever.

"You did?" Despite my best intentions, I couldn't keep my disbelief from my voice. I decided not to care. Torrin would say what he thought regardless of the consequences. I had learned something from my time with him. "You don't even like me."

Brent shot forward in his chair. "What? Of course I do. You're my twin sister. I like you very much. And I'll like you even more when I don't have to worry that you're about to drop dead. I want you steady and healthy. Then we can figure out what's next for you."

No one had ever asked me what I wanted. The machines beeped loudly, and Brent stared at them. "Bianca, I need you to calm down."

The doctor approached fast and fiddled with buttons. They were going to knock me out to calm me down. "No," I said to the healer. "Not now." I forced myself up to a sitting position. "Those men that you called savages, they're my husbands. I love them, and they love me. Where are they now? What did you do with them?"

Brent looked at the doctor sharply. "Give us a second, and if you repeat a word she just said to even your religious confessors, I will have your whole family killed."

The doctor turned and ran from the room. There was the Brent I knew well.

He turned hard eyes on me. "Whatever happened on that planet, it will stay where it happened. Do you understand? Your so-called husbands are going to find themselves handled by a true government now. Military and settlers are on their way there to take over and bring the locals in line. Savages fighting each other like this is something out of history. I have no tolerance for it. They will find the true way. Or they will die. Either way, they will never see you again, and you will never tell a soul that you were married or any of the other things you did down there." He rose. "Get some rest. Your new heart will be a new start. A real one. Love them. What a ridiculous concept."

That last was a mutter under his breath as he swept from the med bay, leaving me alone. I pulled in another breath, and it was slightly less painful this time. They must have knocked me out for quite a while to stabilize me. This last attack had been worse than all the others, and I'd been sure it was the last one. I'd been resigned to my fate, to my death, even though the idea of leaving my men made me so, so sad. Our time together had been bright at least, the best ending I could imagine for someone like me.

Only, right now, watching the sliding door vibrate with the aftershock of Brent's slamming it closed, I realized something even brighter.

I didn't want to die. Not like this. Not alone, away from them.

I needed to find them, save them. We were a family. And besides, damn it, I still had first nights pending with Astor and Mattis. Not to mention a thousand nights with all of them, and days, too. A whole lifetime crammed with possibilities stretched out in front of me. I'd never let myself believe before, but they had shown me that nothing is impossible.

I sat up, waited for the spinning and the burst of nausea to settle, and went to work pulling needles out of my skin. I would go to Jooron fucking Five and get the metal heart. And then I would go back. Home. He couldn't stop me.

Just wait for me, my loves. I'm coming home.

ASTOR

"Come on, we can't hold the last transport any longer. We gotta go," Mattis said, ducking into the lab. Astor crammed a couple more books into his pack. He'd gotten distracted, remembering her reading them, teaching him. Her voice.

And his own stupid, stupid plan for saving her, which looked like it was failing in the most spectacular way.

He grabbed one more item, didn't even look at it, and shoved it into the pack. "Yeah, coming."

The tunnels leading down had collapsed in the first orbital bombardment after the invaders took Bianca. Some of their people had been trapped, had suffocated in the dark. The ancient throne of skulls had most likely been crushed, turning the whole history of their people to mere dust. Astor took every hit, every death, every destroyed building and animal and hope onto his conscience. Guilt was eating him alive, and it was everything he managed not to just sit down right there in the middle of his mostly ruined lab and wait for the next bombardment, which would end him, too.

"So *coming* usually means *moving*. Like with your feet? Come *on*."

Astor peered at Mattis, almost expecting a grin to match the lighter tone, but even Mattis had lost his joy lately. Even he couldn't summon a smile. Shit had to be bad.

"Torrin will kill me if I don't get you out of here, man. So you got a death wish, fine, but at least evacuate so *I* don't get squashed."

"He wouldn't do that," Astor said, but he made himself move. For Mattis' sake. "He doesn't want to see any more death."

Torrin had taken it worse than any of them—her leaving, the attacks from the sky that followed. He'd uncharacteristically shut down there for a while, had been unable to make any decision in the moment. Mattis had to physically drag Torrin from the ancient spaceship tower where they'd— where *Astor* had—signaled to the stars in a last-ditch effort to save their Bianca.

He still believed she had been saved, because if his plan had worked and if she lived, he could endure. He just wished he had proof, anything. Some reason to care.

Mattis reached out and grabbed the pack, hauling Astor along with it, and Astor let himself be led. On the surface, in the wide cavern where they kept the transports, he pulled up short.

"Wait a minute. Where's Dreama? Is she already at the farms?" At Nox's urging, they were regrouping in the farmland. They'd won the land fair and square for the entirety of the season, which might give them enough time to rebuild somewhere else, where the sky people couldn't find them. In this worst of all possible moments, Nox was stepping up and proving that leadership wasn't inherited. It was earned. Astor was so proud of him. They all were.

"No," was all the answer he got to his questions, and it

came so late that Astor had almost forgotten what he asked. Mattis' face looked set and serious, but Astor's mind was moving so slowly, was in such a fugue, that they were already on the transport and rolling out of the only home he'd ever known before he caught the full meaning of that word.

"Wait!" he called out to the driver. "We have to go back. My sister is there. Dreama. We have to—"

A female hand settled on his arm, and he was shocked to see it belonged to Sorcha. But her hand wasn't demanding or grasping. It was light and meant to comfort, though her eyes were sad. "No one has seen Dreama since the first bombardment. My father disappeared at the same time. We have to assume... I'm sorry, Astor."

Hell, it sounded like she meant it.

Too much loss. Too much change. He couldn't handle it. He closed his eyes, unable even to summon the energy to move Sorcha's hand.

His sister dead, his brother broken, his people homeless and hopeless, his home destroyed. And Bianca...

He had to believe she was alive. He had to believe she was coming back.

He centered that belief in his mind, running a hand over the top of his pack and shape of her broken wrist device, the last thing taken from the still-burning ruins of the City-State.

I don't know how, but I will find you, Bianca from the Sky. This cannot be the end.

The End.
Please don't worry, we are hard at work on the next story coming soon. Please turn the page to learn more about us, our books, and where you can learn more about us!
Rebecca and Vivien

ABOUT VIVIEN JACKSON

Vivien Jackson writes fantastical, futuristic kissing books. Her debut science fiction romance, *Wanted and Wired*, was an Amazon Best Book of 2017, a Romance Writers of America RITA finalist, and an SFR Galaxy Award winner. A devoted fangirl and inveterate gamer, Viv lives in Austin, Texas, and watches a lot of football.

She'd love to hear from you on the web, Twitter (@Vivien_-Jackson), or Facebook.

The Tether Cyberpunk Romance Series
Wanted and Wired
Perfect Gravity
More Than Stardust

ABOUT REBECCA ROYCE

As a teenager, I would hide in my room to read my favorite romance novels when I was supposed to be doing my homework.

I am the mother of three adorable boys and I am fortunate to be married to my best friend. I live in Austin Texas where I am determined to eat all the barbecue in town.

I am in love with science fiction, fantasy, and the paranormal and try to use all of these elements in my writing. I've been told I'm a little bloodthirsty so I hope that when you read my work you'll enjoy the action packed ride that always ends in romance. I love to write series because I love to see characters develop over time and it always makes me happy to see my favorite characters make guest appearances in other books.

In my world anything is possible, anything can happen, and you should suspect that it will.

I'd love to hear from you! Please visit my website at www.rebeccaroyce.com to sign up for my newsletter and learn about my books!

Here's where you can find me online:

Rebecca's Randomness Reading Group https://www.facebook.com/groups/RebeccasRandomness/

https://www.rebeccaroyce.com

https://www.facebook.com/authorrebeccaroyce/

www.twitter.com/rebeccaroyce

Instagram: rebeccaroyce79

Cheers!!
Rebecca

OTHER BOOKS BY REBECCA ROYCE...

Redheads

Redhead on the Run https://amzn.to/2Nb3RcH

Redheaded Redemption (Coming Soon)

Wings of Artemis (completed series)

Kidnapped By Her Husbands https://amzn.to/2BQdUxy

Rescued by Their Wife https://amzn.to/2Rr9as4

Crashing Into Destiny https://amzn.to/2VkyXRL

Meeting Them https://amzn.to/2BLPaXm

Reclaiming Their Love https://amzn.to/2GKAw8E

Loving Them https://amzn.to/2BKDmEK

Ship Called Malice https://amzn.to/2BNputj

Saving Them https://amzn.to/2SsrBtH

Dark Demise https://amzn.to/2VidXv3

Light Unfolding https://amzn.to/2GO6Yqr

Still Waters https://amzn.to/2CFePT8

Rising Tides https://amzn.to/2MCdTlM

Lost Star https://amzn.to/2X8hcZA

Pointed Arrow https://amzn.to/3gK9tYH

Last Hope (completed series)

Tradition Be Damned

Past Be Damned

Destiny Be Damned

Compassion Be Damned

Future Be Damned

Dragon Wars (completed series)

Forever

Eternal

Always

Evermore

Endless

Wards and Wands (completed series)

Hexed and Vexed

Curse Reversed

Meow, Baby (novella, co-written with Ripley Proserpina)

Tragic Magic

Safe Haven

Everywhere and Nowhere

Dimension X (coming soon)

More coming soon....

Soul Bound

Prisoner of the Dragons

More coming soon....

Shadow Promised

Strange Days

Weird Nights

Bizarre Years

More coming soon...

The Warrior (completed series)

Initiation

Driven

Subversive

Redemption

Justice

Warrior World (spin off of The Warrior, completed series)

Deacon

Micah

Jason

The Westervelt Wolves (completed series)

Her Wolf

Summer's Wolf

Wolf Reborn

Wolf's Valentine

Wolf's Magic

Alpha Wolf

Angel's Wolf

Darkest Wolf

Lone Wolf

Fallen Alpha

Alpha Rising

Alpha's Strength

Alpha's Sacrifice

Alpha's Truth

Alpha Enticing

Hidden Alpha (coming soon)

Illicit Minds

Illicit Senses

Illicit Connections

Illicit Alliance (coming soon)

The Outsiders

Love Beyond Time

Love Beyond Sanity

Love Beyond Loyalty

Love Beyond Sight

Love Beyond Expectations

Love Beyond Oceans

Love Beyond Flames

Love Beyond Lies

Love Beyond Death (coming soon)

Cascade (completed series)

Haunted Redemption

Phoenix Everlasting

Fragility Unearthed

Persuasion Enraptured

Reverse Harem Story (completed series)

Unconventional

Unexpected

Undeniable

Kiss Her Goodbye (completed series)

Hard Truths

Dark Truths

Deadly Truths

Shifter World

Planet Bear

Planet Wolf (coming soon)

The Swamp

Hidden

Pursued

Caught

Stand Alone Titles

Under The Lights

No Quitting Allowed

Mr. Wrong

Bite Marks

Bitten Surrender

The Vampire and The Virgin

Demon Within

Crimson Lust

Call Me Crazy

The Men of Elite Metal

The Storm (writing with Ripley Proserpina**) completed series.**

Lightning Strikes

Thunder Rolling

The Deluge

Heart of the Nebula (writing with Heather Long**) completed series**

Queenmaker

Deal Breaker

Throne Taker

Stranded Hearts (writing with Vivien Jackson)

The Girl Who Fell From The Sky

The Girl Who Crossed The Stars (coming soon)

Stupid Boys (writing with C.R. Jane)

Stupid Boys

Dumb Girl

Crazy Love

Through the Gates (writing with Skye MacKinnon)

Purgatory City

Infernal Land

The Coveted (writing with Ripley Proserpina)

Eyes in the Darkness

Voices in the Darkness

Return to the Darkness

Prison Princess (part of the Prison Princess world, writing with CoraLee June)